The Ratbridge Chronicles

VOLUME 1

HERE·BE·MONSTERS!

AN ADVENTURE INVOLVING

MAGIC, TROLLS, AND OTHER CREATURES

·Mactavish·Charts·&·Maps·

Maps and Charts for every trip and educational purpose.

1). The Solar System
2). The Planets
3). The Earth
4). Continents
5). Towns and Cities
  A). Grimethorpe
  B). Radstock
  C). Chibley
  D). Morgan-Freestanding

Coming soon from Mactavish-

MONSTER LOCATION
Both Terrain and Below

For the traveler of nervous disposition and those who wish to travel in dangerous parts.

diagram .15/1067

Wart-off
"See Tru-Sprout
(below)

Mud-shoes
Slip into Mud

BLOB

WANTED

£10,000 REWARD
FOR THE CAPTURE AND DELIVERY TO TRIAL

The above scoundrel is wanted for attempted poisoning, and avoiding arrest. His whereabouts are not at present known, but if encountered, should be apprehended and brought before the justices of this town.

BY ORDER *Sidney Quezy*

TRU–SPROUT

HERMAN'S OIL OF BRUSSEL IS THE PURE ESSENCE OF THE KING OF VEGETABLES. THOUGH FOUL-SMELLING. THIS OIL HAS POWERS BEYOND THE UNDERSTANDING OF MERE MORTALS. BUY SOME FOR EVERY ILL!

S.S. HOPELESS

The good ship **"HOPELESS"** shall sail forth upon the 18th day of this month, in our good Queen's year 1803, in search of the Edge of the World, by way of "New Lands" (*if found*). Passage will be offered in exchange for the sum of **40** guineas. It is expected that the voyage will be of 18 months and that it will be of some amusement to those aboard. Apply at **the Sign of the Black Crow**, by the hour of 11 afore noon on the day of sailing.

GNOMES

"Gnome with fish"

AN EDUCATIONAL CRUISE *featuring*
"GNOMES OF THE FJORDS"

Departing the 12th of this month for 3 weeks to **Scandinavia**. Upon the newly refurbished Luxury Cruiser- **"MoonBeam** *(Ex. Sprat Factory)"* of Whitby, we shall take in the heritage of Gnome culture and history, to the accompanyment of a discourse by Dr. R.G. Fingle *(Radstock School of Gnomistry)*.

Charge.	
1st	£3.18/-6d
2nd	£2.5/-6d
3rd	£1.12/-11d
Self Catering Stoker	7/-

TICKETS AVAILABLE FROM FINGLE & DOG ltd.   no refunds or returns

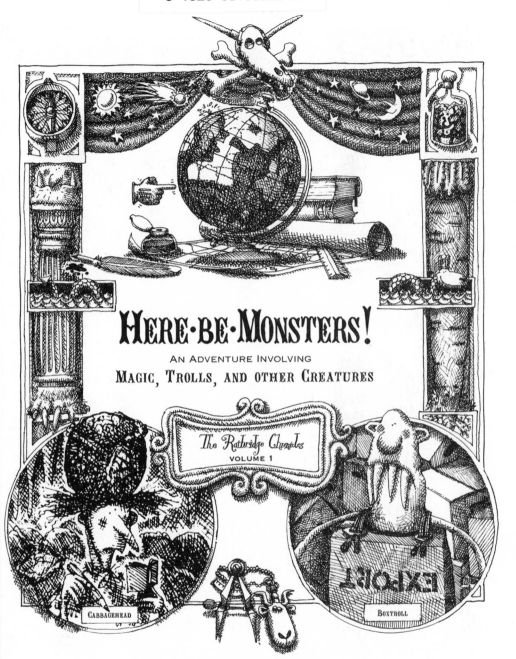

Here·be·Monsters!

AN ADVENTURE INVOLVING

MAGIC, TROLLS, AND OTHER CREATURES

The Ratbridge Chronicles
VOLUME 1

CABBAGEHEAD

EXPORT

BOXTROLL

WRITTEN AND ILLUSTRATED

by Alan Snow

ATHENEUM BOOKS FOR YOUNG READERS

NEW YORK   LONDON   TORONTO   SYDNEY

Atheneum Books for Young Readers • An imprint of Simon & Schuster Children's Publishing Division • 1230 Avenue of the Americas • New York, New York 10020 • Copyright © 2005 by Alan Snow • First published in Great Britain in 2005 by Oxford University Press • This book is a work of fiction. Any references to historical events, real people, or real locales are used fictitiously. Other names, characters, places, and incidents are products of the author's imagination, and any resemblance to actual events or locales or persons, living or dead, is entirely coincidental. • All rights reserved, including the right of reproduction in whole or in part in any form. • Book design by Alan Snow • The text of this book is set in Old Claude. • The illustrations of this book were rendered in pen and ink. • Manufactured in the United States of America • 10 9 8 7 6 5 4 3 2 1 • First U.S. Edition 2006 • Library of Congress Cataloging-in-Publication Data • Snow, Alan. • Here be monsters! / written and illustrated by Alan Snow. • p. cm.—(The Ratbridge chronicles ; #1) • Summary: While gathering food to bring to his grandfather, young Arthur becomes trapped in the city of Ratbridge, where he and some new friends try to stop a plot to shrink the monsters of Arthur's home, the Underworld, for a nefarious purpose. • ISBN-13: 978-0-689-87047-7 • ISBN-10: 0-689-87047-7 • [1. Fantasy.] I. Title. • PZ7.S6805Her 2006 • [Fic]—dc22 • 2005024438

The Ratbridge Chronicles

VOLUME 1

HERE BE MONSTERS!

IN WHICH WE LEARN A LITTLE
ABOUT ARTHUR, BOXTROLLS,
CABBAGEHEADS, AND STRANGE
GOINGS-ON IN RATBRIDGE

To Edward,
and with enormous thanks to everyone
who has helped along the way

HERE·BE·MONSTERS!

AN ADVENTURE INVOLVING
MAGIC, TROLLS, AND OTHER CREATURES

CONTENTS

Johnson's Taxonomy
of Trolls and Creatures

Aardvark

Aardvarks are invariably the first animals listed in any alphabetical listing of creatures. Beyond this they have few attributes relevant here.

Boxtrolls

A sub-species of the common troll, they are very shy, so live inside a box. These they gather from the backs of large shops. They are somewhat troublesome creatures—as they have a passion for everything mechanical and no understanding of the concept of ownership (they steal anything that is not bolted down, and more often than not, anything that is). It is very dangerous to leave tools lying about where they might find them.

Cabbageheads

Belief has it that cabbageheads live deep underground and are the bees of the underworld. Little else is known at this time, apart from a fondness for brassicas.

Cheese

Wild English Cheeses live in bogs. This is unlike their French cousins who live in caves. They are nervous beasties that eat grass by night, in the meadows and woodlands. They are also of very low intelligence, and are panicked by almost anything that catches them unawares. Cheeses make easy quarry for hunters, being rather easier to catch than a dead sheep.

Crow

The crow is a very intelligent bird, capable of living in many environments. Crows are known to be considerably more honest than their cousins, magpies, and enjoy a varied diet, and good company. Usually they are charming company, but should be kept from providing the entertainment. Failure to do so may result in tedium, for while intelligent, crows seem to lack taste in the choice of music, and conversational topics.

Freshwater Sea-cow

Distant relative of the manitou. This creature inhabits the canals and drains of certain West Country towns. A passive creature of large size and vegetarian habits. They are very kind to their young and make good mothers.

Grandfather (William)

Arthur's guardian and carer. Grandfather has lived underground for many years in a cave home where he pursues his interests in engineering. All the years in a damp cave have taken their toll, and he now suffers from very bad rheumatism, and a somewhat short temper.

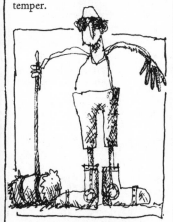

The Man in the Iron Socks

A mysterious shadowy figure said to be much feared by the members of the now defunct Cheese Guild. He is thought to hold a dark secret as well as a large "Walloper." His Walloper is the major cause of fear, but he also has a sharp tongue, and a caustic line in wit. History does not relate the reasoning behind his wearing of iron socks.

The Members

Members of the secretive Ratbridge Cheese Guild, that was thought to have died out after the "Great Cheese Crash." It was an evil organization that rigged the cheese market, and doctored and adulterated lactose-based food stuffs.

Rabbits

Furry, jumping mammals, with a passion for tender vegetables and raising the young. Good parents, but not very bright.

Rabbit Women

Very little is known about these mythical creatures, except that they are supposed to live with rabbits, and wear clothes spun from rabbit wool.

Rats

Rats are known to be some of the most intelligent of all rodents, and to be considerably more intelligent than many humans. They are known to have a passion for travel, and be extremely adaptable. They often live in a symbiotic relationship with humans.

Trotting Badgers

Trotting badgers are some of the nastiest creatures to be found anywhere. With their foul temper, rapid speed, and razor-sharp teeth, it cannot be stressed just how unpleasant and dangerous these creatures are. It is only their disgusting stench that gives warning of their proximity, and when smelt, it is often too late.

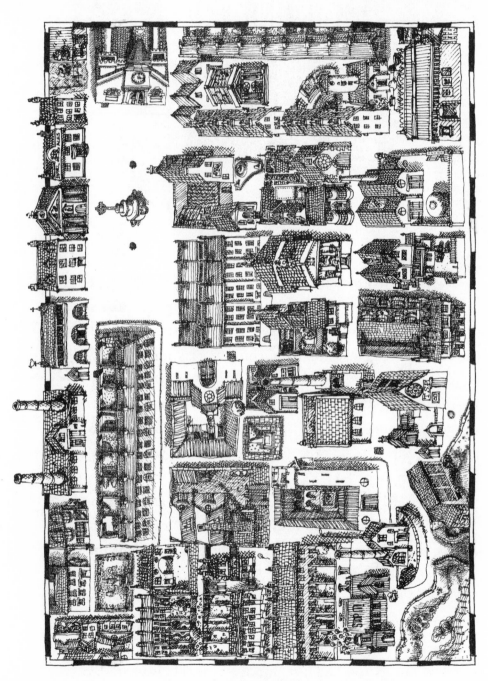

Ratbridge town center.

chapter I

COMING UP!

Ratbridge.

It was a late Sunday evening and Ratbridge stood silver gray and silent in the moonlight. Early evening rain had washed away the cloud of smoke that normally hung over the town, and now long shadows from the factory chimneys fell across oily puddles in the empty streets. The town was at rest.

The shadows moved slowly across the lane that ran behind Fore Street, revealing a heavy iron drain cover set among the cobbles.

Then the drain cover moved. Something was pushing it up from below.

One side of the cover lifted a few inches, and from beneath it, a pair of eyes scanned the lane. The drain cover lifted further, then slid sideways. A boy's head wearing a woven helmet with nine or ten antennae rose through the hole and glanced around. The boy shut his eyes, and he listened. For a moment all was quiet; then a distant dog bark echoed off the nearby walls. Silence returned. The boy opened his eyes, reached out of the hole, and pulled himself up and out into the lane. He was dressed very

A pair of eyes scanned the lane.

oddly. In addition to the helmet, he wore a large vest knitted from soft rope, which reached the ground, and under that a short one-piece suit made from old sugar sacks. His feet were wrapped in layers of rough cloth, tied with string.

Fixed about his body by wide leather straps was a strange contraption. On his front was a wooden box with a winding handle on one side, and two brass buttons and a knob on the front. A flexible metal tube connected the box to a pair of folded wings, made from leather, wood, and brass, which were attached to his back.

The boy slid the drain cover back into place, reached inside his under-suit, and pulled out a toy figure dressed just like him. He held the doll out and spoke.

"Grandfather, I am up top. I think I'll have to go gardening tonight. It must be Sunday; everything is shut. The bins behind the inn will be empty." He looked at the doll.

There was a crackle of static, then a thin voice came from the doll. "Well, you be careful, Arthur! And remember, only take from the bigger gardens—and only then if they have plenty! There are a lot of people who can only survive by growing their own food."

Arthur smiled. He had heard this many times before. "Don't worry, Grandfather, I haven't forgotten! I'll only take what we need, and I *will* be careful. I'll see you as soon as I am done."

Arthur replaced the doll inside his suit, then started to wind the handle on the box. As he did, the box made a soft whirring noise. For nearly two minutes he wound, pausing occasionally when his hand started aching. Then a bell pinged from somewhere inside the box and he stopped. Arthur scanned the skyline, crouched, and then pressed one of the buttons. The wings on his back unfolded. He pressed the other button and at the same moment jumped as high as he could. Silently the wings rushed down and caught the air as he rose. At the bottom of their stroke, they folded, rose, and then beat down again. His wings were holding him in the air, a few feet above the ground.

Arthur reached for the knob and turned it just a little.

"Grandfather, I am up top."

As he did so, he tilted himself a little forward. He started to move. Arthur smiled. . . . He was flying.

He moved slowly down the lane, keeping below the top of its walls. When he reached the end, he adjusted the knob again and rose up to a gap between the twin roofs of the Glue Factory. Arthur knew routes that were safe from the eyes of

He was flying.

the townsfolk, and would keep to one of them tonight on the way to the particular garden he planned on visiting. When it was dark or there was thick smog, things were easy. But tonight was clear and the moon full. He'd been spotted twice before on nights like this, by children, from their bedroom windows. He'd got away with it so far, as nobody had believed the children when they said they had seen a fairy or flying boy, but tonight he was not going to take any chances.

Arthur reached the end of the gap between the roofs. He dipped a little and flew across a large stable yard. A horse started and whinnied as he flew over. He adjusted his wing speed and increased his height. The horse made him feel uneasy. At the

He adjusted the knob.

far side of the yard he rose again, over a huge gate topped with spikes. He crossed a deserted alley, then moved down a narrow street flanked with the windowless backs of houses. At the far end of the street he slowed and then hovered in the air. In front of him was another high wall. Carefully he adjusted the knob and rose very gently to the point where he could just see the ground beyond the wall. It was a large vegetable garden.

A horse started and whinnied as he flew over.

Across the garden fell paths of pale light, cast from windows of the house. One of the windows was open. From it Arthur could hear raised voices and the clatter of dominoes.

That should keep them busy! he thought, scanning the garden again. Against the wall farthest from the house was a large glass lean-to.

He checked the windows of the house again, then rose over the wall and headed for the greenhouse, keeping above the beams of light. He came to rest in front of the greenhouse door.

Dark leafy forms filled the space. As Arthur entered, he recognized tomato plants climbing the strings, and cucumbers and grapes hanging from above.

He moved past all these and made his way to a tree against the far wall.

It was a tall tree with branches only at its top. Dangling from a stem below the branches was what looked like a stack of huge fat upside-down spiders. It was a large bunch of bananas. As Arthur got closer, he caught their scent. It was beautiful.

Arthur could hardly contain his delight. Bananas! He tore one from the bunch and ate it ravenously. When he finished, he looked over at the house. Nothing had changed. So, he reached inside his under-suit, pulled out a string bag, then grabbed a hold of the banana bunch and gave an eager tug. It wasn't as easy to pick the full bunch as it had been to pull off a single banana, and Arthur found he had to put his full weight on the bunch. A soft fibrous tearing sound started, but still the bunch did not come down. In desperation Arthur lifted his feet from the ground and swung his legs. All of a sudden there was a crack, and the whole bunch, along with Arthur, fell to the ground. The tree trunk sprang back up and struck the glass roof with a loud crack. The noise sounded out across the garden.

"Oi! There is something in the greenhouse," came a shout from the house.

Arthur scrambled to his feet, grabbed the string bag, and looked out through the glass. No one was in the garden yet.

It looked like a stack of huge fat upside-down spiders.

He rushed to collect up as many of the bananas as possible, shoving them into the bag. Then he heard a door bang and the sound of footsteps. He ran out of the greenhouse.

Clambering toward him over the rows of vegetables was a very large lady with a very long stick. Arthur dashed over to one of the garden walls, stabbed at the buttons on the front of his box, and jumped. His wings snapped open

A very large lady with a very long stick.

and started to beat but not strongly enough to lift him. He landed back on the ground, his wings fluttering behind him. Arthur groaned—the bananas! He had to adjust the wings for the extra weight. He wasn't willing to put the bananas down and fly away empty-handed—they were too precious. He grabbed at the knob on the front of the box and twisted it hard. The wings immediately doubled their beating and became a blur. Just as the woman reached the spot where Arthur stood, he shot almost vertically upward. Furious, she swung her stick above her head and, before he could get out of range, landed a hard blow on his wings, sending him spinning.

"You little varmint! Come down here and give me back my bananas!" the woman cried. Arthur grasped at the top of the wall to steady himself. The stick now swished inches below his feet. He adjusted the wings quickly and made off over the wall. Shouts of anger followed him.

Arthur felt sick to the pit of his stomach. Coming up at

night to collect food was always risky, and this was the closest he'd ever been to being caught. He needed somewhere quiet to rest and recover.

I wish we could live aboveground like everybody else! he thought.

Now he flew across the town by the safest route he knew—dipping between roofs, up the darkest alleys, and across deserted yards, till finally he reached the abandoned Cheese Hall. He knew he would be alone there.

The Cheese Hall had been the grandest of all the buildings in the town and was only overshadowed by a few of the factory

The Cheese Hall.

chimneys. In former times, it had been the home of the Ratbridge Cheese Guild. But now the industry was dead, and the Guild and all its members ruined. The Hall was boarded up and deserted. Its gilded statues that once shone out across the town were blackened by the very soot that had poisoned the cheese.

Arthur landed on the bridge of the roof, and settled himself among the statues. As he sat catching his breath, it occurred to him that maybe he should inspect his wings for damage. The woman had landed a fairly heavy blow, but Arthur decided it would be too dangerous and awkward to take his wings off high up here on the roof, and besides, they seemed to be fine. Then something distracted him from his thoughts—a noise. It sounded like a mournful bleat, from somewhere below. He listened carefully, intrigued, but heard no more. When he finally felt calm again, he stowed the bananas behind one of the statues, climbed out from his hiding place, and flew up to the best observation spot in the whole town. This was the plinth on the top of the dome, which supported the weather vane and lightning conductor.

A complete panorama of the town and the surrounding countryside, broken only by the chimneystacks of the factories, was laid out before him. In the far distance he could just make out some sort of procession in the moonlight, making for the woods. It looked as though something was being chased by a group of horses.

The plinth on the top of the dome.

North East Bumbleshire.

chapter 2

THE HUNT

Three large barrel cheeses broke from the undergrowth.

Strange sounds were filtering through the woods—scrabblings, bleatings, growlings, and, strangest of all, a sound closely resembling bagpipes, or the sound bagpipes would make if they were being strangled, viciously, under a blanket. In a small moonlit clearing in the center of the woods, the sounds grew louder. Suddenly there was a frantic rustling in the bushes on one side of the clearing, and three large barrel cheeses broke from the undergrowth, running as fast as their legs would carry them. Hurtling across the clearing, bleating in panic, they disappeared into the bushes on the far side of the clearing, and for a moment all was still again.

Suddenly a new burst of rustling came from the bushes where the cheeses had emerged, along with a horrid growling noise. Then a pack of hounds burst out into the open. They were a motley bunch, all different shapes and sizes, but they all had muzzles covering their snouts, and they all shared the awful reek of sweat. The hounds ran around in circles, growling through their muzzles. One small fat animal that looked like a cross between a sausage dog and a ball of wire wool kept his nose to the ground, sniffing intently. He gave a great snort, crossed the clearing, and dived onward after the cheeses. The other hounds followed.

They were a motley bunch, all different shapes and sizes.

The weird bagpipe sound grew closer, accompanied by vaguely human cries. Then there was a louder crashing in the undergrowth, and finally the strangest creature yet arrived in the clearing. It had four skinny legs that hung from what looked like an upturned boat made from a patchwork of old sacking. At its front was a head made from an old box, and on this the features of a horse's face were crudely drawn. A large, angry man rode high on its back.

"Which way did they go?" the man screamed.

An arm emerged from the sacking and pointed across the clearing. The rider took his horn (made from some part of a camel) and blew, filling the clearing with the horrible bagpipe-like sound. Then he raised the horn high in the air and brought it down hard on his steed.

"Hummgggiff Gummmminn Hoofff!" came muffled cries of pain from below.

The creature started to move in a wobbly line across the clearing, picking up speed as the rider beat it harder. More men on these strange creatures arrived in the clearing, following the sound of the horn. They were just in time to catch the lead rider disappearing. They, too, beat their mounts. As they did, shouts of "Tallyho!" and "Gee-up!" could be heard over the cries from the beasts below.

The front legs of the last of these creatures came to a sudden halt. However, the back legs kept moving and, inevitably, caught up with the front ones. There was an *Ooof!* and a sweaty, red face emerged from the front of the creature. The head looked up at the rider and spoke.

A large, angry man rode high on its back.

"That's it, Trout! I have had enough! I want a go on top."

"But I only got a turn since the start of the woods, and you had a long go across the fields," moaned the rider. Another face

now emerged from the back end of the creature and joined in.
"Yes! And Gristle, you tried to make us jump that gate!"

A sweaty, red face emerged from the front of the creature.

"Well, I'm not going on, and I'll blame you two if we get in trouble for getting left behind," said the face at the front.

"All right then!" the rider said with a pout.

He jumped down, and as he took off his jacket and top hat, the creature's body lifted to reveal two men underneath. The man at the front unstrapped himself, and the rider took his place.

The creature's body lifted to reveal two men underneath.

The body lowered itself, and the new rider put on the jacket and hat and climbed with some difficulty into the saddle.

"Don't you dare try going through the stream," the back end of the creature demanded.

"All right, but make sure we catch up," said the new rider. "You know the rules about being last!"

He then grabbed a large twig from an overhanging branch, snapped it off, and belted the back end of his mount. With a short scream and some cursing, the creature set off. Quiet returned to the clearing.

With a short scream and some cursing, the creature set off.

The woods now disgorged a weird procession. First the cheeses, then after a few moments the hounds, followed by the huntsmen. Baying filled the night air as the hounds got a clear sight of their quarry. Fear drove the cheeses faster. The hounds gained on them, and as they did, the cheeses' bleating became ever more mournful.

Then the first of the cheese-hounds struck. One of the smaller

A weird procession.

cheeses was trailing a few yards behind the rest. It was an easy target. In one leap, the hound landed its front paws on the cheese. Whimpering and bleating, the cheese struggled to get free, but it was no good. Its legs buckled, and it collapsed on the grass. The dog rolled the cheese onto its side with its snout and held it down firmly with his paws. Most of the other hounds raced after the other fleeing cheeses, but a few dogs paused long enough to worry the trapped cheese, growling threateningly. As they did so, the leader of the hunt arrived on his mount and clonked it mercilessly with his horn.

"Back to the chase, you lazy dairy-pugs!" he yelled. "Gherkin! Deal with this 'ere cheese!"

In one leap, the hound landed its front paws on the cheese.

"Yes, Master!" replied a stubby rider close behind. He slowed his mount, stopped close to the cheese, and climbed down. Throwing a piece of dried bread to the ground to distract the hound, Gherkin put a boot on the cheese to keep it pinned down, then took some string from his pocket and tied it firmly to the cheese's ankle. Keeping a tight hold on the string, Gherkin climbed back onto his mount.

"Right. My boys, it's a gentle ride home for us," said Gherkin, stirring his mount back toward the town.

"Gherkin! Deal with this 'ere cheese!"

"It might be a gentle ride home for you, Gherkin, but it's a damnable long walk for us!" a muffled voice grunted from under the saddle. Still, off they set with the cheese in tow. The hunt was now in the distance, picking off the rest of the cheeses. Their mournful cries were replaced by a resigned silence.

Off they set with the cheese in tow.

The Cheese Hall.

chapter 3
FROM ON HIGH

He grabbed his doll from under his suit.

Arthur watched it all from his perch on top of the Cheese Hall. The procession drew closer to Ratbridge, and now he could make out most of the creatures involved. It slowly dawned on him what was happening. It was a cheese hunt!

He grabbed his doll from under his suit and raised it to his mouth.

"Grandfather! Grandfather! It's Arthur. Can you hear me?" There was a crackling and his grandfather replied.

"Yes, Arthur, I can hear you. What's happening?"

"I think I see a cheese hunt!"

There was a pause; then Grandfather spoke again. "Are you absolutely sure? Cheese hunting? Where are you?"

"I am sitting on top of the Cheese Hall. I am . . ."—Arthur decided to gloss over earlier events—". . . having a break. I can see the whole thing. Riders and hounds chasing and catching cheeses."

"But they can't! It's cruel and it's illegal!" Grandfather sputtered. "Are you sure there are riders on horses?"

"Yes, Grandfather. Why?"

"Because all the cheese-hunting horses were sold off to the Glue Factory after the Great Cheese Crash."

"They do seem to be riding horses."

"Well, they do seem to be riding horses . . . but there's something rather odd about them," Arthur told him.

"What is it?"

"They're very ungainly and somewhat oddly shaped. I can see that even from here. Who do you think is doing the hunting?"

"I am not sure," said Grandfather. "Where are they now?"

"They are approaching the West Gate."

"Well, they must be from the town then. If we could find out who was responsible, perhaps we could do something to put a stop to it. Do you think you could have a closer look without being seen?"

"Yes, I think so," Arthur said, starting to feel excited.

"Well, keep up on the roofs, and see if you can follow them." Grandfather paused. "*But . . .* be very careful!"

"Don't worry; I will be."

"And call me if you find out anything."

"All right. I'll speak to you later. And, Grandfather . . . I've got some bananas."

"Err . . . well . . . err . . . I rather like bananas. . . ." Grandfather's voice trailed off.

Arthur put the doll away and wound his wings again. Here at last was a chance for some real adventure.

Here at last was a chance for some real adventure.

The hunt wove its way into town.

chapter 4
INTO THE TOWN

He pulled out a large, black iron key.

By the time the Hunt reached the West Gate, they had nine cheeses in tow. The hounds were exhausted. As the chase was over, their muzzles had been removed. Snatcher, the leader of the hunt, maneuvered his mount till he was within arm's length of the thick wooden gate. He pulled a large, black iron key out of his topcoat, leaned over, and unlocked it. Gristle, on the horse behind him, dismounted and swung the gate open.

Arthur flew from the Cheese Hall to a rooftop near the gate and settled out of sight behind a parapet. He looked down.

In the street below, the hunt wove its way into town. It was a terrifying sight. Strange four-legged creatures were carrying very ugly men in very tall hats. A pack of manky hounds sniffed around behind them, and just visible in the shadows were tubby yellow cheeses tied with pieces of string to some of the riders. A cheese stumbled on the cobbles and let out a bleat.

"Quick!" hissed Snatcher. "Muffle 'im!"

One of the riders threw a large sack over the cheese and it fell silent. The rider scooped up the sack and the procession continued on its way.

He looked down.

Arthur moved along the parapet till he reached the end of the building. An alley divided him from the next house. He pressed the buttons on the front of his box, rose silently, and flew toward the next house. He was proud of himself—he had not made a single sound that attracted their attention. But what he had not accounted for was the position of the moon. As he crossed the alley, his shadow fell across the street.

The procession continued on its way.

Arthur's flapping shadow was too much for them.

Cheeses have many predators, but the one that they fear most is the Cheese Hawk. The merest hint of anything large and winged will send cheeses into a blind panic. Arthur's flapping shadow was too much for them. All hell broke loose.

One cheese let out a sharp cry. This set off the other cheeses. The riders, caught off guard, had the strings ripped from their hands as the cheeses bolted . . . straight under the

They, too, all piled into the heap.

legs of the "mounts." Two of the mounts tripped over the cheeses and collapsed, throwing their riders to the ground. The riders following them were unable to halt their mounts, and they, too, all piled into the heap. The hounds now went crazy. In their excited state, with no muzzles to hold them back, they set upon all the available human limbs sticking out

Just above Snatcher.

of the heap. This caused much screaming and wailing. In the middle of the confusion, only Snatcher and his mount were left standing. He looked up and caught Arthur in his stare.

"What do we have 'ere?" he said with a mixture of malice and curiosity.

Arthur watched the commotion in shock. Then, suddenly, his right wing gave a jerk. He twisted around and saw a large tear in it, and his heart sank. The banana woman's blow had left its mark.

Arthur started to drop. He grabbed for the knob and twisted it hard. Still he fell, his right wing dragging limply above him like a streamer. Snatcher was driving his mount toward the ground below him. In a last desperate attempt, Arthur reached for the handle on the side of the box and started to wind for all he was worth. The remaining wing sped up. Harder and harder he wound. His descent slowed to a stop . . . just above Snatcher.

His arm aching, Arthur wound even harder. Then he felt

something grab his ankle. He tried to pull away. There was a cackling from below.

"'Ow ingenious! I always rather fancied flying," came a voice.

"Let me go!" cried Arthur.

"I shall not!" came the reply, and Arthur felt a sharp tug swinging him around, and the tip of his broken wing poked Snatcher in the left eye.

"Wwwwaaaahhhh!!" Snatcher cried, releasing his grip on Arthur's ankle and putting his hands to his eye. As soon as he was released, Arthur rose a little. Still winding he kicked off from one of the walls and started down the alley. Behind him he could hear a very pained Snatcher.

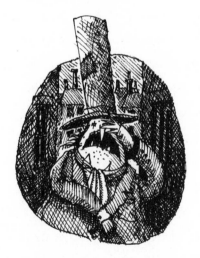

"Wwwwaaaahhhh!!"

"Get the little tyke!" screamed Snatcher.

Though he kept winding, it was impossible for Arthur to get high enough to escape over the roofs with the broken wing. He'd have to make his way through the streets and alleys to get

Snapping below.

back to the drain, he thought wildly. But the cheese-hounds were now snapping below him, and he wound faster still, trying to keep above their reach. . . .

Ahead of him the alley faded into darkness, and he turned through an archway into a yard beyond. With a start of relief, Arthur realized he knew where he was. The yard backed onto the lane where the drain—and the way home—was. He had a chance of getting there if his wings would just hold out. The wall dividing him from the lane was just a few feet higher than he was flying. He might just make it. The barking grew louder again. Arthur wound and adjusted the knob at the same time, twisting it with all his might and willing himself over the wall.

But the remaining wing could not take any more. With a sharp tearing noise, the leather tore away from the wing spars. Arthur frantically reached out for the wall, but it was no good. He was falling—and the cheese-hounds were waiting for him

below. Dropping to the ground, he spun around to face the drooling hounds, bracing himself for the worst. There seemed to be no way he could fight them off. Then he noticed the flailing wing spar. He tore it from his back and spun around to confront any dog that seemed to be getting closer. Then he

The drooling hounds.

noticed a water cask in the corner of the yard, next to the back wall. Perhaps if he could manage to get onto that, he might have a chance. Fending off the dogs, he moved toward the cask. The hounds moved with him. Then Arthur's heart sank again. Snatcher entered the yard. He quickly dismounted and walked toward Arthur, holding a hand over his injured eye.

"No, you don't, you little vermin. I have plans for you! And for your wings!" he wheezed.

The man's eye now was so swollen that it had closed.

"It's just as well that you poked me in me glass eye,"

Snatcher hissed, "or I'd have had to come up with something even more unpleasant than what I've got planned for you!"

"No, you don't, you little vermin."

Snatcher made a lunge for Arthur. Arthur jumped back and bumped into the cask. He was completely cornered.

"Now, boy, give me those wings of yours. I am very interested in contraptions! Take 'em off now! Now!" Snatcher ordered.

Arthur slowly reached for the buckle on one of his shoulders.

"Faster, boy!" Snatcher snapped. "Get 'em off quick, or I'll be setting the hounds on yer!"

Arthur released one buckle, then another, and finally the last one at his side. The wings were now loose.

"Give 'em 'ere!" Snatcher hissed.

Arthur slipped the wings over his head, and as he did so, Snatcher grabbed them.

Snatcher grabbed the wings.

"Clever, very clever . . . might well be useful!" Snatcher mused as he turned the remains of the wings over in his huge hands.

Arthur stood with his back against the water cask, glancing from the snapping dogs to Snatcher. Grandfather had warned him so many times about being careful. Now, having made just one mistake, he was in real trouble for the first time in his life. The dogs took their chance and moved closer.

Then one of the larger hounds made a lunge for him. Arthur kicked out just in time and caught the dog's nose with his toe. The dog pulled back with a whimper, and Snatcher looked up.

Arthur kicked out just in time.

"You just keep him there, me pugs." He smirked and turned back to his inspection.

Arthur slowly moved his hands back onto the cask, then stealthily, always keeping an eye on Snatcher, he pulled himself up till he was sitting on the edge of it. The hounds started to growl and strain forward, but Snatcher, absorbed in the wings, absentmindedly shushed them. Careful not to make a sound, Arthur raised his knees till his heels were resting on the edge of the cask.

The hounds started to growl and strain forward.

He glanced up at the top of the wall. One of the hounds let out a bark. Snatcher looked up and realized what was happening. He let out a cry of rage just as Arthur jumped up, grabbed the top of the wall, and pulled himself over it.

He fell flat to the ground on the other side. For a few seconds he lay there, his heart pounding, trying to catch his breath. Shouts of anger and barking emanated from over the wall.

"Get round the back and 'ave 'im, you mutts!" Snatcher bellowed. There was the sound of leather on dog and then a loud howling.

He fell flat to the ground.

Arthur scrambled to his feet and started for the drain cover at the far end of the lane. Then he heard the hounds coming around the corner. He wasn't going to make it. He ducked into a doorway in the wall, then peeped back out. Snatcher, surrounded by hounds, stood by the drain cover. There were more footsteps and the rest of the riders appeared.

"I think he went down here! Must live down below! Go and get the glue and an iron plate!" Snatcher ordered. A group of the hunters disappeared.

Snatcher, surrounded by hounds, stood by the drain cover.

Snatcher turned and scanned the alley. "Okay, the rest of you search the alley, just in case."

The men stood for a moment while hounds sniffed the air. Then the little dog that looked like a cross between a sausage dog and a ball of wire wool started to make his way down the alley directly toward Arthur. Arthur pressed his back against the door. This time there really was no way out. A shiver of fear went through him at the thought of what Snatcher would do when he got hold of him. Suddenly he felt the door give way behind him. Something grabbed him around the knees and pulled him through the doorway, and the door slammed shut.

Arthur pressed his back against the door.

The shop.

chapter 5

HERE BE MONSTERS!

It framed a boxtroll.

Arthur found himself standing in total darkness. The overwhelming relief at having got away from Snatcher and his hounds was mixed with the awful fear that he might have been dragged into something even worse. Who or what had pulled him through that door and why? A soft gurgling noise came from somewhere behind him. He turned round toward it and trod on something. There was a squeak, a scuffling of feet, and the sound of a doorknob being turned. Light broke in as a door opened. It framed a boxtroll, its smiling head protruding from its large cardboard box.

Arthur had seen boxtrolls before, underground. He had occasionally come across them as he explored the dark passages, caverns, and tunnels. Boxtrolls were timid creatures and always scuttled away as soon as they noticed his presence. Arthur had heard that boxtrolls loved everything mechanical, and he'd seen their work everywhere underground—draining the passages and shoring up the tunnels and caves. This was the first time

Arthur had seen one close at hand, and it now stood smiling and beckoning to him.

Arthur walked toward it hesitantly. The boxtroll turned and scampered up a huge heap of nuts and bolts that covered the floor of the room ahead. As it reached the top, it stopped and picked up a handful of the nuts and bolts. Arthur stared as it lifted them to its mouth and kissed them. It then sprinkled them back over the heap and grinned.

Then, beckoning to Arthur again, the boxtroll turned and scuttled out of the doorway on the other side of the room. Arthur clambered over the heap and followed it into a small hallway. Ahead of them was a paneled door. The top panels

The boxtroll turned again to Arthur and smiled.

were made of glass, and through them a warm yellow light shone. The boxtroll knocked on the door.

"Come on in, Fish!" a muffled voice replied.

The boxtroll turned again to Arthur and smiled. Then it opened the door, walked a few steps into the room, and cleared its throat.

"Well, what is it, Fish? What treasures have you brought to show us this evening?" a man's voice said from somewhere inside the room. "Come on then, let's have a look!"

The boxtroll reached back. It took Arthur's hand and led him into the room.

The old man sat in a high-backed, leather armchair.

Arthur's jaw fell open. From among the cages, tanks, boxes, old sofas, clocks, brass bedstead, piles of straw, heaps of books, and who knew what else, stared four pairs of eyes. There were two more boxtrolls sitting on a shelf, a small man with

a cabbage tied to the top of his head, and an old man. The old man sat in a high-backed, leather armchair. He was wearing half-glasses and a gray wig and was smiling at Arthur.

"Hello. Who do we have here?" the old man inquired in a gentle voice.

Arthur blinked. The old man waited patiently.

"I'm Arthur!" he finally said.

"Well, Arthur, are you a friend of Fish's?" the old man asked.

Two other boxtrolls made spluttering noises. The boxtroll holding Arthur's hand turned to him, squeezed his hand, and made a happy gurgling sound.

"Yes," said the old man, "I think you are!" He looked sternly at the two boxtrolls on the shelf. "And Shoe and Egg should know better than to snigger at Fish!" The two boxtrolls fell silent, their faces turning bright red.

The two boxtrolls fell silent, their faces turning bright red.

Arthur looked around the room. It was packed to overflowing. If you took a junk shop, added the contents of a small zoo, then threw all your household possessions on top, it would start to give you an idea of what it was like. It smelled a little of compost. But it was warm and quiet, everyone looked friendly, and, best of all, there were no hounds snapping at him.

He had no idea where he was, but he did know that he felt safe. Safe enough to ask a question himself.

"Please, sir, may I ask you who you are?" asked Arthur.

"Certainly, young man!" The old man grinned. "I am Willbury Nibble, Queen's Counsel . . . Retired! I was a lawyer, but now I live here with my companions."

Arthur looked about. "What is this place?"

"Oh, this was once a pet shop, but now I rent it to live in. And these are my friends," Willbury said, looking around at the creatures. "You have met Fish already it would seem, and these two reprobates"—he nodded at the other boxtrolls— "are Shoe and Egg."

The boxtrolls on the shelf smiled at Arthur. Then the old man turned to the last creature—the little man with the cabbage on his head. "And this is Titus. He is a cabbagehead."

The cabbagehead scurried behind the old man's chair.

"I am afraid he is rather nervous. He'll get used to you, though, and then you will find him charming."

"I am afraid he is rather nervous."

A cabbagehead! Grandfather had told Arthur stories about cabbageheads. Legend had it that they lived in the caverns deep underground. It was said that they grew strange vegetables there and worshiped cabbages. This had something to do with why they tied cabbages to their heads. Even Grandfather had not seen a cabbagehead, they were so shy.

They lived in the caverns deep underground.

Arthur thought for a moment, then asked, "Your friends are all underlings, so, well, why do they live with you?"

Willbury smiled with bemusement. "What do you know about underlings, Arthur?"

"I know that the boxtrolls look after the tunnels and plumbing underground. But I don't know much about cabbage-heads," Arthur admitted.

"Well, I am not sure I entirely approve, but our boxtroll friends here act as scouts." Willbury gave the boxtrolls a funny look.

"Scouts?" asked Arthur.

"Yes. It would seem that the boxtrolls have a need for certain supplies to help with their maintenance of the Underworld. So Fish, Shoe, and Egg wander the town looking for . . . 'supplies.' When they find them, they 'prepare' the item for removal—loosen it, unbolt it, unscrew it, whatever. That's why there is such a large heap of nuts and bolts in the back room. God help me if I am ever visited by the police."

"They 'prepare' the item for removal."

He looked rather severely at the boxtrolls, then resumed speaking. "They leave signs for the other boxtrolls. You may have seen strange chalk marks on the walls about town. These are there to guide the other boxtrolls to the supplies so they can make a quick getaway."

A quick getaway.

Arthur looked at Fish, who grinned and nodded.

"Well!" said Willbury, rather sternly. "I don't think I approve at all. Our friends the boxtrolls have a rather strange attitude toward ownership. Have you not noticed that most of your arrows point at someone else's property?"

The boxtrolls looked rather guilty. Arthur felt a little guilty himself remembering the bananas he had left on top of the Cheese Hall. He decided it'd be safer to change the subject. "And your friend Titus?"

Willbury beamed. "He is researching gardening. The cabbageheads are always trying to improve their methods of cultivation. So occasionally one of them spends some time up here studying human gardening methods. Egg and Shoe discovered him one night sleeping in a coalbunker and brought him back. He's been here for a few weeks writing up a report. When he's finished, he'll go back to the Underworld."

Willbury looked behind his chair and said coaxingly, "Titus, I think our new friend might like to see your report if you would like to show it to him."

The cabbagehead shot from behind Willbury's chair to a barrel that stood in one corner of the shop. There was a hole cut in its side just big enough for Titus to clamber through. He disappeared and re-emerged carrying something. He ran back and hid behind the chair. A hand offering a small green notebook appeared.

Willbury took the notebook and opened it. Arthur leaned over to look. The pages were covered with tiny writing and the most beautiful drawings of plants.

A squeak came from behind the chair. Willbury closed the notebook, winked at Arthur, and passed it over his shoulder to an outstretched hand. The notebook disappeared.

The pages were covered with tiny writing and drawings.

"Now, Arthur, please sit down if you wish." Willbury lifted his feet from a footstool and pushed it toward Arthur. "So what brings you here?" he asked.

Arthur suddenly felt overwhelmed. He sat. He didn't know where to begin. Fish came forward and started talking. "Hummif gommmong shoegger tooff!!!"

Arthur suddenly felt overwhelmed.

"I think it would be better if Arthur himself explained what's happened, Fish," said Willbury. He smiled encouragingly at Arthur. "Are you in trouble?"

"Yes," whispered Arthur. There was a pause.

"Well, let's hear what kind of trouble it is. We'll try to help you if we can. I have spent my whole life sorting out trouble for other people," said Willbury.

Arthur hesitated, then decided he could trust Willbury. "Yes, I am in trouble. They've blocked my hole back. It's the only way I know to get home. And they have taken my wings!" Speaking the words aloud made Arthur realize fully what a terrible situation he was in.

"All right," said Willbury, leaning forward, looking both confused and concerned. "I think you better tell me the full story."

Arthur started. "I'm from the underground . . . well, I have lived there since I was a baby."

Willbury looked curious. "Underground?"

"Yes. Me and my grandfather live in a cave . . . well, three caves, actually. One we use as a living room and kitchen, another is Grandfather's bedroom and workshop, and the smallest is mine. It's my bedroom." Arthur looked around the shop. "It's warm and cozy, a bit like this place."

"Well, three caves, actually."

"But why do you live underground?" Willbury asked in a puzzled voice.

Arthur paused for a few moments. "I'm . . . I'm not really sure. Grandfather always tells me he'll explain when I'm older."

"And what about your parents?"

Arthur looked sad. "I don't know. . . . I am a 'foundling,' I think."

"But your grandfather?"

"Oh . . . he's not my real grandfather; he just found me abandoned on the steps of the poorhouse, when I was a baby, and took me to live with him. He's raised me like he is my father, but because he's so much older than my father would be, I call him 'Grandfather.'"

"So, has he always lived underground?"

Arthur thought for a moment. "No, he said he lived in the town when he was younger. But he doesn't talk about it. . . ."

Willbury seemed to realize he was upsetting the boy with so many personal questions, so he asked next: "You say 'they' have blocked your hole back to the underground and taken your wings? Who are 'they'?"

Arthur grew instantly animated. "I saw these men hunting cheese and I went to have a look, but my wings broke and the hunters took them, and then I escaped and was trying to get back down underground when they blocked up my hole."

"But what were you doing aboveground? And what wings? I don't understand," said Willbury.

Arthur decided to tell Willbury all. "I was gathering food." His face grew red, but he continued. "It's the only way we can survive. My grandfather is so frail now that I have to do it. And he made me some wings so I could get about the town easily."

"Your grandfather made you *wings*?"

"Yes, he can make anything. He made my doll as well so I

could talk to him from anywhere." Arthur reached inside his under-suit and pulled out the doll to show Willbury.

Willbury's eyes grew wide. "Do you mean to say that you can talk with your grandfather, using this doll?"

"Yes," said Arthur.

"Does it still work?" asked Willbury.

"Yes . . . I think so." Arthur looked at the doll closely—it didn't look damaged in any way.

Arthur looked at the doll closely.

"When did you last speak to your grandfather?"

"An hour or so ago, when I was sitting on top of the Cheese Hall."

"On top of—oh, never mind. Does he know what's happened to you or where you are?"

"No . . . ," said Arthur.

"Well, I suggest you speak to your grandfather right now to let him know you are all right and that you are here," Willbury insisted. All the eyes in the room fixed on Arthur and the doll. "I should like to talk to him also, if I may?" he added.

Arthur nodded. He wound the tiny handle on the box on the front of the doll. There was a gentle crackling noise, and then grandfather's voice broke through.

"Arthur, Arthur, are you out there?"

"Yes! Yes! It's me! Grandfather, it's me! Arthur!" Arthur yelped. It was such a relief to hear his voice.

"Arthur! Where are you? I've been so worried. Are you all right?" Grandfather's voice sounded shaky.

"I followed the cheese hunt like you told me to. I did try to be careful, Grandfather, but the huntsmen tried to catch me. They took my wings! And sealed up the drain! But I've escaped and found a safe place . . . and someone who can help me!" Arthur reassured him. "I'm in an old shop, with a man called Willbury. He wants to speak to you."

"Certainly—please pass the doll to him," Grandfather told Arthur. Arthur gave the doll to Willbury, who had been looking at it a little uneasily. Willbury cleared his throat.

"Good evening, sir."

"Good evening, sir. This is Willbury Nibble speaking. I have Arthur with me in my home. I haven't heard the full story, but it sounds as if he has had a terrible time. I would just like to say that you have my word, as a gentleman, that while your grandson is in my charge, I shall do all within my power to keep him safe. I shall also endeavor to help him return to you as soon as may be!"

"Thank you, Mr. Nibble!" replied Grandfather. "If you could help Arthur get back to me safely, I would be very grateful!"

Arthur moved closer to the doll. "Grandfather, how am I going to get back now that the huntsmen have blocked up the drain?"

For a moment there was just a gentle hissing and crackling from the doll; then they heard Grandfather's voice again. "I know there are other routes between the town and the Underworld. But I don't know where they are. They belong to other creatures." There was a mixture of frustration and worry in his voice, and Arthur grew even more glum—he hated to cause his grandfather worry.

"Sir," replied Willbury, "I have a number of boxtrolls and a cabbagehead living with me. They may know of a way!" He looked around and was met by nodding heads. Even Titus had come out of hiding and was nodding.

"Yes! It seems they do," Willbury said. "I will have them guide Arthur back to you!"

"Thank you!" came the voice from the doll.

Arthur looked at the creatures gratefully. Of course—it was such a simple answer. He needn't have been so worried. Then Willbury spoke again.

"I think it might be a bit risky with these blackguards who chased Arthur roaming about. I suggest we wait till early tomorrow morning, then Fish and the others can find Arthur a hole."

"I agree, Mr. Nibble. I think Arthur has had enough excitement for one evening." Then Grandfather paused for a moment. "Getting Arthur back is my first concern. But I am worried about his wings. Without them, he won't be able to collect food for us safely. . . ."

"I understand your concern, sir. I am not sure where they are or how we might get them back, but I will think on it. Do you have enough food for the moment?" asked Willbury.

"Yes, I have several large clumps of rhubarb growing under the bed," said Grandfather.

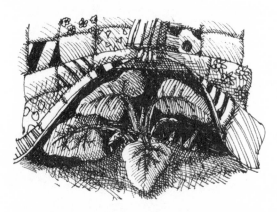

"I have several large clumps of rhubarb."

"Good. We'll give Arthur a good supper, and there is plenty of space for him to sleep here."

"Thank you so much, Mr. Nibble. And, Arthur, look after yourself. . . . I need you back!" said Grandfather.

"I will, Grandfather. Good night."

"Good night, Arthur, and I shall see you in the morning."

The doll fell silent, and Arthur took it back from Willbury. He kissed it and tucked it back in his under-suit.

"Why don't we have a little something to eat, and Arthur can finish telling us his story," Willbury suggested, looking at Arthur. Then, turning to Titus, he said, "Titus, get the big forks!"

A huge smile shot across Titus's face, and he disappeared back inside the barrel for a moment. He returned, carrying massive three-foot forks. Willbury leaned down and Titus whispered in his ear.

"Yes, Titus! Go and get the buns . . . and the cocoa bucket," Willbury said.

Titus bounded out of the door at the back of the shop and returned carrying a huge plate of buns and a large zinc-plated bucket full of cocoa. He set them by the fire, and the other creatures, Willbury, and Arthur gathered around him. Willbury hung the bucket on a hook over the fire, and after a few minutes it was slowly bubbling. Everybody took a fork and started to toast the buns. When the buns were crisp, they dipped them in the cocoa before eating them.

Arthur finished his story as they ate. He told of how he would come up every night to gather food, usually from trash bins from behind stores and restaurants. Grandfather said it was shocking, the food people threw away! But because when Arthur came up today and realized it was a Sunday, he had to go "gardening." Then, rather shamefacedly, he told of his raid on the greenhouse and how he had been struck by the woman;

of his flight to the Cheese Hall and how he had seen the hunt and had tried to spy on them; then of all that had followed.

The boxtrolls listened in awe as they sucked on their buns, and Titus got so caught up in the story that he hid behind Willbury when Arthur mentioned the hounds. Arthur finished his tale and looked toward Willbury, who was staring into the fire.

"It has been quite an adventure, Arthur. You poor lad. Let's get you a big drink of cocoa, then off to bed with you. A good night's sleep will do wonders," Willbury said, taking the cocoa off the fire. When it had cooled a little, they all took turns drinking straight from the bucket. Arthur felt much better.

Drinking cocoa straight from the bucket.

"Now, let's get our heads down. We need to be bright and fresh for the morning!" said Willbury.

The creatures found places for themselves around the room and nestled down while Willbury made up a bed for Arthur under the shop counter, out of old velvet curtains. Arthur took

off his hat and climbed in. Willbury tucked another curtain around him.

"You sleep well, Arthur. I have an idea where we might make inquiries about your wings in the morning."

Willbury left Arthur to settle, and the light in the shop went out. Arthur pulled the soft velvet covers over his head. The curtain felt heavy and gave off rather a comforting dusty smell. Arthur lay quietly in the darkness and started to think. *It will be good to get back to Grandfather tomorrow. But my wings . . . I can't lose those. . . . I wonder what Willbury meant when he said he had an idea?*

His thoughts became slower as sleep overtook him. Soon all that could be heard was gentle snoring.

Soon all that could be heard was gentle snoring.

Snatcher.

chapter 6
THE CEREMONY

Snatcher raised the pole.

Across the town from where Arthur slept, deep within the heart of the Cheese Hall, the huntsmen and their mounts were getting changed. They stripped down to their long johns and, from cases stored under the benches that bordered the room, they took out furry capes, hats, and some battered musical instruments. They donned the clothes, picked up the instruments, and made their way through a small wooden door into a hexagonal chamber. The chamber was some twenty feet across, about thirty feet high, with a vaulted ceiling. In the center of the floor was a deep circular hole. If one had looked into the hole, one might have seen a bubbling mass of sticky yellow cheese far below. This was the Fondue Pit.

Watching from a balcony was Snatcher. He was dressed in the same furry robes and hat as the other huntsmen, but in his hand he held a wooden pole. At its tip was a gilded duck. A piece of string went from the duck's head to Snatcher's hand. When the huntsmen had settled down, Snatcher raised the pole and waved it

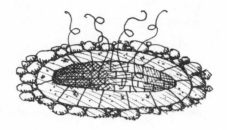

The Fondue Pit.

slowly over his head. The huntsmen started to play on their instruments. Some had drums, and others, strange horns. The noise was awful and grew louder and louder, till Snatcher pointed his duck stick at the hole and pulled the string. The huntsmen immediately stopped playing. The duck's mouth opened and emitted an eerie quack. The quack faded away, leaving only the sound of bubbling molten cheese. Snatcher spoke.

"Members of the Guild, we are on our way to wreaking revenge on this appalling town. Soon we will be unstoppable!"

The men assembled in the chamber cheered. Snatcher raised his duck stick and the crowd grew silent.

"It is time to feed the Great One! Gristle, lower the cage," Snatcher's voice boomed.

From somewhere above, there was a clanking of chains and the bleating of a cheese. Slowly a cage came into view. In it was one of the cheeses gathered from the hunt. The crowd watched

The duck stick.

in silence as the cage went lower and lower until it disappeared into the pit. After a few more seconds the bleating became more frenzied. Then suddenly it stopped, and the chain went slack.

There was another clank from high above, the chain tightened, and the cage emerged from the pit. It was empty except for a few strands of cheese, which stretched, then broke from the bottom of the cage.

Slowly a cage came into view.

Snatcher raised the duck stick. Again it opened its mouth and quacked.

"More cheese, Mr. Gristle!" Snatcher ordered, and gave an evil chuckle.

A model of Ratbridge.

chapter 7
WHICH HOLE?

He sat up and banged his head.

Arthur woke up with a start. He sat up and banged his head on the wooden shelf above him. Then he remembered where he was. Pale daylight filled the space between the counter and the wall behind it. A face popped into view and smiled at him.

"Good morning, Fish!" Arthur said, rubbing his head.

Fish gurgled in a friendly way and disappeared. He returned a moment later carrying the cocoa bucket. Arthur swung himself from under the counter and took the bucket—there were only a

He returned a moment later carrying the cocoa bucket.

couple of inches of the rich, dark liquid in the bottom. Obviously, he realized, he must be the last one up. He lifted the bucket and drank the lot. Fish giggled, then took the bucket back. Arthur wiped his mouth on the hem of his string vest and burped.

"Thank you. I needed that."

Willbury appeared behind the counter wearing a worn dressing gown of green silk.

"Good morning, Arthur. I hope you slept well! I think we had better get ready. It's still early, but it's market day, so the streets will get busy quite soon, and I know the underlings prefer it when there are not many people about."

Arthur followed Willbury and Fish out from behind the counter and almost walked into a pile of books. A complex

"We have made a model of the town."

He handed them each a silver coin.

pattern of books covered most of the floor. The other creatures stood around its edges.

"What's this?" asked Arthur.

"It's Ratbridge," replied Willbury. "My friends here don't really understand maps, so we have made a model of the town with all its buildings and streets. This way we can plan our expedition."

Arthur looked again at the books on the floor. There before him lay every street and building, defined by books and other objects from the shop. It was astonishing! He looked about and got his bearings. Then he pointed to a small dictionary. "That's where we are!"

"Yes!" said Willbury, laughing. "It works quite well, doesn't it?"

"Well, where have we got to go?"

The underlings started chattering, and each of them pointed at a different part of the "town." There seemed to be some difference of opinion.

"Hmmm. There are more holes than I imagined, and it seems the underlings each has a favorite one," said Willbury. He turned to them. "I will give each of you a six-groat coin, and I want you to place it where your hole is." He handed them each a silver coin. The creatures carefully leaned over the model and placed down their coins. Willbury surveyed the positions of the holes.

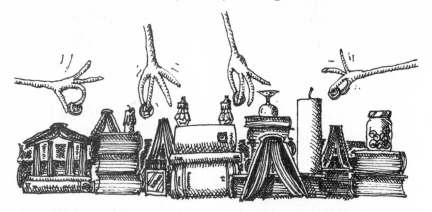

The creatures placed down their coins.

"I rather like the idea of Titus's hole. It's nice and close," he finally declared. The boxtrolls all laughed. Willbury looked at them, puzzled.

"What is it? What's wrong with Titus's hole?" he asked.

The boxtrolls squeaked and made signs at Arthur and Titus.

"Oh, of course," said Willbury. "Titus's hole *would* be too small for Arthur." He turned to Titus. Titus reluctantly nodded.

Willbury turned back to the boxtrolls. "Well then, what do you suggest?" Fish seemed the most insistent. He kept pointing at his coin, which was placed among books that made the shape of houses and gardens near the edge of town.

Willbury's eyes traced a route from the shop to Fish's coin. "It seems to me that Fish may have a point. Arthur should have no trouble fitting down a boxtroll hole, and we could get there very quietly down these back streets." Willbury indicated the route with a walking stick. "If we find there are too many people about, we can always divert and make our way to one of the other holes. We'll set off right after breakfast." He turned to Arthur. "I am sure your grandfather is anxious to see you again."

Arthur paused. "But what about my wings?"

"Yes . . . well . . . ," replied Willbury. "I told you I had an idea. Based on what you said about the man who took them, it occurred to me that he must be someone who knows about mechanical things and the like. I know a person who knows most people in that line. Finding her may take some time as I have not seen her about recently, so I think it better that we get you back to your grandfather first."

Arthur's heart sank. "But . . . if I go back without his wings, Grandfather will be so disappointed in me. . . ."

"Well, you don't need to worry about that. I'll go to the market this morning and get you some food. I have to go anyway as we are out of buns." Willbury looked around indulgently at the creatures. He turned back to Arthur. "Come back tonight and I will have plenty for you to take back to the Underworld."

Then Willbury gave Arthur a rather disapproving look. "Mind you, I don't hold with taking other people's things. None of this would have happened if you hadn't helped yourself to that lady's bananas. Now, everybody collect up these books and put everything away, and I'll make breakfast."

"I don't hold with taking other people's things."

Arthur, the boxtrolls, and Titus set about tidying the floor, then hovered around the fireplace where Willbury was using the cocoa bucket to make porridge.

"I am afraid it may taste a little chocolaty," apologized Willbury.

"I think I should rather like that," replied Arthur, and the other creatures nodded in agreement.

Willbury grinned. "Well, then I shall add more cocoa and sugar. It will cut out the need to make cocoa afterward. Titus, would you be so good as to fetch the bowls and spoons?"

After finishing the cocoa porridge, which everyone declared a success, Willbury excused himself and reappeared a few minutes later, fully dressed. Then he unbolted the front door, and the little band set off through the deserted streets.

Willbury was using the cocoa bucket to make porridge.

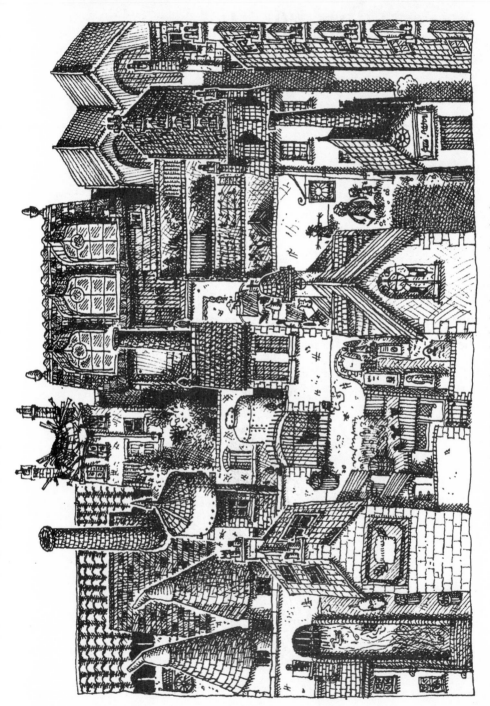

The group made their way through the back streets of Ratbridge.

chapter 8
SEARCH FOR A HOLE?

The boxtrolls trotted ahead.

The boxtrolls trotted ahead as the group made their way through the back streets of Ratbridge. At each corner the boxtrolls checked for humans, then waved the group on. As yet they had the town to themselves. When they passed a carpentry workshop, Willbury pointed to some blue chalk marks on the cobbles.

At each corner the boxtrolls checked for humans.

"I think Fish has been here recently," he said to Arthur. Arthur's eyes followed the direction of the arrow drawn on the street. It pointed to a pale strip of brickwork where a drainpipe had once been fixed. "Yes, I really must have words with him," Willbury added.

The group moved on. Within ten minutes they were approaching the site of Fish's hole.

Fish stopped by a door in a garden wall.

Fish, taking the lead, stopped by a door in a garden wall. He signed to the others to keep quiet and follow him. He pushed at the door and they all made their way into an overgrown garden. It was clear that the house that it belonged to was deserted. They followed Fish up the garden path, carefully avoiding brambles. He led the way to a brick outbuilding, and opened its door. Then he let out an anguished squeak.

The others crowded around to see what had upset him.

A large, rusty iron plate covered the floor inside. Dried black glue bulged from around its edges.

Dried black glue bulged from around its edges.

Fish started to make gobbling noises.

"Confound it!" said Willbury. Then he looked at the boxtrolls. Shoe and Egg were comforting Fish.

"Let's see if we can lift it," said Willbury. "If we get a large stick, we could try to force it under the edge."

An old spade.

Arthur spotted an old spade in the brambles and hurried to fetch it. Willbury smiled. "Good thinking, Arthur. I think Fish is the strongest one here. Give him the spade and let him try." Fish tried to push it under the edge of the iron plate, but the glue was so hard that even after a great deal of effort, he made no impression.

He made no impression.

"I don't think we should worry too much, Fish. The hole must have been found when someone was doing repairs on the house, and they just covered it up," said Willbury consolingly. "Let's try another hole."

Fish frowned. He threw the spade down in a rather bad-tempered way.

"Fish! That is not the sort of behavior I expect from a boxtroll. Pick that up and leave it neatly against the wall, please," Willbury said sternly.

Fish looked huffy but did what he was told.

"Shoe, I think your hole is the closest one to here. Let's go there," Willbury continued. Then he put his hand on Arthur's shoulder. "Don't worry. We'll have you back home before you can say 'Jack Robinson.'"

The group set off again, this time following Shoe. Fish

trailed behind, muttering to himself and kicking every pebble he found in his path.

The butcher's shop.

They passed through a few more streets, then arrived outside a butcher's shop. Shoe led them up the side alley next to the shop and into a walled yard. On one side was a derelict pigsty. Shoe looked about to check that nobody was watching them, then opened the pigsty's gate and went inside. He came back out looking distraught. He took Willbury's hand and led him into the sty. Arthur and the others followed. Old straw had been pushed up around the edges of the sty, revealing another large iron plate.

On one side was a derelict pigsty.

"Oh dear!" muttered Willbury. "This looks bad. Two holes both sealed up!"

"Three if you count mine," said Arthur.

"You're right, Arthur. This seems more than a coincidence," said Willbury, sounding worried.

Arthur was also starting to feel worried. He moved forward and took a long look at the iron plate. "This is how the huntsmen sealed up my hole last night." Getting home suddenly did not seem so straightforward after all.

Willbury rubbed at his chin. "I'm beginning to suspect these things could be connected. We had better go and check the other holes forthwith," he said.

Egg now came forward and gurgled to Willbury.

"Yes, Egg! Let's check your hole. Hopefully we'll have more luck there."

A few people were now out and about, pushing handcarts toward the market. The boxtrolls looked uneasy. Titus nervously tried to keep Arthur between himself and the humans.

Egg led them quickly to a rubbish heap behind the Glue Factory, where he immediately started pulling pieces of junk away from one end of the heap. After a few moments he stopped. Sunlight glinted off an iron plate. . . .

In silence Egg turned and looked back at them. The boxtrolls started to make an agitated mewing sound. Willbury walked over to the iron plate and stared. Arthur joined him, feeling increasingly alarmed.

"Why would anyone do this?" he asked.

"I am not sure . . . but I have a very bad feeling about it. We should check Titus's hole to see if the same thing has happened there." Willbury turned and spoke to Titus, who was trembling all over. "Can you show us your hole please?"

Titus nodded his head and the group set off again, this time at a real pace. The streets were now filling and the little group was getting a lot of stares. Titus was so concerned about getting to his hole that he hardly noticed the onlookers and even dared to lead them.

He hardly noticed the onlookers.

They went up and down so many streets that Arthur wasn't sure where they were anymore. Titus moved more and more quickly. Then he disappeared around a corner into an alley. The others turned the corner to see Titus in the distance, running toward a drain. Before he reached it, he stopped.

The others caught up to find Titus whimpering to himself. This time, for several seconds no one said a word. They just stared at the large iron sheet covering the drain. Finally Willbury spoke. "I'm so sorry, Arthur, but I'm not sure what to do. This is terrible . . . and I don't think we know of any more holes."

Arthur did not know what to say. The thought of never going home again was too much to bear.

Willbury took Arthur's hand and gave it a squeeze. Then Fish made a noise.

"GeeeGoooW!"

"GeeeGoooW!"

The other boxtrolls turned to look at him and repeated the noise. "GeeeGoooW! GeeeGoooW! GeeeGoooW!"

Fish turned to Willbury and started to jump up and down. The other boxtrolls joined in. Even Titus was nodding eagerly.

"What is it?" asked Willbury.

The underlings all pointed down the street.

Willbury grasped Arthur's arm. "I think they know of another hole, Arthur."

The underlings nodded.

"Well, let's go!" said Willbury. And they began to run.

The wet dry dock.

chapter 9
THE WET DRY DOCK

A freshwater sea-cow.

Not far from the back of the Cheese Hall was a disused dry dock. This was connected to the canal by a short channel. It was no longer dry, as its huge wooden gates were open and hanging from their hinges. The hulks of several boats were partially submerged in the murky water, and the occasional bubble rose up and broke the weedy surface. If you listened very carefully, you might have heard a low, rumbling, mooing sound coming from its depths.

Willbury and Arthur looked expectantly at the boxtrolls. The boxtrolls peered into the water. Then some more bubbles broke the surface. The boxtrolls grinned and clapped their hands excitedly. Fish looked up and down the footpath and spotted a clump of grass. He pulled it up and tossed it into the water, near where the bubbles had emerged. It sank slowly. And just as slowly, something large moved under the water.

Arthur was startled. "Quick, Willbury! Did you see that?"

"Yes, I did. . . . I'm not sure what it is."

Fish spotted a clump of grass.

Fish, Shoe, and Egg were now running up and down the bank, gathering vegetation. When they had a small heap, they nodded to one another, gathered it up, and threw it into the water. They all waited.

A large, hairy, pink muzzle broke the surface of the water, right in the middle of the floating vegetation.

"Oh my word!" said Willbury. "I have never seen one of *those* before."

"What is it? What is it?" Arthur asked impatiently.

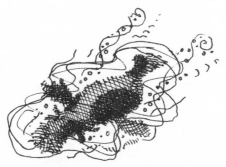

Something large moved under the water.

"I believe it's a freshwater sea-cow!"

The boxtrolls nodded. The freshwater sea-cow lifted its head above the water, revealing two large, gentle eyes and a pair of

short horns. The creature was huge. Arthur stared in awe at its enormous black-and-white body floating beneath the water. It began to vacuum up the greenery with its huge floppy nose. With a couple of breathy sucks the food was gone. The sea-cow sank back down till only its eyes and horns were visible above the water. It looked very sad.

A large, hairy, pink muzzle broke the surface of the water.

Fish crept closer to the water's edge, crouched down, and held out some dandelion leaves. Slowly the sea-cow moved toward him, raised its head, and sucked in the leaves. Fish's hand got covered in slobber, but he kept very still. Then very carefully he reached out with his other hand and patted the sea-cow's nose. The group watched in silence.

Fish made gentle gurgling noises as he stroked the pink muzzle, and the sea-cow held still. Then it let out a deep sigh. Fish made a mewing sound and the sea-cow replied with another sigh.

Arthur tugged on Willbury's arm. "I think he's talking to it!"

Fish and the sea-cow continued to gurgle and sigh at each other, then the sea-cow sunk back into the water and vanished. Bubbles rose from the pool and then all was still.

Fish stood back up. He looked very upset.

"What is it, Fish?" asked Willbury.

Fish started to jabber. As he did so, Willbury leaned down so Titus could whisper a translation. Willbury looked more and more uneasy. When Fish had finished, Willbury turned to Arthur, his face pale. "Something tragic has happened. That poor sea-cow!" he said, his voice trailing off.

"What is it?" whispered Arthur.

"Well, the freshwater sea-cows live in waterways under the town. They use a tunnel that extends from the dry dock to come out into the canal to feed. That sea-cow has three calves. A few days ago she left them here to play while she went off to forage in the canal. When she returned, the calves were gone, and the tunnel blocked."

Fish held out some dandelion leaves.

Fish slowly nodded. The group stood very still.

"What can we do?" asked Arthur.

"I'm not sure, Arthur. I'm not sure," said Willbury very quietly. Then he turned to the underlings. "Do you know of any more holes?"

The underlings slowly shook their heads.

Willbury gazed into the water for a while, tutting to himself, then said, "I really have no idea what is going on. I think it best if we all go back to the shop."

Fish's hand got covered in slobber.

He headed back up the path. The others followed in silence. As they trailed through the now crowded streets, Titus gripped Arthur's hand. Things did not look good.

Willbury.

chapter 10

The Return

"Grandfather! Are you there?"

As soon as they were inside the shop, Willbury told Arthur to call his grandfather. "He needs to know what's going on." Arthur nodded in agreement.

He reached under his shirt for the doll, wound the handle, and soon the familiar crackling could be heard.

"Grandfather! Are you there?"

Grandfather's voice came back straightaway.

"Arthur, where are you? Are you underground yet?"

"No . . . I'm not," Arthur replied. "We've tried, but all the underlings' holes have been blocked up."

There was a pause. Then they heard Grandfather again.

"Where are you now?"

"I am back at the shop with Mr. Nibble."

"Can you let me speak to him, please?"

Arthur passed the doll to Willbury.

"Hello, sir," said Willbury.

"Every entrance has been sealed up."

"Hello, Mr. Nibble. This doesn't sound good at all. Have you any idea what is going on?"

"Frankly . . . no. We have tried five entrances to the Underworld, and every one has been sealed up. With Arthur's, that makes six."

"Do you think that lot who chased Arthur last night are sealing up the holes to stop Arthur from getting back underground?"

"I don't think so. Some of the holes have been sealed up for some time. It's not just about Arthur. . . ."

There was another pause.

"Do you have any clue who this bunch of ruffians are?" asked Grandfather.

Willbury thought for a moment. "I don't, but there is someone I know who is well up in the world of inventions. She knows everyone with an interest in mechanics in Ratbridge. She might know the man who took Arthur's wings."

"If you could follow up that lead, I would be very grateful."

"I'm going to the market for food and will visit my friend after that," replied Willbury.

"Thank you, Nibble." Then he asked, "This business with the cheese hunting? It's been illegal for years now. In the old days it was the Cheese Guild that did the hunting, but the Guild was said to have died out when the trade was banned."

"Do you think the blocked holes might be something to do with that?" asked Willbury.

"Years ago, when I lived aboveground, there were *rumors* about the Cheese Guild. Nothing specific . . . just the odd story of 'goings-on' . . . secret meetings and the like."

Willbury looked pensive. "If you don't mind me asking— why *do* you live underground?"

There was a long pause.

There was a long pause. When Grandfather finally replied, there was a steely tone to his voice that Arthur had never heard before. "I was accused of a crime that I did not commit. I have had to take refuge here ever since."

Arthur felt his skin prickle. This was the closest he had ever come to finding out the reason for their life underground. Would Grandfather say more? What sort of crime could have driven him underground for so long? He looked up and found Willbury's gaze upon him. Then Grandfather continued.

"I've kept it from Arthur as I felt he was too young to understand. But please believe me when I say you have my word as a gentleman that I am an innocent man."

"I believe you, sir," said Willbury. Then nodding at Arthur he added, "We shall leave it at that. I think Arthur may be old enough to understand. But I also think it better he hears this sort of thing from you face-to-face."

"Thank you."

Willbury looked at Arthur one more time, then asked another question. "On a more immediate matter: Do you have enough food?"

"Yes. The rhubarb seems to be thriving. I think I have a few days' supply."

"Well, hopefully we can get this matter sorted out very quickly."

"I do hope so," said Arthur quietly.

"Yes. I am sure my friend will be able to help," said Willbury.

"Can you call me as soon as you know anything?"

"I'll make certain of it."

"Thank you. And Arthur. . . . *You take care*, my boy."

"All right, Grandfather!" said Arthur. He took the doll from Willbury. "I will be very careful. And I will be back . . . soon!"

Arthur was trying to sound positive, but he actually felt less sure than ever of when he was going to get home.

"Speak to you later then," said Grandfather.

"Good-bye . . . till later!" Arthur put the doll away.

"Right!" said Willbury firmly. "I think we need a good feed. I can always think better on a full stomach. Let's draw up a shopping list." Though Willbury's voice sounded chipper, his face looked grim.

Arthur could tell that Willbury was as worried as he was but that he was trying to keep everyone's spirits up. If he could put a brave face on the situation, then Arthur would too. The boxtrolls and Titus needed him to be strong, so he tried to raise a smile as they all sat down around the shop. Willbury took out a quill and a scrap of paper from under his chair.

Then there was a knock.

Willbury took out a quill and a scrap of paper.

A rather grubby man.

chapter 11

A Visit

Everyone turned to the door.

Everyone turned to the door. Through the window they could see the tall shadow of a figure standing outside.

Willbury put his finger to his mouth. "Quiet!" he whispered. "It may be the hunters looking for Arthur. Arthur, quick, hide behind the counter."

Arthur obeyed without hesitation. He never wanted to see the huntsmen again if he could help it. The memory of their leader's sneering face still made him shudder. He got back down into the space where he had slept the night before. There was a crack in the woodwork, and by placing his eye close to it, he could still see the shop door. He watched as Willbury unlocked the door and stepped back.

A rather grubby man wearing a frock coat and a top hat stood on the doorstep. He held a large box in his arms, and on the ground by his side was a bucket.

"Excuse me, sir," he said in an oily voice. "My name is Gristle, and I represent the Northgate Miniature Livestock

A bucket.

Company. I was wondering if you might be interested in buying some rather small creatures?"

Willbury looked quizzically at the box and then stared at the bucket. "Err ... umm ... you know this is not a pet shop anymore?" he said slowly. "What are they?"

"They are the very latest thing! Miniatures! Little versions of some of the pet industry's bestsellers."

Mr. Gristle put down the box and, with a flourish, took off the lid. Willbury took a look at the contents of the box and couldn't help smiling.

"You wouldn't like to do a swap, would you?"

"They're beautiful!" he said, squatting down. Then he frowned. "But they don't seem very happy."

"No," replied Gristle. "I think it's a by-product of the breeding."

The underlings had become curious. They shyly moved closer.

"You wouldn't like to do a swap, would you? I'm looking for *big* creatures," Gristle said, eyeing up Willbury's companions. All the big creatures pulled away and hid behind Willbury.

All the big creatures hid behind Willbury.

"Certainly not!" Willbury blurted, outraged. Then his curiosity got the better of him. "What's in the bucket?"

Arthur was also immensely curious, but the underlings were obscuring his view. He would have to wait, he told himself.

"A little spotty swimming thing. I believe it's from Peru," said Gristle.

"How much do you want for them?" asked Willbury.

"How would five groats sound?" said Gristle in a hopeful
sort of way.

"It would sound very expensive!" replied Willbury.

"Well, three groats, five farthings. It's my last offer. I can
always take them to the pie shop." Gristle smirked.

Willbury looked shocked. The underlings gasped collec-
tively. Willbury took out his leather coin bag and gave Gristle
the money.

Willbury took out his leather coin bag.

"Thank you, squire! Are you sure you don't want to part
with any of your *big* friends?" Gristle asked again.

"Absolutely not! Now, be off with you!" Willbury had
taken a distinct dislike to Mr. Gristle. He lifted the box and
the bucket off the doorstep and into the shop and closed the
door on the salesman.

The letter box flipped open.

"I really am very interested in your *big* friends, sir. I'm sure
we could come to some arrangement?" came the disembodied
voice of Mr. Gristle.

"Go AWAY!" said Willbury, starting to get angry.

The letter box closed for a moment, and then a ten-groat
banknote appeared, held by two long, thin, grubby fingers.

"Pretty please," whispered Gristle.

The fingers started to wave the note. Willbury took a lone cucumber from the vegetable box that was on the floor.

"I'm warning you. GO AWAY! I do not sell friends!" Willbury was turning red.

Another banknote held by another pair of fingers slipped through the letter box and started waving.

"Oh, go on! Twenty groats. They are only dumb old underlings," the voice said.

"Oh, go on!"

This was too much for Willbury. He raised the cucumber and brought it down on the letter-box flap. There was a *Splut!* as the cucumber hit the flap, a *Snap!* as the flap closed on the fingers, and a scream from outside. The fingers and the banknotes disappeared.

"You'll be sorry for this!" came a muffled shout. Then they heard the sound of footsteps hurrying away.

A silence settled over the shop.

"You can come out now, Arthur," Willbury finally said.

Arthur joined the group huddled around the box and

bucket. He peered into the box. The bottom was covered with straw, with half a turnip, covered in tiny bite marks, lying

Arthur joined the group huddled around the box and bucket.

in one corner. Standing on the straw were a number of tiny creatures. There was a cabbagehead and a boxtroll, both about five inches high, and three trotting badgers. Most trotting

Three trotting badgers.

badgers were the size of large dogs, but these were the size of mice. All the creatures in the box were shaking with fear.

Fish leaned over the box and made a low, cooing noise. The tiny boxtroll looked up and started squeaking. Fish looked puzzled. He looked up at Shoe and Egg, who also seemed puzzled. It was obviously a boxtroll, but they couldn't understand what it was saying. Shoe grunted softly. Fish nodded, raced out of the room, then raced back in again. In his hand was a brass nut and bolt. He laid them in the straw next to the tiny boxtroll. It made some more squeaking sounds, then picked up the nut and bolt, kissed them, and gave them a hug. The big boxtrolls smiled.

The tiny boxtroll.

A small splash came from the bucket. Everyone turned to see ripples spreading over the surface of the murky green water.

"I wonder?" Willbury muttered to himself.

He reached for a small piece of the shattered cucumber and dropped it into the bucket. For a moment it hung just below the surface. Then a tiny head emerged from the murk and started to nibble the cucumber. As the creature fed, more of it came into view. Its body was short and stout. It had horns and a large, floppy nose, and its skin was white with black patches.

"Oh my!" said Willbury. "It's a tiny freshwater sea-cow."

"It's so small!" said Arthur. "You don't think it's one of the calves the mother lost?"

"No, no. They would be much bigger than this," Willbury said. Then he muttered to himself. "Peru, did he say? I didn't think that they had them in South America."

He looked up at Fish. "Will you and Titus go and get the old fish tank from the back of the shop? Fill it with fresh water. We need to get this little one out of that dirty bucket."

Fish and Titus fetched the tank, placed it on the counter, then started to fill it with jugs of water. Willbury laid an old stoneware jar on its side in the tank. There was some pond-weed in the bucket, so he took that out and placed it in the tank too. When the tank was three-quarters full, Willbury told Fish and Titus that they could stop. Then he lifted the bucket onto the counter, rolled up his sleeves, and gently lifted the sea-cow out and into the tank. With a *plop* the little creature entered the water. It swam straight to the bottom of the tank and disappeared into the jar. They all stood around the tank and watched. After a minute or so, a nose emerged.

"Keep very still," said Arthur quietly. He was practically holding his breath, not wanting to disturb the tiny creature.

Slowly the sea-cow swam out and started to explore its new home.

"Now we must find new homes for our other friends," Willbury said. "I want Fish, Shoe, and Egg to look after the little boxtroll, and Titus, you're in charge of the tiny cabbagehead."

The big boxtrolls looked very happy. Willbury picked up

The sea-cow started to explore its new home.

the little boxtroll (who was still hugging the nut and bolt) and passed him to Fish. The other boxtrolls crowded around. After a great deal of billing and cooing, they set off around the shop to give their new friend a tour.

Titus, however, looked nervous. Willbury lifted the tiny cabbagehead up to his nose. He took a sniff and smiled, then offered it to Titus to smell. Titus leaned forward and took a tiny sniff.

After a moment Titus's face broke into a smile too. He then lowered his face to the tiny cabbagehead and allowed it to smell him. The tiny cabbagehead gave a little squeak and jumped onto his shoulder.

"Why don't you show him where you live?" suggested Willbury.

Titus's eyes grew bright. He clutched the tiny cabbagehead to his chest, shot across the room, and disappeared through the hole in his barrel.

Willbury picked up the little boxtroll.

Willbury smiled. "Titus really needed a companion!"

Suddenly there was a scuffling from the box, and the trotting badgers scurried across the floor and disappeared into a mouse hole in the baseboard.

"Oh dear!" said Willbury.

Arthur picked up the box and turned it over. One corner had been chewed away.

"That's the problem with trotting badgers! They are really wild—and have *really* sharp teeth," said Arthur. "Grandfather always warned me to stay away from the outer caves and tunnels where they live. He says that you can get in serious trouble with a trotting badger!"

"Oh! Well, do you think these little ones will be all right?" asked Willbury.

"If they are anything like the big ones, they should have no problems. It's the mice in that hole that I feel sorry for; trotting badgers will eat anything."

"Well, we'll leave out some milk and biscuits for them later. Maybe if we keep them fed, they'll leave the mice alone. I don't think there is anything else we can do," said Willbury looking at the hole in the baseboard.

He picked up the quill and paper from his chair. "Now, I think we should finish this shopping list, get to the market, and then find my friend."

Arthur and Willbury sat down again. As soon as the boxtrolls realized what was going on, they joined them.

"How are you getting on with your new friend?" Willbury asked them.

Fish gurgled and pointed at a matchbox on the mantelpiece, then at the little boxtroll who Shoe was now holding.

"Oh! You have called him 'Match.' How very appropriate," said Willbury.

The boxtrolls and Arthur giggled.

"Now, what would everybody like to eat?" asked Willbury.

Shoe nudged Egg, who then reached inside his box and produced a folded piece of paper. He handed it to Willbury. Arthur watched as Willbury unfolded it. Drawn very neatly on the paper were pictures of all the foods that the boxtrolls wanted, grouped together by type.

"Thank you, Egg!" said Willbury, studying the pictures. "I notice that you are rather light on vegetables. You know they are good for you."

The boxtrolls moaned. Willbury turned toward the barrel in the corner. "Titus! Could you come out? I think we need some help with the shopping list."

Titus with the tiny cabbagehead.

Titus appeared, carrying the little cabbagehead, and took up position standing next to Willbury.

"So, Titus, do you have any suggestions for vegetables?"

The boxtrolls looked glum while Titus's eyes lit up. He leaned over and started to whisper in Willbury's ear. Willbury was soon struggling to keep up. The list grew very long. The boxtrolls looked increasingly unhappy. Then Willbury raised a hand and Titus stopped. "I think that is enough vegetables. Thank you, Titus."

Titus looked at the little cabbagehead and whispered again to Willbury.

"Yes. I am sure I can get your friend a Brussels sprout." Willbury caught the boxtrolls making faces at each other. "You could take a few tips from cabbageheads on diet. Boxtrolls cannot live by . . ."—Willbury looked back down at the paper they had given him—". . . cake, biscuits, treacle, boiled sweets, toffee, shortbread, pasties, anchovies, pickled onions, raspberry jam, and lemonade alone!"

The boxtrolls looked rather guilty. Willbury turned to Arthur. "What would you like to eat?"

"Do you think we could have some more cocoa and buns?" he asked rather sheepishly.

Willbury raised one eyebrow. "Well, only as part of a properly balanced diet," he began. Then he giggled. "I was going to get them anyway."

Arthur smiled.

"And I think I shall get myself a few pies," Willbury announced, finishing the list and putting down his quill. "Right, we had better get going. I think it best if we leave the underlings and their new friends here."

"We had better get going."

Willbury put on his coat while Arthur stood waiting by the shop door. Arthur had never been to market, and he was excited by the idea. But when Willbury opened the door, there was an immediate shock. The street was thronging with people.

Arthur was astonished. He had never been aboveground in the middle of the day before. He never dreamed that there could be so many people in the world. Suddenly he felt rather frightened.

"Keep close; I don't want to lose you," said Willbury.

And off they set.

Three men in top hats and mufflers, sitting on a large cart.

What they failed to notice was that across the street were three men in top hats and mufflers, sitting on a large cart. As Willbury and Arthur headed toward the market, the men climbed down. One lifted a large metal bar from the back of the cart. The other two took out some old sacks. The men then walked shiftily toward the shop, all the while checking to see that nobody was watching them.

The men then walked shiftily toward the shop.

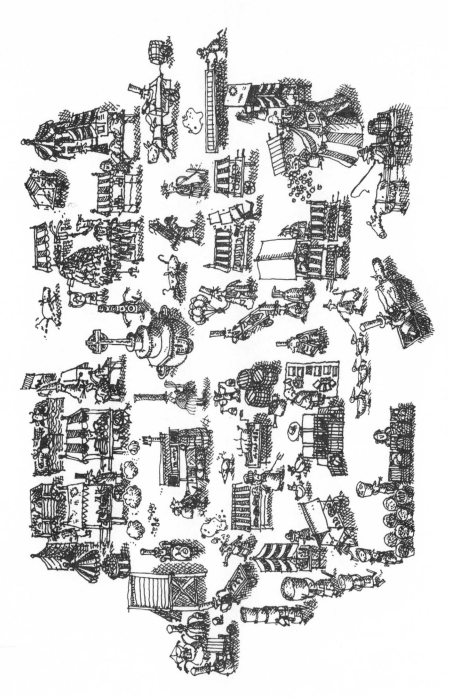

Early morning in Ratbridge market.

chapter 12

The Market

Willbury led Arthur through the streets of Ratbridge.

Willbury led Arthur through the streets of Ratbridge toward the market. Arthur had never been anywhere so crowded. There were tradespeople, farmers, shopkeepers, dogs, chickens, pigs, street sellers, street performers, and more children than he had ever seen in his life. On his nighttime expeditions he had rarely seen children, and when he had, he hid. But now they took no notice of him as they played. Some of them were kicking about a leather ball the size of a cabbage, while others were chasing each other or fiddling with sticks in puddles. Arthur felt a little jealous at the easy way they laughed and spoke with one another.

"Willbury?" asked Arthur.

"Yes, Arthur?"

"What do children do?"

"You know. Play with friends and go to school and the like . . ."

Arthur was not sure he did know. He looked at the children. "I don't think I have any friends."

Willbury stopped and turned to him. "I think you do! What about Fish . . . and Egg and Shoe . . . and Titus . . . and me?"

Arthur smiled, and they walked on. It was so noisy! There was shouting, barking, horses' hooves on cobblestones, the rumble of cart wheels, and over everything was the cackling of the fashionable ladies.

There were an awful lot of ladies doing an awful lot of cackling.

There were an awful lot of ladies doing an awful lot of cackling. And as they cackled, they tottered slowly down the streets, their bottoms wobbling behind them. Arthur had not seen bottoms like these before. From the way the ladies paraded their *derrieres*, it seemed that to have an interesting behind was very much the thing! Round ones, cone-shaped ones, pyramidal ones, cuboid ones, and some that defied description. All, large and wobbling like jellies.

The ladies seemed perturbed by the bottoms of their rivals and kept taking furtive looks at the competing behinds. And they had plenty of time for these observations, as they moved so slowly. This was because they wore ridiculously high-heeled shoes, which seemed to have been specially designed to make walking close to impossible.

Arthur could not help overhearing the conversation of two of the ladies.

"Hark at her," said one to another.

"Which one do you mean? That Ms. Fox?" replied the other.

"Yes! Coming on hoity-toity with her new hexagonal buttocks," said the first, with more than a hint of jealousy.

"No! And on shoes like that! She thinks she's the bee's knees, and she doesn't even realize that hessian went out weeks ago!"

They were met by a wall of rather shabby people.

Arthur had no idea what they were talking about. He looked up at Willbury, slightly bewildered. Willbury smiled, leaned toward him, and whispered, "Fashion victims!"

Approaching the market, the streets became even more and more crowded. Arthur found it very exciting. As they entered the market square, they were met by a wall of rather shabby people.

"Hang on tightly to my hand, Arthur!" said Willbury as he pushed into the throng.

Arthur grabbed Willbury's hand and hung on. Slowly they squeezed their way through the jostling mass of bodies. Arthur could see very little except when there was a break in the crowd, and for a moment he caught sight of the stalls. He was amazed! He had never seen such a profusion of things. Stacks of sausages, bundles of new and secondhand clothes, strange tools and gadgets, bottles of grim-looking medicines, stacks of broken furniture, toys, clocks, pots and pans. . . . The list went on and on. Even when he couldn't see much about him, the smells kept flooding into his nostrils. Some were familiar, some new, some sweet, and some very, very unpleasant. Arthur felt boggled by it all. How strange the town seemed by day.

Occasionally Willbury guided them toward a particular stall where he would buy food, and then again off they would set on their journey. As the supplies amassed, Arthur helped Willbury carry the bags.

Finally they broke free of the crowds, and Arthur found himself by the intersection in the very center of the market.

Willbury led him toward a pie stall that stood near the intersection. Around it was a group of people wearing oily overalls, chewing on pies, chatting, and drawing on black-boards attached to the stall. Built into one side of the stall was a strange copper drum with a chimney. A man behind the stall was shoveling coal into the drum through a door in its base.

Around it was a group of people wearing oily overalls, chewing on pies.

"Are you hungry?" Willbury asked Arthur. "The pies here are simply the best in Ratbridge. Would you like to try one?"

Arthur looked at the group around the stall tucking into their pies and decided that he was very hungry indeed.

"Yes, please!" he answered.

The man behind the stall looked up and smiled at Willbury. "Good day to you, Mr. Nibble, sir. Is it the usual? A nice turkey and ham special for yourself?" the man asked Willbury. "And what would the young man like?"

"Yes, a turkey and ham would be very nice, thank you, Mr. Whitworth," replied Willbury. "I recommend that you try one as well, Arthur."

"Yes, please!" said Arthur again.

Mr. Whitworth opened a door in the top of the copper drum and scooped out two large steaming pies with his spade. He flipped them onto a stack of newspapers on the counter, put down the spade, and then wrapped a few sheets of the newspaper around the pies.

Mr. Whitworth scooped out two large steaming pies with his spade.

"Will there be anything else, Mr. Nibble?" asked Mr. Whitworth.

"Just a bit of information. I am trying to get in touch with Marjorie. Do you happen to know where she is?" replied Willbury.

"Haven't you heard? She's been camping down at the Patent Hall for weeks, ever since they lost her application."

"Lost her application?" Willbury sounded alarmed.

"Yes. Marjorie took her application and prototype for some new invention of hers for approval, but the man who was checking them went for lunch with them. And never came back. Now Marjorie's stuck there—if she leaves the queue, she could lose her invention forever!"

"How awful! We must go and see her straightaway." Willbury hesitated for a moment. "I'll take her six of your finest pork and sage, please! She'll need to keep her strength up. How much is that?" asked Willbury, offering a silver coin.

"They are two groats each, Mr. Nibble. But I'll not be taking your money. We are all doing what we can to help poor Marjorie. It may be a small thing, but pies are vital to keeping one together. If you take them down to the Hall for her, I'll not be charging you for the pies for you or for the boy, either."

Mr. Whitworth pulled six more pies and a small cake from the oven, wrapped them, and placed them in a sack with the two turkey and ham pies.

"The cake is for you, young man." Whitworth winked at Arthur.

"Thank you!" said Arthur. Cake! He'd heard of cake!

Mr. Whitworth pulled six more pies and a small cake from the oven, wrapped them, and then placed them in a sack with the two turkey and ham pies.

"Yes! It is very kind of you, Mr. Whitworth. Thank you, indeed!" said Willbury.

Mr. Whitworth passed the sack to Arthur. "You look like a strong lad. If you run out of energy, you can always eat one."

Happily Arthur took the sack and swung it gently over his shoulder. Then with a parting wave to Mr. Whitworth, they picked up the shopping bags and set off into the crowd again.

IS THAT THEOREM CAUSING CONFUSION?
IS THAT HYPOTHESIS BEFUDDLING YOUR BRAIN?

You need brain food! Try a pie!! From

WHITWORTH'S SCIENTIFIC PIES

Choose from today's finely balanced range:

Turkey and ham

Turkey and ham in precisely equal quantities with a catalyst
of four-sevenths of a teaspoon of the strongest English mustard

Pork and sage

The finest Ratbridge Old Spot pork combined with a compound
formed of four-fifths fresh sage, one-tenth ground cloves, and
one-tenth ground black pepper

Venison and red currant jelly

A combination of venison with a precisely set jelly
formulated from nineteen red currants per pie

Rhubarb and ginger

An amalgam of rhubarb and ginger, with one-third of an ounce of cardamom,
and heated for forty-seven minutes to a temperate 108 degrees centigrade

All pie vessels are formed from pastry, which has been made from flour
specially milled to a density of thirty-six pounds per cubic foot.

Madame Froufrou.

chapter 13
Madame Froufrou

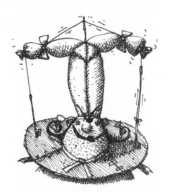

A very strange woman.

Arthur and Willbury set off for the Patent Hall, Arthur trying to keep up with Willbury as they pushed their way through the crowds again. As they reached the edge of the market, the crowds became even denser, until finally they could no longer find their way through and were forced to come to a stop.

They were in the middle of a large crowd of ladies, all of whom seemed in a state of high excitement. It was clear there was something unusual going on.

"What's happening?" Arthur had to raise his voice to make himself heard.

"I am not sure. There seems to be a platform with someone on it," Willbury called back.

Willbury then guided Arthur in front of him. The crowd parted a little, and Arthur could see a high wooden platform. On it stood a very strange woman. She wore a dress that looked as if it were made from skinned sofa and cardboard, an enormous pink wig, and a pair of rubber gloves. She also had a patch over one eye.

"Who is that?" asked Arthur. Despite never having seen a woman dressed in such a way before, Arthur thought the woman looked oddly familiar, but for the life of him, he didn't know where from.

A woman standing next to them overheard Arthur's question. "Don't you know? It's Madame Froufrou, the fashion princess!"

Willbury and Arthur looked at each other, shrugged their shoulders, and turned back to watch.

The strange woman raised her arms to quiet the crowd, and the din died down. The ladies were now all aquiver, and some let out squeals of delight.

"What has she got this week?" one whispered.

"I heard it's something really special . . . and totally new," replied another.

"I can hardly bear it," said the first. "I missed out last week, and they haven't let me in the tearooms since."

The woman on the platform glowered at the crowd. A silence fell but was broken by the sound of a large wooden box being slid up onto the stage. The woman started to speak.

"Today, my little fashion friends, Madame Froufrou 'as a real treat for you."

Little cries of "*Magnifique!*" "*Wunderbar!*" "I must have one," and "I must have two" came from the crowd.

The lady on the platform gave a smirk. She leaned over to the box, opened a door in its lid, and reached in with her large rubber-gloved hand. She paused, then looked about the crowd and gave them what was supposed to be a look of delight. Then she slowly pulled out a tiny creature. It was a miniature boxtroll.

Then she slowly pulled out a tiny creature.

The crowd let out a gasp of admiration. Arthur turned to Willbury. They both looked shocked.

"It's just like the ones that man brought to the shop this morning! What do you think is going on?" asked Arthur.

"I am not sure, but I don't like it!" replied Willbury. "Let's watch."

Madame Froufrou started to speak again. "'Ere I 'ave a tiny lap creature, just the very sort the finest ladies of Pari are clamoring for as we speak. I 'ave a very limited supply, and I'm afraid that some 'ere will be left in a sad and lonely fashion backwater."

She paused and stared at the crowd. A pitiful moaning started from all around Arthur and Willbury.

"I cannot 'elp this, but it is for you to decide whether you are a woman of tomorrow or merely an ugly frump ... with no sense of taste ... or chance of social position!"

At this, the ladies of the town started a desperate squeaking.

Then someone cried, "Me, me, sell one to me!"

Others immediately joined in the cry. "ME, ME, ME! NO! ME, ME!"

The noise grew so loud that Arthur had to put down his packages and put his hands over his ears until Madame Froufrou raised a hand and halted the cries. All that could be heard was the snapping of purses opening, and coins being counted.

A fashionable lady of Pari.

"I cannot be kind to you all. . . . My supplies are very limited."

Someone in the audience let out a miserable whimper.

"Should Madame Froufrou choose the ladies at the front to give the opportunity to buy these sweet treasures?"

Cries of "No! No! No!" came from the back of the crowd.

"Should I choose only those who are wearing this week's pink?" asked Madame Froufrou, grinning.

"No! No! No!" came the cries from all but those who wore pink.

"I think I shall do as they do in Pari," said Madame Froufrou.

"Yes! Yes! Yes!" cried the ladies. "Do what they do in Pari!"

"Yes, I shall do what they do in Pari. I shall do what is the latest thing . . . and select only from those who are . . . fashionably . . . RICH!" Madame Froufrou came to a halt and several ladies in the crowd fainted.

She scanned the crowd. "Now, there is a question you must ask yourselves. Am I fashionably *rich*? If you are not . . . you must cast yourself from this world of glamor and retire to your true miserable and rightfully low position." She glowered at the crowd.

There was silence for a moment, then cries of "I am rich! I am rich! I am rich!" filled the air.

Again Madame Froufrou raised her hand and silence returned.

"What a joy it is to be in such fashionable company.

But . . . I have a feeling that hiding among us are some . . . DOWDY FRUMPS!"

A dowdy frump!

Arthur noticed that the women around him started to tremble.

Madame Froufrou paused a long time for dramatic effect, then spoke again. "I shall have to weed them out . . . *but how?*" There was another very long pause as she peered around the crowd. "I have an idea . . . an idea that will show up the dowdy frumps hiding among us!"

Several more ladies in the crowd fainted.

Madame Froufrou started again. "Could the fashionable ladies here please raise their hands and display the most fashionable quantities of money they can. . . . And please do check that those around you are fashionable!"

Hundreds of hands shot up and started to wave money.

Hundreds of hands shot up and started to wave money. The ladies looked nervously around. Madame Froufrou now took out an enormous pair of binoculars and started to scan her audience.

"As I look at this crowd, I am shocked that one whole area is obviously harboring the dowdy trying to pass themselves off as fashionable. . . ."

Nervous twitching broke out.

"I shall turn my back for a moment and let them crawl away . . . for if they are still here when I turn back . . . I shall POINT THEM OUT!" With that, she turned her back on the crowd.

The ladies now struggled to find every last penny to hold up in an attempt to avoid being labeled a frump.

Madame Froufrou turned slowly back and smiled. "Ah! I see they have fled! It is only the stylish that remain."

"Yes! Yes!" cried the crowd in relief.

"Well, it is time for us to impart the new and ultimate

accessory upon those who deserve it! Come hither, Roberto and Raymond."

Two men dressed in dirty pink suits climbed onto the stage.

Two men dressed in dirty pink suits climbed onto the stage.

"These are my French fashion specialists, and they are here to help me select those who are the most fashionable. Roberto and Raymond, please take out your fashion scopes and wands. . . . Divine those who are most promising!"

Arthur watched in amazement as Roberto and Raymond pulled out what looked like binoculars made from toilet rolls, and fishing rods with small buckets hung on the end. Looking through their binoculars, they started to scan the crowd.

Roberto's gaze fixed upon a particularly full hand, and he turned to Madame Froufrou. "Madame, I think I see a fashion angel," he said, indicating the "angel" in the crowd.

Looking through their binoculars, they started to scan the crowd.

"Yes, it is true! A woman of grace and virtue! Now, my angel, if you would place your offering in the bucket affixed to our fashion wand and take a numbered ticket, I shall invite you to collect your very precious, new lifestyle accessory from the stage, and lo . . . You shall be a queen among women!"

Roberto took out a grubby ticket from his pocket and put it in the bucket at the end of his wand. Then he swung the wand out over the crowd to the angel's outstretched arm. The woman pushed all of her money into the bucket, took the ticket, and squeaked as she made her way toward the stage. Looks of hatred and envy followed her. The bucket swung back over the crowd and disappeared. When the angel had made her way to the stage, Madame Froufrou passed the tiny boxtroll down to her in exchange for the ticket.

Roberto and Raymond began selecting more members of the crowd, while Madame Froufrou stood by the wooden

box and handed out more miniature boxtrolls. The crowd of ladies rapidly thinned as they handed over their cash, collected their new pets, and set off in small groups to parade them.

Madame Froufrou passed the tiny boxtroll down to her.

Only three ladies were left. They still held their handfuls of cash aloft, fighting back tears.

Madame Froufrou saw Arthur and for a moment fixed him with a rather steely gaze, before focusing her eye on the ladies.

"Do you know her?" whispered Willbury.

"I am not sure, but there is something about her. I get the feeling that I have met her before," Arthur muttered nervously.

"And from the look of it, I think she thinks she knows you!" Willbury replied.

Madame Froufrou addressed her remaining customers.

"We have, I am afraid, sold out of our little friends in the box, but it is not my way to let you *poor* ladies go home . . . with no chance of social position. It seems I have a late special offer."

The remaining ladies let out their breath. Roberto and Raymond disappeared down behind the stage, and after a few moments three large zinc buckets were passed up.

Arthur stared at the buckets, then turned to Willbury. "You're not thinking what I'm thinking about those buckets, are you?"

Willbury frowned. "If I am, this is definitely more than a coincidence!"

"Come closer, ladies. In these vessels are some very special creatures that have only come into fashion in the last few minutes," Madame Froufrou whispered.

The remaining ladies happily made their way to the front of the stage.

"Yes! The very, very latest. Freshwater sea-cows! Dredged from the banks of the Seine. These creatures are the very height of chic in the bathrooms of Pari and Milan."

The ladies started to giggle, and Willbury gathered up his shopping bags. "Quick, Arthur. Grab your things. I am going to have words with this Madame Froufrou."

Arthur picked up his sacks and followed Willbury toward the platform.

"Excuse me, madam!" called Willbury. Madame Froufrou looked from Willbury to the ladies, then back at Willbury.

"I am sorry, ladies, but I have to go." She snatched the money from the outstretched hands. "Help yourselves to the buckets." Then she turned and jumped off the back of the stage.

"Excuse me, madam! Where do you think you are going?" shouted Willbury. "I want a word with you!"

Arthur followed Willbury as he ran around to the back of the platform.

Madame Froufrou and her assistants were gone.

Willbury looked quizzically at Arthur. "You said she looked familiar to you. Do you know where you might have seen her?"

"I'm not sure, but, well, I know it's strange, but I got the same feeling when I was looking at her that I got when the leader of the cheese hunt cornered me. She could have been his twin sister."

"Very strange indeed. . . ." Willbury paused to think. "Something is very wrong . . . and weird. I think we had better go and find Marjorie. Maybe she can throw some light on things."

Madame Froufrou and her assistants were gone.

Outside the Patent Hall.

chapter 14
The Patent Hall

A miniature French poodle.

As they made their way up the side streets toward the Patent Hall, Willbury became increasingly excited.

"Before today I'd never seen, nor even heard of, miniature boxtrolls, cabbageheads, sea-cows, or trotting badgers. And now there are miniatures everywhere!" said Willbury.

"I suppose there are different types of creatures in different countries," Arthur suggested.

"True. I've heard of miniature French poodles, so I guess France might be the home of a lot of small things," Willbury said pensively. "All the same, I don't like something about what's going on. . . . Think how unhappy those poor creatures were when they arrived at the shop. And as for Madame Froufrou . . . Well! The less said about her, the better!"

"Except, well, she makes me nervous," Arthur admitted, bewilderment in his voice.

Willbury looked at the bag. "Arthur, I wonder . . . This

business of the hunt leader and Madame Froufrou looking like brother and sister is strange. Do you suppose all this bother is tied up in some way?"

Arthur gave a slight shrug. "Do you think your friend might be able to help?" he asked.

"Well, she might not be able to shed any light on this matter of the miniature creatures, but as for getting you back to your grandfather with your wings, maybe she can help. As I said, Marjorie knows pretty well everybody in the town who has anything to do with mechanics."

"Who *is* Marjorie?" asked Arthur.

"Marjorie was my clerk."

"Marjorie was my clerk. Very bright woman. She used to deal with patent claims mostly. Invariably she could understand most inventions better than their creators, so when I retired, she decided to go into inventing rather than sticking with law. She has a natural aptitude for it. A lot of the legal stuff can be very boring so I was not surprised. Anyway, with all the legal work she did with patents and now with her own inventing, she knows everybody who has anything to do with machines and the like." At that, Willbury nodded his head vigorously as though agreeing with himself. Then he leaned close to Arthur and added, "Though it is quite a secretive world, if you are trusted like she is, you do get to hear what is going on."

"So do you suppose she might have heard where my wings are?"

"That is what I'm hoping, but even supposing we do get your wings back, we still have to get you back underground." Willbury sighed.

"Yes . . . I have been thinking about Grandfather . . ."

Willbury put a hand on Arthur's shoulder. "There have to be other ways to get you back."

A trotting badger.

"There are," said Arthur. "But I just don't know where!"

Willbury stopped in his tracks. "What do you mean? Have you heard of other routes?"

"Well, lots of creatures live underground, and not just under Ratbridge. Some of their tunnels link up. It might be possible to go down one of the tunnels outside Ratbridge and get back to Grandfather. But I just don't know where the other tunnels come out aboveground. And it might be dangerous," Arthur replied.

"Dangerous?" Willbury sounded surprised.

"Yes. I was always warned to stay away from the outer tunnels. Trotting badgers live in some of them . . . and they can be very, very nasty. Grandfather lost a finger to one when he was younger."

"And what about the other creatures?" asked Willbury.

"There are rabbits . . . and rabbit women."

"Rabbit women? I thought they were just a myth."

"Oh, no! They exist. I saw them once when I was exploring . . . well, not actually them . . . I found a home cave," replied Arthur.

"Home cave?"

A rabbit woman knitting rabbit wool.

"It's a place where they live. You can tell it's a home cave by the things they leave about—scraps of food, ash, rabbit droppings, and suits the rabbit women have knitted from rabbit wool."

"So do you know where the rabbit women's holes are? Could we find one?" asked Willbury.

"No." Arthur's face fell. "I don't think so. They tend to be rather private and keep very much to themselves. They have to . . . to avoid the trotting badgers." He paused. "Besides, the rabbit women are so good at tunneling that their holes could be miles away."

It had started to drizzle. They trudged glumly along until they came to a small crossroads. Willbury pointed down one of the streets. "This way. The Patent Hall is not far now."

"By the way, what exactly is a patent?" asked Arthur.

"Oh! That was my speciality as a lawyer." Willbury perked up a little. "A patent is a legal certificate given by the government to the inventor of some new device or idea or process. The patent says that because it is their idea, they are the owner of that invention. This gives them the right to use their invention without others copying it without their permission. The patent will last for some years, and that way, inventors can profit from their inventions."

"Does that mean that if I had invented string, I could charge everybody who made or sold string?"

"Yes, Arthur, if you had invented string, you would be a very, very rich man." Willbury chuckled.

"So what happens at the Patent Hall?"

"It's a government office where the inventors go to get patents. They have to prove that their ideas work and are totally new."

They turned up another side street, and there in front of them stood the Patent Hall. It was a fine building with a frontage that looked like a Greek temple. Arthur had noticed it before when he had been flying, but approaching it on foot, it seemed far bigger than he remembered. There was a queue of inventors that started in the street, led up the steps and past the pillared entrance, and disappeared through a huge pair of oak doors. The members of the queue all carried carefully wrapped bundles and looked nervously at Arthur and Willbury as they passed.

"Why are they looking at us like that?" asked Arthur.

"They are worried that someone might steal their ideas before they are registered and patented," said Willbury. "There are people that come here specifically to try and get their hands on new ideas and rob the poor inventors of their patents."

Willbury led Arthur up the steps of the Patent Hall. Just inside, a man was handing tickets to people in the queue, which led into a large crowded hall. A series of tents, each with a number on it, lined the hall. The tents were made of thick canvas that had seen better days and were now covered in burns and a multitude of stains. Strange noises and the odd flash of light emanated from several of the tents. Outside each of these tents stood a queue of even more nervous-looking inventors.

"That is where the inventors have to give their initial demonstrations. If they get through that, they are sent upstairs to have their inventions checked for originality," said Willbury, walking toward the tents.

A group of very shifty-looking men stood at the far end of the hall. Arthur caught Willbury glaring at them.

"Failed Patent Acquisition Officers! Scum!" Willbury muttered, to Arthur's surprise.

"Who are?" asked Arthur.

"That lot at the foot of the stairs!" Willbury pointed an accusing finger. "They are the very scum of the mechanical

"The very scum of the mechanical world."

world. Technical vultures! They hit a man when he's down, and by the time he recovers, they have either made off with his invention or have him so tied up in contracts that he either has to buy them off or hand the whole thing over to them. Vermin! They should be locked up!"

"How do they do that?" asked Arthur, peering nervously at the men.

"Well, if an inventor isn't granted a patent because his idea is not fully developed or the patent officers just don't understand it, the inventor can get very upset and disheartened, and that lot . . ."—Willbury pointed his finger again at the group at the bottom of the stairs—". . . that lot move in on him."

The Failed Patent Acquisition Officers spotted Willbury pointing at them and were now trying either to hide behind the tents or slide along the walls and out the exit.

Willbury's voice grew louder. "Every day they assemble

there, waiting for their chance to spring. They watch for unhappy faces leaving the tents, then, with all the slime they can muster, they approach the person and offer him 'sympathy.' They might take him around the corner for a cup of tea, offer him a biscuit or piece of cake, tell him they might have a few bob to help him take his project further, ask him to just sign a little document to show they are pals and will be willing to have fun together . . . and before he knows what's hit him, he doesn't own the clothes he stands up in! The scum then turn the screw. They make the person finish his project under the threat of legal action, then sell it once it's patented . . . without a single penny going back to the inventor."

Willbury took a turnip from his shopping bag and threw it.

Willbury's voice could now be heard throughout the hall. He was more agitated than Arthur had ever seen him, yet

Arthur was even more surprised when Willbury took a turnip from his shopping bag and threw it at the last of the Failed Patent Acquisition Officers, who were sneaking out the main doors.

There was a yelp from outside, and some of the older inventors cheered.

"Very satisfactory!" said Willbury, rubbing his hands. "When I was a lawyer, it was a favorite pastime of mine to break the grasp of that filth. I have very happily kicked their posteriors on a number of occasions! And if there was one thing that would persuade me to come out of retirement, it would be the opportunity to kick a few more."

Arthur simply stared at Willbury.

"Now," said Willbury, "come, my boy." He grasped Arthur's arm. "Let us find Marjorie!"

Willbury walked over to one of the queues, and when he asked about Marjorie's whereabouts, several arms pointed up to the balcony on the second floor. Arthur and Willbury set off up the stairs. When they reached the top, Willbury led Arthur to a small tent at the far end of the balcony where a very unhappy-looking woman sat hunched in a deck chair, reading a book of mathematical tables. Willbury coughed and the woman looked up.

"Good morning, Marjorie," said Willbury. "How are you? I would like you to meet a good friend of mine, Arthur."

The woman dropped the book of tables to her lap and immediately ranted, "Not well, Mr. Nibble. Not well. I have been stuck here for months, and things are not looking good!"

She paused for a moment, then stood up and reached out a hand to Arthur. "I'm sorry. How very impolite of me. I am pleased to meet you, Arthur." She gave him half a smile. "It's just everything has gone wrong for me."

In a deck chair sat a very unhappy-looking woman.

Arthur shook her hand and gave her a sympathetic smile back.

"I did want to ask you for some help, but before we get on to that, please, tell me what has happened here," said Willbury.

"I came here three months ago with my new invention, did my initial demonstration downstairs, and then was sent up here to see a Mr. Edward Trout. He had to check the machine for originality. I was a bit dubious when he said he was taking it away for inspection. Then he didn't come back!"

"What! He never came back?" asked Willbury.

The receipt.

"Yes! That's right. I can prove that I gave him a machine because I've got a receipt, but because my receipt has no description of my machine on it, I can't prove what it is that he has of mine. They keep trying to get rid of me by sending out junior clerks with any old rubbish they can find in the warehouse, but I won't leave until they give me back my invention!" By now Marjorie was in such a rage, she was standing.

A junior clerk with a piece of rubbish from the warehouse.

"Oh dear, dear me!" said Willbury. "This is terrible. So you've camped out here ever since?"

"The other inventors have been very good about it. They bring me food when they can . . . and this tent and chair. But I can't spend the rest of my life here."

Willbury looked very concerned. "No . . . no you can't."

Marjorie continued on. "The clerk who disappeared has apparently now left the employment of the patent office, and I am very scared that he just ran off with my invention."

"Do you suppose it was so good that he's . . . stolen it? What was it?" asked Willbury.

Marjorie furtively looked around, then she whispered to Willbury, "I know I can trust you, Mr. Nibble . . . but at this point I think it better that no one else knows! I will tell you that it is fantastic. It is the culmination of the last two years' work. But in the wrong hands, it could be very dangerous . . . and now it has either been stolen or lost!" Marjorie looked so sad that Willbury took her hand in his.

Arthur caught Willbury's eye and pointed to the sack.

"I know it may be of little comfort, but we have brought you some pies from Mr. Whitworth," said Willbury. "Arthur, why don't you get them out while I go and have a word with the head patent officer, Mr. Louis Trout."

"Louis Trout?" said Marjorie. "It was an Edward Trout that went off with my machine."

"I had heard that Louis Trout's son had joined the office.

It must have been him," said Willbury. "I am sure that he will know exactly what has happened."

"You'll never get in to see him, Mr. Nibble," said Marjorie. "I have been trying for weeks!"

"You'll never get in to see him, Mr. Nibble!"

"I think I shall. He knows me from a certain legal case. And if I let one or two things drop in conversation with his receptionist, I think he will see me very quickly."

With that, Willbury left Arthur and Marjorie and opened the grandest of the doors along the balcony.

Marjorie's eye fixed on the sack. "Err, um . . . what flavor pies are they?"

"We've got six pork and sage, a couple of turkey and ham, and Mr. Whitworth gave me a cake as well. You can share that with me if you want," offered Arthur.

Suddenly Marjorie looked a lot more perky. "It's not one of Mr. Whitworth's mulberry cakes, is it?"

"I am not sure," replied Arthur. "Why?"

"You wouldn't be offering to share it if it was," Marjorie jested.

Arthur reached inside the sack, pulled out the smallest of the bundles, and unwrapped it. The cake was pink and dotted with small pieces of fruit.

"It is!" declared Marjorie. "Joy upon joy. Do you really not mind sharing it?"

Arthur grinned. "I don't mind." And he broke the cake in two and passed half to Marjorie. She stared at the cake and after a few moments closed her eyes and took a bite. Arthur watched her, then did the same. As soon as the cake entered his mouth the flavor burst over his tongue. Marjorie was right—it was a joy. He opened his eyes to see Marjorie stuff the rest of her half of the cake into her mouth at one go.

"Now I remember food! My stomach thought that my throat had been cut. Do you mind if I get stuck into a pork and sage pie . . . or two?"

Arthur reached inside the sack again and pulled out the rest of the parcels. He unwrapped one; it had a pig made of pastry on the top. "I guess this must be pork and sage then?"

"Yes. Whitworth always puts a sign on his pies so you can recognize what's inside." Arthur passed her the pie. "I have to thank you for bringing these to me. It is very kind."

Something occurred to Arthur. This was the first woman

he had ever spoken to and he felt a little bashful. He watched as Marjorie tucked into the pie, then there was a noise from the other end of the balcony. Willbury was storming down the hall, looking flushed and angry.

Arthur ran to meet him. "What's the matter, Willbury?"

"Pack up your things, Marjorie! The Head Patent Officer, Mr. Louis Trout, has taken early retirement and gone off to set up a new business with his son . . . the man who disappeared with your invention!"

Marjorie lowered the pie from her mouth and hastily swallowed. "So, they *have* stolen my machine!"

"So, they have *stolen my machine!"*

"I am sorry, but it looks as if it might well be that way," said Willbury.

Then he added gently, "I think the chance of getting your machine back here at the moment is almost nil. Your last chance is to file an official complaint. Come on to my shop, and I will help you draft one. And besides, I think we need your help. If you come with us, I'll explain why."

They collected their things and set off back across town to the shop. Marjorie was muttering about what she might do if she ever caught up with the Trouts, Arthur was worrying about Grandfather and his wings, and Willbury had a face like thunder. And then things got worse. . . .

Willbury, Arthur, and Marjorie stood in the doorway of the shop and just stared.

chapter 15
GONE!

Even Willbury's armchair had been broken and upended.

Willbury, Arthur, and Marjorie stood in the doorway of the shop and just stared. The door had been ripped from its hinges, and inside, the comfortable untidiness had been reduced to shambles.

"Oh no!" Willbury said in barely a whisper. "What's happened?" The color had gone from his face completely.

Arthur felt fear wash over him. The bookcases were overturned, the curtains were torn, and newspapers were scattered over the floor. Even Willbury's armchair had been broken and upended. The room was a pitiful sight.

Willbury suddenly grasped Arthur's arm. Then he called out, his voice shaky, "Fish! Titus! Egg! Shoe! Where are you?" He was met with silence. He called again; then he turned to Arthur. "Where are the creatures?"

Arthur broke free of Willbury's grip and ran across the room. He looked behind the counter; then he ran to the back room and hall. He returned looking very glum. "They're not here."

Willbury walked forward into the center of the shop and stopped. He reached down and picked up the torn piece of cardboard, raised it to his nose, and sniffed.

He picked up the torn piece of cardboard and sniffed.

"Fish!" he muttered, and clutched the piece of cardboard to his chest. "Arthur, something awful has happened!"

That's when Arthur felt something soggy beneath his feet. He looked down and saw the fish tank on its side. In the shadow of the earthenware jar lay the miniature sea-cow. It didn't move, and Arthur was not sure if it was still alive. Willbury dropped to his knees.

"Quick, Arthur, fetch a jug full of water!"

When Arthur returned with the water, Willbury righted the tank and filled it slowly. The sea-cow floated on the surface of the water. They all stared at her, hoping they were not too late. To their joy, after a few moments it twitched and started to move.

Willbury righted the tank and filled it slowly.

"Thank God!" cried Willbury. "I hope it's going to be all right. Arthur, go and get more water." He gently lifted the tank and placed it back on the counter, and Arthur soon had the tank filled.

Now that one calamity was averted, they focused again on the underlings. "Where do you think they could be?" asked Arthur.

Willbury looked about hopelessly. "I am not sure. . . ." He lifted a bookshelf upright. "Would you see to that water?" He pointed at the damp patch on the carpet. "Use the newspapers to soak it up."

Arthur lifted a handful of them and let out a gasp. There, huddled beneath the papers, shaking uncontrollably, was the miniature boxtroll.

"It's Match!" cried Arthur.

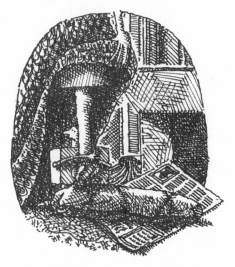

The tiny boxtroll threw its arms around Arthur's ankle.

The tiny boxtroll ran straight at Arthur and threw its arms around his ankle. Arthur squatted down to pick the creature up, and something shiny caught his eye. It was Match's nut and bolt. Arthur gently scooped up Match, then with his other hand, picked up the nut and bolt and passed it to Match's outstretched arms. Match took the nut and bolt and snuggled into Arthur's palm.

Marjorie looked at the miniature boxtroll, then walked over and looked in the tank. She did not say a word but looked very uneasy.

"What is it, Marjorie?" asked Willbury.

"Nothing." Marjorie paused. "It's just . . . where did these tiny creatures come from?"

"I bought them this morning from an awful man called Gristle." Willbury stopped. "He wanted to buy Fish and the other big creatures. He was desperate to get his hands on them.

Why, why? I wonder if he was behind this? If so, he is going to pay for it!"

"And we saw miniature creatures today at the market, too," Arthur said. "Willbury, do you think that Gristle is working with Madame Froufrou?"

"It's certainly suspicious . . . and I can't help feeling Fish and the others are in terrible danger." He looked around the room again and his eyes fixed on the barrel in the corner. "Titus!" he exclaimed, and rushed to the barrel. Willbury got down on his knees and peered through the hole in the side of Titus's barrel.

"Oh dear, you poor thing!" murmured Willbury. He reached inside the barrel and pulled the tiny cabbagehead out. "Titus may be gone . . . but his little friend is still with us."

Willbury held the miniature cabbagehead in his hand and gently stroked it.

Willbury held the miniature cabbagehead in his hand and gently stroked it. It, too, was shaking. "Poor, poor thing," Willbury said mournfully.

As Willbury, Arthur, and Marjorie fussed over the tiny cabbagehead, there was a sudden coughing from the shop doorway. They spun around, fearful of who they would see there. But the sight that greeted them was quite unexpected— it appeared to be a large basket full of dirty washing supported by a pair of legs.

A large basket full of dirty washing supported by a pair of legs.

"Good morning! Need any washing done?" The washing lowered itself to the floor, and from behind it stepped a smiling man with a platform made of sticks fixed to his head. On the platform sat a large, friendly looking rat wearing a spotted handkerchief tied around his head.

"This is Kipper," the rat announced cheerfully, indicating the man below, "and my name is Tom. Business card, please, Kipper!"

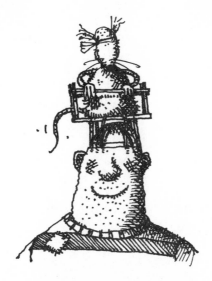

On the platform sat a large, friendly looking rat.

The man pulled out a tiny business card from his pocket and passed it to the rat, who then held it out. Willbury took the card uneasily and read it.

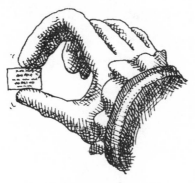

A tiny business card.

FIRST MATE TOM, R.N.L.
THE RATBRIDGE NAUTICAL LAUNDRY
WE WASH WHITER AND BOIL THINGS BRIGHTER
NO LOAD TOO BIG OR FILTHY

Willbury was not sure whether to address the rat or the man beneath.

"It's all right," said the man called Kipper. "I'm just the muscle around here. You deal with the boss."

"Boss?" cried the rat. "Not boss! This is a working cooperative. We are all equal in the Ratbridge Nautical Laundry. It *is* true that I deal with the customer interface and you deal with the load management. But you know very well that last week when we tried it the other way around . . . it all went horribly wrong!"

"True enough, Tom. You're rubbish at shifting things and I am rubbish at organizing stuff. Anyway, sir," Kipper said, turning to Willbury, "if you would like to deal with Tom here, as he is the brains of this outfit, I shall just stand beneath until required."

"Yes," said Tom the rat. "Now, may we be of any service to you? You are very lucky as this week is our 'Big Smalls Promotion.' As we are new in this area, the Ratbridge Nautical Laundry is offering a special introductory offer to new customers. As much underwear as you would like boil washed, free . . . if you get two shirts and a pair of trousers laundered . . ."

Tom stopped. Kipper had just poked him in the ribs.

"I think our friends here have more on their minds than cheap deals on getting their underwear washed," said Kipper.

Tom looked about the shop.

"Oh my Gawd! What's happened here? Closing-down sale?" he asked.

"No, I think we have been raided and our friends snatched," replied Willbury.

"Oh!" said Tom. "Please excuse my patter." He looked genuinely concerned. "When did this happen?"

"In the last hour or so. We've just got back from town, and this is what we found on our return," said Willbury.

"Did you say your friends are missing?" asked Kipper.

Willbury gently stroked the miniature cabbagehead. "Yes, our dear, dear friends are missing."

"How many were there?" asked Tom.

"Four," Arthur said. "Fish, Shoe, Egg, and Titus."

"They're three boxtrolls and a cabbagehead," added Willbury.

"Oh, dear!" said Tom. "How terrible!"

Then Kipper added, "We've had three of our crew disappear in the last couple of weeks."

"What?" cried Willbury. "This has happened to you as well?"

"Yes, when the first one disappeared, we thought he might have just run away, but last week two more disappeared, and we're sure that something bad has happened to them. The last two were good mates . . . not the type to run off," Kipper told him.

"What happened?" asked Arthur. "Did you have a break-in like this?"

"No—the first to go was a very unpopular rat called Framley. He was a nasty piece of work, so nobody was sorry to see the back of him. He just disappeared one day from the Laundry," said Kipper.

The first to go was a very unpopular rat called Framley.

"That Framley . . . If he hadn't gone, I think he would have been booted out anyway," added Tom. "We were all a little wary of him, to be honest—felt he could turn violent at any time. But then last week we lost two more rats, Pickles and Levi. They were really good blokes. Never came back from a shopping trip."

"This is very peculiar!" said Willbury, frowning. "Have you got any idea where they might have gone?"

"I think you should talk to the captain," said Tom. "He's started an investigation. Why don't you come with us to the ship?"

Kipper looked up at Tom, and Tom corrected himself. "Er . . . laundry?"

"Well . . ." Willbury looked around the shop. "I know it's a mess, but it'll have to wait."

"Don't worry about clearing this place up. We can send a party from the Laundry to tidy up for you," said Kipper.

"That's very kind of you, but . . . ," said Willbury.

"Not at all. We insist!" replied Kipper. "The crew really enjoys cleaning. It's all those years at sea." Tom nodded in agreement.

"Well, thank you," said Willbury. "Could we go and talk to your captain right now then?"

"Certainly! Follow us," replied Tom. "Up Kipper and home! And don't spare the horses!"

As Kipper picked up the huge laundry basket and pulled its straps over his shoulders, Arthur tapped Willbury on the shoulder. "What about Match, the sea-cow, and Titus's little friend?"

"Right! Let's take them with us. We can't leave them here." Willbury slipped the tiny cabbagehead into the top pocket of his jacket.

"Marjorie, would you put the sea-cow back in the bucket with some water?"

"Certainly," said Marjorie.

Once Marjorie, with a bit of gentle fussing, managed to get the frightened sea-cow out of the tank and into the bucket, they set off for the Laundry. As they walked, Arthur held Match close and murmured, "Don't worry, Match, we'll get the others back. It's all going to be all right."

Match seemed comforted by Arthur's words, but Arthur wondered if they were true.

The Ratbridge Nautical Laundry.

chapter 16

PANTS AHOY!

The pink and white ensign when washing is on the boil.

The canal ran along the backs of factories. Once it had been Ratbridge's main commercial link with the outer world. Barges had brought coal and other raw materials to the town and had taken goods manufactured there out to the world. The canal had bustled with life. But since the coming of the steam railway, it had not been much used, except by unambitious fishermen and small boys with model boats. Then a few weeks ago a large ship had somehow lodged itself under the canal bridge, and as its crew needed an income, and because of their limited skills, they had "launched" the Ratbridge Nautical Laundry. The crew was unusual in that it consisted of a mixture of sailors and rats, working together as equal partners. Rumor had it that they had a long and interesting history, and that before they turned their hands to laundry, they had been an altogether less respectable crew, but nobody in Ratbridge knew that much about them yet.

Rain was just starting to fall as the little group turned onto the towpath. Ahead of them was a very peculiar sight. The aft end of the wooden sailing ship filled the canal. Steam rose from a tall chimney positioned on the main deck and wafted through what looked like ragged sails that fluttered from the rigging. As they drew closer, they could hear a rhythmic hissing and throbbing of machinery. A vaguely minty smell wafted through the air. Arthur felt Match twitching.

"What is it, Match?" The miniature boxtroll pointed toward the steam and squeaked excitedly.

There was something large and green moving slowly up and down among the steam.

"You've got a beam engine!" exclaimed Marjorie, almost dropping the bucket with the freshwater sea-cow in it.

Kipper beamed. "Yes. And it's a really big one!"

"Where on earth did you get it?" Marjorie said excitedly.

Kipper looked around nervously, and Tom spoke up. "Err . . . we acquired it . . . on a recent trip to Cornwall. . . ."

"How do you acquire a beam engine?" asked Marjorie.

"With a great deal of pushing and shoving. . . ." replied Kipper.

"Can't say much, but it was superfluous to the needs of its owners," said Tom.

"And we won't be going back there on holiday anytime soon," Kipper added. Tom glanced away as Willbury gave them a rather suspicious look.

"What's a beam engine?" Arthur asked.

"It's a sort of steam engine, but it usually stays fixed in one place. Instead of moving things like a railway engine does, it uses its power to work machines," Marjorie explained. Her eyes were shining. "It's a most incredible invention."

They were approaching the ship's gangplank. Arthur looked up and realized the "sails" were in fact hundreds of pieces of washing, pegged onto the rigging and flapping in the breeze.

"All aboard!" cried Kipper, and the group climbed the plank up onto the deck of the Ratbridge Nautical Laundry. Sitting on the rails were some twenty miserable-looking crows.

Miserable-looking crows.

"What's up, Mildred?" Tom asked one of them.

"Rain!" answered Mildred. "We just got this load hung when it started."

"Aren't you going to take it in?" asked Tom.

"Doesn't seem much point as it is already wet," said Mildred. "Besides, where are we going to put it? The hold is full of dirty washing, the bilges have got another load in, and the crew quarters are packed with boxes of washing powder."

"Where is everybody else?" asked Kipper.

"Either down in the bilges working on the next load or delivering and collecting," replied Mildred.

"What about the captain?" asked Tom.

"Not seen him! Drinking tea somewhere dry, I expect!" complained another crow.

"All right for some!" Kipper commiserated.

Tom turned to his guests. "I'll take you down below to try to find the captain, but first I need to check in this washing. Kipper . . . the hatch!"

Kipper walked to a large hatch set in the deck and stamped three times. The hatch opened and a friendly looking rat jumped out.

"Morning, Kipper! Morning, Tom! Got the list to go with this lot?" the rat asked as he pointed to the washing in the basket. Kipper produced a long strip of paper and handed it to the rat.

"Can you be careful with those big woolly underpants, Jim?" said Tom. "Wool has a tendency to shrink, and the lady who the pants belong to can only just get them on as it is."

Jim saluted. "Aye, aye. Me and the boys will take it from here!" Then he called down the hatch. "Oi! Lads! Another load . . . and keep an eye on the big pants!"

Suddenly ten more rats jumped out of the hatch and maneuvered the basket of washing down through the hole. The hatch door closed.

"Have you seen the captain?" Tom asked Jim.

*Suddenly ten more rats jumped out of the hatch
and maneuvered the basket of washing down through the hole.*

"Yes. He's in his cabin sorting out the invoices. Follow me!" Jim walked aft toward another hatch. The others followed.

As they made their way down the steps in the hatch, Arthur asked Tom who the birds were.

"Oh, the crows deal with drying and folding. They are part of the crew. They're very fussy and even fold socks properly. What happens is that some of us go into town and collect the clothes in baskets. As we collect the washing, we write it all down on a list so we know who everything belongs to. Then we bring it all back to the ship. Jim here then collects the lists, and the rats he works with divide the washing into different color and fabric loads. That's so we don't get colors running or clothes shrinking. Then the bilge crew put the loads into the bilges, and we pump water in from the canal. We add soap powder and about half a barrel of peppermint toothpaste and then stoke up the beam engine. When the wash is finished, the bilge crew pass the washing up on deck and the crows hang it out to dry. When it's dry, the crows fold it and the rats pack it back into baskets to be delivered to its owners."

Arthur was impressed.

The party reached the bottom of the stairs, and now made their way along a narrow passageway. Jim pointed to a series of portraits that hung on the walls.

"These are our captains," he announced proudly.

"There are rather a lot of them," replied Arthur, looking from picture to picture to picture.

"Yes. We elect a new one every Friday," said Tom. "We are very democratic. There is a long tradition of pirates . . . err . . ."—Tom stopped midsentence, looked embarrassed, and corrected himself—". . . laundries electing their own captain."

They reached the end of the passage and Jim knocked on the door.

"Come in!" came a cry. Jim opened the door, and there, behind a desk covered in charts and laundry slips, sat a rat with a huge hat on.

"I've got the latest list for you, Captain," Jim said, handing it over. "And these are some visitors that Tom and Kipper have brought back."

"Aye, Aye!" said the captain, surveying the group. "Who do we have here? Not a complaint about washing I hope?"

"No, Captain. These good people," said Tom, pointing at Arthur, Willbury, and Marjorie, "have had a spot of bother. Some friends of theirs have disappeared."

"Oh dear! We have got something in common then," said the captain, frowning.

"We may have, indeed," said Willbury. "May I introduce myself and my friends here. I am Willbury Nibble, and this is Arthur, and Marjorie."

Match gave a squeak. Willbury had forgotten to introduce the tiny creatures.

The captain.

"Oh, I am very sorry. And this is Match . . . and err . . . a cabbagehead friend in my top pocket here . . . and there is a tiny freshwater sea-cow in Marjorie's bucket."

"Good to meet you all," said the captain, doffing his hat. He looked curiously at the miniature creatures for a moment, then asked, "How many friends have you lost?"

"How many friends have you lost?"

"Four. Some boxtrolls and a cabbagehead," Willbury answered. "They disappeared . . . or, rather, were snatched sometime after Arthur and I went to the market and to find my friend Marjorie this morning."

"How sure are you that they have been snatched?" asked the captain.

"I am very sure. When we got back to the shop where they lived with me, the place was wrecked. It looked as though there had been a struggle," answered Willbury.

"When our 'colleague' Framley disappeared, there were no real signs of a struggle. But it was hard to tell, as his corner of the crew's quarters is always such a mess. He was a right lazy critter . . . and unpleasant with it," the captain told Willbury.

"His corner of the crew's quarters is always such a mess."

"He's about the biggest, ugliest, laziest rat you have ever seen!" Kipper chimed in.

The captain went on. "It's only his expertise in the sorting of laundry that we really miss!"

Tom, Kipper, and Jim nodded in agreement.

"When did you notice that he'd gone?" asked Willbury.

"It's only his expertise in the sorting of laundry that we really miss!"

"On Friday nights we always have a meeting. We elect a new captain and do the profits share."

"If there is any money," said Kipper glumly.

"We have been making a few groats, but so far most of our money has gone back into washing powder and toothpaste. Framley is very, very fond of money and had been making noises about going off because he wasn't making enough here. That week after the share out, we realized that a few coppers were left over, so we took a roll call and found Framley was missing."

"Tom mentioned that a couple of other rats have gone missing as well?" said Willbury.

"Yes, Levi and Pickles. About a week after Framley disappeared, they went shopping and never came back. We miss them. . . . Pickles is my brother," the captain said, his voice cracking. He cleared his throat and added, "We sent out search parties, but there was no sign of them."

"Do you have any clues as to who might have got them?" asked Willbury.

"This is what I have been investigating. At first I didn't think we had any enemies as we lead such a quiet life, but there was an incident a few weeks back. We had a visit from a rather odious man by the name of Mr. Archibald Snatcher, and a couple of his sidekicks. He said he wanted to welcome us to Ratbridge on behalf of the 'new' Cheese Guild. The captain that week was a man called Charley. He greeted the visitors and gave them tea and biscuits. Over tea this Snatcher asked if the crew would like to join his guild. Only he was not interested in us rats joining the guild, only the humans! He was really rather unpleasant about rats. Talked as if we weren't even in the room. Said we couldn't be trusted in the presence of cheese. He called us vermin! Awful he was! So we showed him and his friends a long walk off a short plank . . . and they took a dip in the canal."

"So we showed him and his friends a long walk off a short plank."

Kipper and the other rats all giggled but stopped when the captain raised a hand.

"There was something else that happened when they first came on board. Framley had been picking on smaller rats and crows all morning, and finally, just as Archibald Snatcher arrived, a fight broke out between Jim here and Framley."

"I was just trying to stop Framley from bullying some of the clothes sorters. He turned on me," Jim said, obviously still distressed. "He got really nasty and went for my throat. If Kipper here had not pulled him off, I don't know what he would've done."

"Anyway, it all blew over, what with the visit from strangers and things. But Snatcher had been watching Framley fighting and afterward said something to him."

"Do you know what he said?" asked Willbury.

"I asked Framley, and he said that Snatcher offered him a job," replied the captain.

"It does seem strange," said Willbury.

"Yes, it does, especially considering his low opinion of rats," said the captain. "But if he was interested in Framley, how come Levi and Pickles disappeared as well? They were perfectly happy."

"What did Snatcher say about this guild of his?" asked Arthur.

"Not very much. Just that it was some sort of organization for the mutual benefit of its members. And he kept making jokes about it having 'big' plans for Ratbridge." Then the captain addressed Willbury. "Could you tell me a little more about what happened to you this morning?"

Willbury paused to think for a moment. "We had an odd

visit this morning before we went shopping. But from the sound of it, it was not from your friend. This was from a slimy man who was trying to sell miniature creatures. He was very interested in buying my friends, but I sent him packing. Said his name was Gristle."

"Gristle!" said Jim. "That was the name of one of Snatcher's sidekicks!"

"Are you sure?" asked Arthur.

"It was me what was serving them tea."

"It was me what was serving them tea. I am sure he called one of them Gristle when he was asking him to pass the sugar," replied Jim.

"Then I think all the disappearances are linked," said Willbury. "What did this Snatcher look like?"

"Big bloke with sideburns . . . and a glass eye," replied Jim.

Arthur looked at Willbury. "It's him! The leader of the hunt!"

"Yes," replied Willbury. "I think we know who has your wings . . . *and* our friends!"

An air of unease filled the cabin.

"Where does this Snatcher hang out?" Willbury asked the captain.

"That's what I have been investigating. Snatcher had mentioned a building called the Cheese Hall. He said he wanted to restore it to its former glory."

"Yes, I know of it," said Willbury. "But it's been deserted for years!"

Arthur looked at Willbury excitedly. "I was there last night on the roof," he said. "I'm quite sure I heard something inside!"

The captain pursed his lips. "Interesting. I had someone go down to have a look at that place. Jim, could you get Bert?" As Jim ran out the door, the captain said, "He can tell you everything he told me. This is getting more curious by the minute."

"Have you contacted the police?" Willbury asked.

There was a sudden silence in the cabin.

"I see," said Willbury. "Does this have something to do with your beam engine?"

"Err . . . yes . . . and a few other things. We have a strange relationship with police," the captain finally said. There was a sudden noise from the corridor, and the captain looked immensely relieved. Jim had returned with Bert.

"Ah! Bert!" the captain cried, waving him in. "Would you like to fill my new friends in on what you told me about the Cheese Hall?"

"Certainly, Guv!" Bert lifted the beret he was wearing and pulled a small notebook out from under it. "Three weeks ago tonight—the second of September at nine thirty-three p.m., I approached the Cheese Hall from the southern side, after instruction to do the same. I was wearing a green vest and had eaten three—"

Bert lifted a beret he was wearing and pulled a small notebook out from under it.

The captain stopped him. "Bert! Get to the point!"

"All right, then!" Bert looked disappointed. "Something is going on in there. The place is boarded up and is supposed to be up for sale, but I saw lights and heard things!"

"All right, then!" Bert looked disappointed.

"What things?" asked Willbury.

"Strange bleating, moaning things!" Bert replied dramatically.

"I heard something like that when I was there," Arthur concurred. "I thought it could have been cheeses."

"Did you manage to have a look inside?" asked Willbury.

"No." Bert sounded sorry that he couldn't be of more help. "There was no way I could get in—the place is built like the Bank of England. It's mouse and rat proof. . . . I asked the local mice. Guess a cheese guild would want to keep its cheese safe!"

"Did you try knocking on the front door, Bert?" asked Willbury.

Bert looked rather embarrassed. "I didn't think of that."

"I find the direct approach often works. It might be well worth a go, and we have little to lose," said Willbury.

"We should storm the place!" Kipper suggested, leaping up.

Willbury shook his head. "We might find ourselves in even worse trouble if we go down that route. . . ."

"So, when do you think we should go?" asked Tom.

"Can't we go now?" Arthur said anxiously. "We've got no idea what they might be doing to our friends."

"I agree," said Willbury. "But if they are up to no good, it might be as well not to raise their suspicions. I think I should go alone and see what I can find out."

"I don't like that idea," said the captain. "Anything could happen to you. If you go to the door, the rest of us can hide out of sight, but we should be at hand, just in case there is any trouble."

"How about we hide in the Nag's Head Inn, opposite the Cheese Hall? We can watch through the windows," said Tom.

"I think we should get the whole crew together for this," said Kipper.

"Well, what are we going to do then?" asked Arthur.

The captain straightened his huge hat. "I suggest that Mr. Nibble waits here for ten minutes to allow the rest of us to get to the Nag's Head, then he comes down and tries knocking on the front door of the Cheese Hall. We'll watch from the pub."

Willbury turned to his friends. "Marjorie, I'm so sorry you've got caught up in this. I promise we'll try to solve your problem as soon as we find our friends. Why don't you and Arthur stay here and look after the tiny creatures while the rest of us go to the Cheese Hall?"

Marjorie shook her head. "I'd like to come. I might be able to be useful, and I—well, I'd like to help if I can."

"I'm coming too," Arthur declared. "Fish and Egg and Shoe and Titus are my friends."

"Very well," said Willbury reluctantly. "But I do think it best if we leave the poor miniatures here on the ship. They could easily get hurt if there is any trouble." He turned to the captain. "Do you have somewhere they could safely stay?"

The captain thought for a moment. "We have a box that used to house the sextant before Kipper dropped it over the side. The boxtroll and the cabbagehead could use that."

Kipper blushed furiously and looked as if he was about to cry.

Kipper dropped it over the side.

"Never mind, Kipper. Nobody knew how to use it anyway." The captain got down off his chair and lifted a pile of papers off a mahogany box on the floor. He opened it, showing them the deep red, padded, velvet lining.

"This should suit your friends here. Will the sea-cow be all right staying in her bucket for the moment?"

"I think so. Maybe we could find something larger for her later," said Willbury. He lifted the tiny cabbagehead out of his pocket from where it had been watching the proceedings and placed it gently in the padded box. It immediately lay down and closed its eyes. Then Arthur leaned down and allowed the boxtroll to join the cabbagehead. Match looked around the box and noticed a number of small spare parts fixed to the inside of the lid. He smiled, put his nut and bolt in one corner of the box, then set about quickly removing all the spare parts and piling them up with his nut and bolt. Then he cuddled up to the pile and closed his eyes.

"Should we leave them anything to eat?" asked Arthur.

"Would ship biscuits do?" asked the captain. "They are a tad bit hard but we could break them up."

"I think they would do very well, if you have any spare," replied Willbury.

The captain climbed back on his chair and opened one of the desk drawers. He took out two biscuits, placed them on the desk, picked up a rock that was acting as a paperweight, and gave the biscuits a sharp blow. The biscuits shattered into small pieces and the captain collected them.

"What should I do now?" he asked.

"If you sprinkle some in the bucket and put the rest in a heap in the sextant case, that would do for the moment," said Willbury.

The captain followed Willbury's instructions, then brushed off his hands.

"Thank you. I am sure they will be very happy now," said Willbury. "If you'll put the bucket down next to the box, Marjorie, I think we can be on our way."

After organizing for a few minutes, the entire crew of the Ratbridge Nautical Laundry, accompanied by Arthur and Marjorie, set off for the pub. Willbury stood on the deck waiting, rain dripping from the washing above.

Four of the largest workers set off in search of a boxtroll.

chapter 17

CABBAGEHEADS

Things were becoming positively soggy.

Meanwhile, far below the streets of Ratbridge, there was also much activity. For the last week or so, the cabbageheads under Ratbridge had been very happy. The water supply had been much better than usual. But now things were becoming positively soggy.

The cabbageheads lived, and gardened, in a vast cavern several hundred feet under the streets of the town, at the deepest point of the network of underground tunnels. It was here that water was collecting. The special low-light cabbages were swimming in water, and it was getting worse.

So a meeting was held, and it was decided that a party would go up and politely ask the boxtrolls to turn off the water for a few days.

Four of the largest workers set off in search of a boxtroll to talk to. As they made their way through the tunnels, it became clear that the boxtrolls had not been doing their job very well. Water was leaking everywhere. The cabbageheads muttered to one another that this was not a bit like the boxtrolls, letting things fall into this state. What could be causing them to neglect their job like this? Perhaps they had acquired some new piece of machinery that they were busy playing with and they were distracted from their duties, the cabbageheads whispered.

After traveling a good distance, they climbed up on a dry rock for a rest and had a cabbage sandwich each. This was their favorite food and was made of a cabbage leaf sandwiched between two more cabbage leaves.

A cabbage sandwich.

As they ate, one of them noticed that the rock they were sitting on was covered in netting. Nudging his companions, he pointed to the netting in puzzlement. All the cabbageheads seemed baffled and twittered nervously to one another.

Then, without any warning, there was a *twang*, and before they could blink, the net whipped up in the air with them all in it.

The cabbageheads hung in the net for hours, trembling as water dripped down on them. They had no idea what or who could have caused this terrible thing to happen. Then they

heard the sound of approaching feet and saw the flickering of candles. The lights got closer, and they could see a group of men, all wearing tall hats and carrying sacks over their shoulders. The cabbageheads trembled even harder.

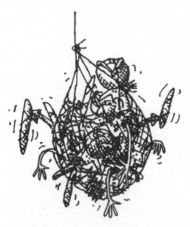

The cabbageheads hung in the net.

The men lowered the net and dumped the cabbageheads in the sacks.

"These ain't going to be enough."

"We got a few boxtrolls in the other traps last time!"

"Let's just hope we ain't caught any more trotting badgers!"

"Too right!" And off the party set. Within moments all that was left in the tunnel were a few uneaten cabbage sandwiches lying on the floor.

Willbury paused, then pulled the knob.

chapter 18

THE CHEESE HALL

A pair of eyes peered out.

The door of the Cheese Hall was made from very solid-looking oak. Large iron studs were fixed at regular intervals across its surface, and at head height was a metal grille that covered a small hatch. Willbury approached it nervously.

It's certainly not very welcoming, he thought. To one side of the door frame was a metal knob shaped like a cheese. Beneath it a dirty brass plaque read PULL. Willbury paused, then pulled the knob. The sound of a cheese bleat instantly rang out. Willbury raised an eyebrow. Of all the knockers and bells he had knocked, pulled, or pushed, this was certainly the strangest. Then he heard steps, the hatch flew open, and a pair of eyes peered out.

"Yes!" snapped a voice. "What d'yer want?"

"I . . . er . . . would like to talk to someone . . . ," replied Willbury.

"You buying or selling?" The voice sounded very annoyed.

Willbury thought this over. "I am not really buying . . . or selling."

"Well, you ain't no interest to us then. Now naff off!" The hatch snapped shut.

Willbury stood for a moment, perplexed, then he looked back toward the pub where the others were hiding. Most of the crew's faces were pressed hard against the window. He waved at them to get them to hide properly, and they reluctantly ducked down.

Most of the crew's faces were pressed hard against the window.

He pulled the knob again. The bleating started but was cut short by the sound of a thump, then the hatch swung open again.

"What d'yer want now?" snapped the voice.

"Would it be possible to talk to someone about cheese?" Willbury asked.

"No! Cheese is our business, and information about cheese is confidential. I told you to naff off, so go on. Take a walk!" The hatch slammed shut.

Willbury was left standing in the rain, staring at the door. He was not quite sure what to do. He had not expected a warm welcome, but nor had he expected this total failure. He looked up at the building. Wooden boards were nailed over most of the windows, but through gaps in the planks several pairs of eyes were staring at him.

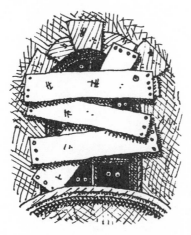

Through gaps in the planks several pairs of eyes were staring at him.

"I am being watched," he muttered. Willbury turned and nonchalantly strolled across the street and into the Nag's Head.

As soon as he walked through the door he was surrounded.

"What'd they say then?" asked the captain.

"Not a lot!" said Willbury.

"Did you ask if they had our friends?" asked Kipper.

"I didn't really get around to that. They were not very chatty," Willbury admitted. "I wonder what our next step is?"

"Storm them with grappling hooks!" said Bert enthusiastically.

"We ain't got no grappling hooks, and anyway, it looks a pretty tough building to storm," Tom said logically.

"Well, we could go back to the ship and get the cannon?" Kipper suggested.

"I don't think the police are going to put up with members of the local laundry letting off cannons in the street," advised Willbury.

"I don't think the police are going to put up with members of the local laundry letting off cannons in the street."

"Yeah. And we ain't got no gunpowder," said Jim regretfully.

"Maybe there is another way in," suggested Arthur, peeping out the window at the Cheese Hall.

"The mice said there's another route, but it's up by the roof," said Bert. "If you look right up there, you can see a pair of doors with a crane that sticks out just above them. It's like one of them Dutch doors they use for lifting pianos into attics and the like. But I don't think there's a way to get up there."

Arthur thought longingly of his wings. *If only . . .*

One of the other rats raised his hand. "'Scuse me, but ain't they got a sewer?"

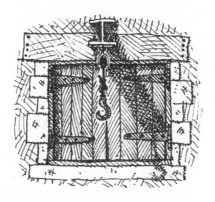

"If you look right up there, you can see a pair of doors."

"The mice say the Cheese Hall has got its own cesspit and well. They're not connected to the main systems. The place is like a fortress!" Bert exclaimed.

"Well, how are we going to find out whether they got our mates then?" asked Tom.

"How about we kidnap one of them and torture 'im!" said Jim.

"Yeah!" agreed Bert.

"I don't think that's quite the right thing to do," said Willbury. "I think we have no choice but to watch the place and see what happens. An opportunity may present itself."

"Does that mean we all get to stay in the pub?" said Kipper hopefully. Tom shot him a disapproving look.

"We just need someone to keep an eye on the entrance. How about we rent a room and set up watch?" said Arthur.

"Sounds like a good idea to me," said Willbury.

"And cheaper than keeping the whole crew in the pub," added the captain.

"We can use the crows to keep in touch," said Tom.

There was a fluttering and Mildred made her way to the front.

There was a fluttering and Mildred made her way to the front.

"I would like to volunteer to act as messenger," she said. "Thank you," said Willbury. "And who would like to take first watch?"

"I will," said Arthur immediately.

"I don't think so," Willbury told him.

"It's not going to be dangerous just looking out of a window," pleaded Arthur. "And besides, it was my idea. I know I can do this, Willbury; please let me."

"All right then, but you are only to watch. And only if someone else stays here with you," said Willbury.

Kipper broke in. "Let me and Tom look after Arthur! We won't let him get into trouble."

"All right. But if anything happens, you are just to send a message back to the Laundry," insisted Willbury. "I need to check that the little creatures are all right."

"Me too," said Marjorie. "The poor little things seemed so frightened. . . ."

Willbury walked over to the bar.

"Excuse me, do you have a room I can rent?" Willbury asked.

"I am afraid we only have a small one in the attic left, as it is market day," answered the landlady.

"Does it have a window on the street?" asked Willbury.

"It does. Who's it for?" she asked.

Willbury pointed out Arthur, Tom, Kipper, and Mildred. The landlady looked uncertain. "The crow will have to perch on the curtain rail, and it will be extra if boots are worn in bed."

"Certainly," said Willbury, and he handed her several bills.

And as the landlady showed Arthur, Tom, Kipper, and Mildred to the room, Willbury, Marjorie, and the rest of the crew returned to the Nautical Laundry.

The landlady.

The Nag's Head.

chapter 19
An Incident Outside the Nag's Head

The sign of the Nag's Head.

Arthur, Tom, Kipper, and Mildred returned downstairs to the bar and ordered some food. Then they settled at a window table. The rain fell, and slowly it grew dark outside.

By ten o'clock they retired to the attic, having finished fourteen games of Old Maid, twenty-seven games of dominoes, and building a large castle from the crusts of toasted sandwiches.

A large castle from the crusts of toasted sandwiches.

"Shall I light a candle?" asked Arthur.

"No," said Tom. "Best not to. But why don't you open

the window. That way we will be able to hear if anything is happening, and we'll be able to put our feet up."

Arthur opened the window and looked down. The streets were empty. Tom and Kipper took one of the two single beds and lay down. Mildred perched on the curtain pole and went to sleep. Arthur stood by the window watching. Soon all he could hear was the rain and Kipper snoring.

Mildred perched on the curtain pole and went to sleep.

Arthur took out his doll and quietly wound it up.

When it was ready, Arthur whispered, "Grandfather. It's Arthur! Are you still awake?"

A sleepy voice broke through the gentle crackling. "Yes, Arthur."

"How are you?" Arthur asked.

"I could be better," came the reply. "It seems to be getting very damp down here. It's playing havoc with my rheumatism. The boxtrolls don't seem to be keeping up with the maintenance. But maybe I am just getting old and grumpy."

"You stay in bed and keep warm."

"What about you, Arthur? What's happening up there?" Grandfather asked.

Arthur told him everything that had happened. When he finished, his grandfather remained silent.

"Grandfather . . . Grandfather . . . are you still there?" Arthur called.

When his grandfather finally spoke, there was not a trace of sleepiness in his voice. "Listen to me, Arthur. You are not to do anything rash. That is an order! I don't want you to do anything but watch. Mr. Archibald Snatcher is a very dangerous man!"

"You know him?" Arthur asked, surprised.

"Oh yes . . . I know him." Grandfather sounded angry. "And he is the reason we live down here!"

"What!" Arthur was shocked.

"Trust me, Arthur. Stay well away from that man."

"But what did he—" Arthur broke off, hearing noise from the street below. "Sorry, Grandfather . . . but something is happening." Arthur peered out the window. Below, in the street, a shaft of light fell from the open door of the Cheese Hall. Slowly a procession of horses and riders were making their way out into the street. It was the hunt.

"I've got to go, Grandfather."

"Arthur! Arthur! Be careful!" Grandfather called.

"I will be. Don't worry. I'll talk to you later."

The doll fell silent, and Arthur tucked it under his suit. Then he shook Kipper and Tom awake.

"Quick! It's the cheese hunt. They're coming out of the hall!" he whispered.

Kipper and Arthur ran to the window.

"It's them I had the run-in with," said Arthur. "But I can't see Snatcher!"

Tom scrabbled up onto the windowsill and looked out. There was a yapping and howling as the hounds appeared. A mild panic broke out among the "horses" as they did their best to avoid the hounds.

Kipper, Arthur, and Tom at the attic window.

"Should we send a message to the Laundry?" asked Arthur.

"Let's wait a few minutes to see what happens," said Tom. "Then we might be able to send more useful information."

Just then, a large figure appeared from the doorway of the Cheese Hall, and the noise in the street subsided. It was Snatcher.

A large figure appeared from the doorway of the Cheese Hall.

A riderless horse walked forward, and one of the members crouched down to form a step for his leader. Snatcher closed the door, stood on the "step," and climbed onto his mount.

Snatcher closed the door, stood on the "step," and climbed onto his mount.

The hunt crowded around Snatcher, who started talking to his men. Try as they might, Arthur, Tom, and Kipper could not make out what he was telling them.

"Quick, let's get downstairs and see what Snatcher's saying," said Tom. "Kipper, wake up Mildred."

Kipper reached up and poked the crow. There was a fluttering, and Mildred settled on his shoulder.

Arthur led the way down into the front parlor of the pub. When they reached the front door, he lifted the latch very slowly and opened the door a few inches, careful not to make a sound. They could hear Snatcher addressing the group.

"The Great One is growing ever greater, and his needs must be met. We must get all the cheese we can tonight. I don't want any slacking. Anybody I catch not pulling his weight may find themselves in 'reduced circumstances.' Get my drift?" Snatcher's oily voice floated over the crowd.

"How much longer are we going to have to go hunting for the Great One?" came a voice.

"The time is very near! Soon we will free the Great One, and revenge will be ours!"

Evil chuckling filled the street. A shiver ran down Arthur's spine. What were these men plotting? Then Snatcher raised a hand.

"Quiet, my boys!" said Snatcher, and the hunt calmed down. "'Tis time to wend our way."

He kicked his horse and led off down the street. The hunt followed.

The hunt making off down the street.

Arthur, Tom, Kipper, and Mildred slipped out of the Nag's Head. There was a quiet flapping as Mildred set off back to the ship to tell about the hunt. Under the cover of the shadows, the others began to follow the hunt down the street. Suddenly there was a shout.

"Hunt! Whoa! I've forgot me Hornswoggle!" It was Snatcher.

"Quick!" Tom said, looking about. "Hide."

Kipper pointed toward an alley behind them. They ran madly for it.

Within moments they could hear a "horse" coming up the street. Arthur sneaked a look. Snatcher dismounted and headed for the door of the Cheese Hall. He unlocked it and went inside.

"Tom!" Arthur whispered excitedly. "Can you distract the horse? I am going to see if I can get inside the Cheese Hall."

Tom hesitated. "It's too dangerous, Arthur!"

Arthur sneaked a look.

"I know. But it may be our only chance to get our friends back," Arthur said beseechingly.

"We'll come with you," said Kipper, looking worried.

"No, I stand a better chance of sneaking past Snatcher on my own," replied Arthur.

Tom and Kipper looked at each other for a moment, then Tom nodded. He scuttled silently toward the horse and made a very convincing bark. The horse started, then Tom jumped as high as he could and bit one of the "legs."

Tom jumped as high as he could and bit one of the "legs."

"AAAAAAAH! Blinkin' hound!" the horse shouted, and it made off down the street.

Tom waved to Arthur, who took a last glance up at Kipper.

"Good luck, Arthur," Kipper whispered. "And don't worry—I'm sure Tom will think of a way for us to help you." Arthur smiled gratefully, then ran to the open door of the Cheese Hall. He looked down the passage. There was no one in sight.

He ran straight through the door just as Snatcher was turning into the passage. Looking around desperately, Arthur spied a very large grandfather clock. He opened its case, jumped inside, and pulled the door closed. As he pushed against the pendulum and chains, the clock made a loud clang. Snatcher stopped in front of it.

"That's odd. It ain't been working for years." He gave the clock a blow with his Hornswoggle, made his way through the front door, and slammed it shut.

A very large grandfather clock.

The entrance hall.

chapter 20

Inside the Cheese Hall

He looked about.

In the passage all was quiet. Then the clock started striking, and as it did, there was also a fair bit of muffled squeaking. The chimes died away and the case slowly opened. A very startled Arthur stepped out. He shook his head and blinked for a moment, then began creeping to the end of the passage. Through an archway was a large entrance hall.

Arthur listened. All was silent; the place seemed deserted. It seemed all the members had gone out hunting, and he would have the Cheese Hall to himself for a while. But perhaps some of them had stayed behind—he'd have to be as careful as he knew how.

He looked about. There was a large marble staircase, several doors, and high up on the walls ran a painted frieze. He studied the frieze in silence. It depicted the cheeses of the world—English cheese frolicked in the fields, cave-bound French cheeses huddled in green and blue mounds, Swiss cheese rolled down mountainsides, Norwegian cheeses leaped from cliffs into fjords, and some Welsh cheeses huddled under a bush in the rain. There were a number of other scenes, but Arthur couldn't work out what countries and cheeses they depicted. He wondered particularly about some small tins being carried by an elephant.

Some small tins being carried by an elephant.

Above the frieze were statues set in alcoves. These he took to be heroes of the cheese world. Most of them looked very miserable, apart from one who was clutching a flaming cheese aloft. This statue had a mad grin on its face. Arthur walked over to the sign below this statue and read:

MALCOLM OF BARNSLEY

1618–1649

"HE LIVES WHO HAS SEEN CHEESE COMBUST BY ITS OWN WILL."

DONATED BY THE

LACTOSE PARANORMAL RESEARCH COUNCIL

Arthur wondered what this meant. Then he noticed that the doors all had small plaques fixed to them. The plaque over the closest door read:

THE MEMBERS' TEA AND CAKE ROOM
LADIES' NIGHT—FEBRUARY 29TH 5:30–6:00 P.M.
NONMEMBERS KEEP OUT!

Malcolm of Barnsley.

The rooms were labeled, Arthur thought curiously. He ran to the next door and read—

THE CHAIRMAN'S SUITE
ENTRANCE BY INVITATION ONLY

At the third . . .

LABORATORY

And at the last . . .

KEEP OUT!

I wonder? Arthur thought, and he reached for the handle. The door creaked open to reveal a long torch-lit passageway. Arthur listened carefully, but all he could hear was a soft bubbling sound from farther down the passage. He listened for another moment, and then his curiosity got the better of him. He crept quietly toward the sound.

At the end, he stopped, gazing in wonderment. Before him was a large, hexagonal stone chamber, with an open shaft in the center of the floor. A large yellow banner hung from the balcony. In the center of the banner was a picture of a wedge of cheese, and beneath it ran the words R.C.G. WE SHALL RISE AGAIN! He looked again at the open shaft and realized that this was the source of the bubbling sound. He started forward and then recoiled. The smell of cheese was overpowering. He held his nose and approached it again. The shaft descended into total darkness, and the bubbling was coming from somewhere below.

He moved back from the hole and looked about worriedly. He wondered where Fish and the others were.

Then Arthur noticed a small wooden door on one side of the chamber. The sign above it read MEMBERS' CHANGING ROOM. He nervously tried the door. It was locked.

"Bother!" Now he'd have to go back to the hall and try the other doors.

Arthur crept back up the passageway to the entrance-hall doorway and once again listened carefully. All he could hear was the bubbling behind him, so he snuck into the entrance hall and looked at the three remaining doors.

He didn't think they would keep the creatures in a tearoom or the chairman's suite . . . so that left the lab. He tried the lab door. It opened.

Arthur found himself at the top of a flight of steps that led down into another vast hall, this one filled with enormous silent machines.

Arthur found himself at the top of a flight of steps that led down into another vast hall, this one filled with enormous silent machines. Stained-glass windows high in the walls cast an eerie light over everything. He decided to risk making a noise.

"Fish . . . Fish . . . are you in here?" he whispered loudly. His voice reverberated alarmingly around the hall before it died away. There was no reply.

As his eyes became accustomed to the gloom, he saw a pale red glow in a far corner of the lab. Arthur strained to see. It was an illuminated sign above some door or passage. It was too far away to read.

Arthur hurried down the steps. The smell of oil and polished brass filled the air. Arthur studied the various machines and apparatuses as he passed by them. He recognized some of the machines from his grandfather's bedroom, but his grandfather's were like toys by comparison. There was a beam engine even larger than the one at the Laundry; lathes and enormous drills; milling machines; rows of glass tanks, filled with liquid, that had metal plates hung in them; a cart with an enormous coil of metal sitting on it; and something very large with canvas sheeting tied over it.

Finally he neared the glowing sign and saw yet another stairway—this one spiraling downward. But he was already in the cellar, wasn't he? He looked up and read—

DUNGEON

Arthur looked back around the hall, and then braced himself. It was very dark down those steps, he thought nervously. Then he swallowed and started down.

He swallowed and started down.

The dungeon.

chapter 21
THE DUNGEON

Arthur reached the bottom step.

Arthur reached the bottom step and stopped. Before him was a corridor lined with three cells on either side. The fronts of five of them were made from iron bars, and each had a door set into the bars. But the last cell on the right-hand side was boarded up. Arthur turned to the first cell and peered inside. Eyes stared back at him from the gloom. He could just make out the shapes of the creatures as they quivered against the back wall.

"Oh, poor things! They're underlings!" he said under his breath.

There was a boxtroll, three cabbageheads, and a rare two-legged lonely stoat. Arthur did not recognize any of them as his friends. Still, he tried the lock, but it was no use. "Don't worry," he whispered through the bars. "I'm a friend. I'll get you out of here if I can!" Then he peered into the cell opposite. That contained only a stack of small cardboard boxes, so he walked on. As he reached the

There was a boxtroll, three cabbageheads, and a rare two-legged lonely stoat.

next cell, there was a flash of movement from the darkness, and suddenly, snarling heads appeared between the bars and snapped at him. Arthur leaped back. They were trotting badgers.

Suddenly, snarling heads appeared between the bars and snapped at him.

Arthur held back till they stopped snapping, quieted down, and finally returned to the back of their cell. Then,

shakily, he turned to inspect the cell behind him. There were three more boxtrolls. For a moment Arthur felt his heart jump, but as soon as he took a better look, he realized none of them were his friends. Again he tried the lock to no avail, and again he whispered some words of reassurance before moving on to investigate the last open cell.

Three very familiar cardboard boxes were stacked on top of one another. Arthur grasped the bars eagerly and whispered, "Fish! Shoe! Egg!"

Three very familiar cardboard boxes were stacked on top of one another.

A head slowly rose from a hole in the top box. It was Fish.

Fish gave a loud gurgle, and heads, arms, and legs sprouted from all three boxes simultaneously. The stack fell over with

a clatter and was followed by a lot of moaning. Titus popped up from behind where the stack had once stood. He smiled at Arthur. Arthur clutched the bars as his friends rushed forward to meet him.

Arthur clutched the bars as his friends rushed forward to meet him.

"Thank goodness you're all right!" exclaimed Arthur. "We've been so worried about you."

Fish, Shoe, and Egg all gurgled excitedly, while Titus squeaked. They reached their hands through the bars, grasping at Arthur, and looked at him very hopefully.

"I'm going to get you out of here!" Arthur said firmly. "I promise." He looked down at the lock. Fish followed his glance.

"I don't suppose you know where the key is, do you?" asked Arthur.

The underlings shook their heads and looked disappointed. Arthur turned round. There was no key visible anywhere, but his eye fixed on the boarded-up cell opposite.

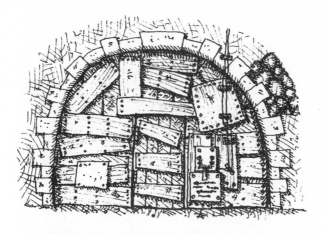

His eye fixed on the boarded-up cell.

The underlings suddenly shuffled nervously. Arthur took a step toward the boarded-up cell but was stopped dead in his tracks. Several pairs of hands were gripping his clothes and holding him back.

"All right, I won't go near it," Arthur assured them.

The underlings let go. Arthur studied the front of the boarded cell. A large switch was fixed to the planks by its door, and underneath it, written in red paint, was—

Beware!
Dangerous Prisoner!
Put switch in upright position
BEFORE entering the cell

"There must be something in there even worse than trotting badgers."

The underlings nodded their heads vigorously in agreement. "What is it?" Arthur asked.

The underlings started jumping up and down and making noises. *Bonk! Bonk! Bonk!*

When they realized that Arthur had no idea what they meant, they gave up.

"Well, I will leave it for the moment. I think I had better concentrate on getting you out of here!" The underlings looked relieved.

"The key must be upstairs somewhere. I'll go and see if I can find it. I will be back soon—I promise!" The boxtrolls and Titus huddled together in the cell and looked at Arthur with pleading eyes. It felt wrong to leave them again, but he knew the only way he could help them was by finding the keys to their cell.

Tearing his eyes away from them, Arthur made for the steps, keeping well away from the boarded cell and the trotting badgers.

*The underlings started jumping up and down
and making noises.* Bonk! Bonk! Bonk!

A huge set of iron doors, set in the floor.

chapter 22

BACK IN THE LAB

Where would they keep the key?

Arthur crept up the stairs, and as he reached the top, he checked again that no one was there.

Where would they keep the key? he wondered, and he started to search the lab. As he tiptoed between the machines, he noticed chains stretching down from the darkness to somewhere near the center of the lab. He headed in that direction and soon found himself standing on a pathway that surrounded a large open area. Beyond waist-height railings were a huge set of iron doors, set in the floor. The chains that he'd seen were fixed to iron rings in the center of the doors. High above hung a strange, giant metal funnel. Its mouth pointed down toward the doors.

Arthur walked around the pathway. On the far side was a box fixed to the railings. It was some kind of control panel. A metal tube ran down from beneath it and through a small hole by the edge of the pathway. He peered into the hole. It was dark and very narrow, but he could just make out a pale light from somewhere deep below. Again he caught the strong smell of cheese. He wondered what could be down there that needed such huge iron doors to contain it.

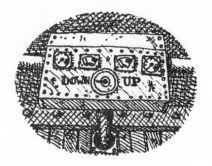

A box fixed to the railings.

He turned back to the control panel. It was covered with an array of dials, and below the dials was a brass disk with a slot for a key. The slot pointed toward the word "down." Across the panel was etched the word "up." Arthur looked over at

He had a bad feeling about it.

the doors, and then up at the chains by the funnel. From the top of the funnel, giant curling wires descended to the roof of what looked like, of all things, an iron garden shed on stilts. Another pair of curly wires emerged from the shed roof and led to a smaller funnel. This was fixed above the roof of a cage that stood on the floor of the lab, next to the shed. The cage was empty. He had a bad feeling about it.

Steps led up to a platform that ran around the shed. Arthur glanced around quickly, then dashed up them. Looking into the shed through its thick glass windows, he saw a workbench covered with bits and pieces and . . . his wings.

Arthur rushed around to the door and tried the handle. It was locked, so he ran to the back of the shed to get a better look. Yes! They were definitely his wings. And the wing spars and leatherwork had been mended. Then his heart stopped. They had taken the box to pieces!

He ran to the back of the shed to get a better look.

"Oh no! What am I going to do now?" he moaned.

He looked frantically at the floor of the lab. On a cart close by were some tools. He rushed down and picked out a sledge-hammer. Returning to the shed, he raised the hammer above his head and swung it at the window in the door.

He raised the hammer above his head and swung it at the window in the door.

The sound reverberated around the lab . . . but the hammer just bounced off the window! Arthur was stunned. He crouched down and waited to see if the noise would bring anyone rushing in. The sound died away and nobody came. Arthur decided to try again. But again the hammer just bounced off.

"Darn it!" he muttered. "I need to find the keys!" Then he had an encouraging thought. Perhaps the keys for the shed and the keys for the cells would all be kept together somewhere.

He glanced about the lab again, but there didn't seem to be anywhere obvious where keys would be kept. Arthur headed

for the Chairman's Suite. The room was very dark, the only light coming from embers in a large fireplace. Arthur could just see the silhouette of a desk across the room. Carefully feeling his way, he crossed to the desk and picked up the oil lamp that was sitting on it. He took a splint from the fire and lit the lamp and instantly felt very uneasy. The faces of generations of Snatchers stared down at him from family portraits on the walls.

"Don't look at them, and you will feel better," Arthur told himself.

"Don't look at them, and you will feel better," Arthur told himself.

He turned his attention to the rest of the room. The desk was huge and cluttered, and behind it, moth-eaten velvet drapes covered the wall. In front of the fireplace were two decrepit sofas and a chaise longue. One of the sofas had an old blanket and a dirty sheet strewn over it, and next to it was a pile of dirty socks. The other sofa was a mess of horsehair and springs. The whole room smelled rather unpleasant.

The desk seemed the obvious place to look, so he started there. In its center a large sheet of paper was laid out, held down at its corners by a paperweight, a dirty cup and saucer, and a pair of old boots. Arthur studied the sheet. It seemed to be some sort of scientific diagram, but any more than that, he could not tell.

Around it were stubs of old pencils, rubber bands, a broken pocket watch, the dried remains of half a sandwich, a ruler, and a broken quill . . . but no keys. Arthur decided to try the drawers. He pulled open the top one.

Socks? Arthur was very surprised. The drawer was filled with socks, only a little less grubby than the pile by the sofa. Reluctantly he put his hand into the drawer and searched to see if there were any keys hidden there. When he decided there were not, he moved on.

Arthur opened the next drawer, and to his disgust, he discovered it contained long johns. He was *not* putting his hand in there. He took the ruler from the desk and used it to empty the drawer. No key there, either. He put the underwear back in the drawer, again using the ruler. Then he closed the drawer very firmly, dropped the ruler as hastily as he could, and shivered.

With a feeling of dread, he opened the next drawer. In this one he found a pink wig.

Arthur recognized it immediately—it was the wig Madame Froufrou had been wearing in the market. So there *was* a connection between her and Snatcher! But there was no time to think about that now—he had to concentrate on looking for the keys.

He lifted the wig out of the drawer, gave it a shake, and then hunted around the empty drawer. No keys!

Arthur replaced the wig and tried the last drawer. This one was so full that he had to pull with all his might. When it finally sprang open, he found a great bundle of fabric crammed inside. He pulled it out and gave another gasp of recognition. It was Madame Froufrou's dress.

It was Madame Froufrou's dress.

Things get curiouser and curiouser, Arthur thought. He checked the drawer fruitlessly for keys, then stuffed the dress back into it. It was not easy and took a certain amount of standing on to make it go back in.

Where next, he wondered.

He went over to a small table by one wall. There was a glass bottle on the table with some objects in it, and Arthur held it up. At the bottom, among some straw, were a tiny piece of cheese and two very small sleeping mice . . . or very, very, very small rats.

As he stood looking at the tiny creatures in puzzlement, he heard a noise from outside the room. Footsteps!—and they were approaching the door. Arthur froze for a second, then

ran to the drapes and flung himself desperately behind them. A moment later someone entered the room and sat down in the chair behind the desk.

At the bottom, among some straw, were a tiny piece of cheese and two very small sleeping mice . . . or very, very, very small rats.

"My poor feet! This blooming rain!" It was Snatcher's voice.

Arthur peeped out from behind the curtains. Snatcher had his feet up on his desk and was unlacing his wet boots. Arthur watched as he took them off and swapped them with the dry

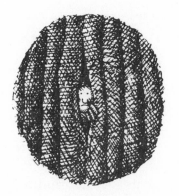

Arthur peeped out from behind the curtains.

pair on the desk. Then Snatcher stood up, walked over to the fireplace, and pulled back his coat. Then Arthur saw them!

Hanging from a short piece of string attached to Snatcher's waistcoat was a large bunch of keys. After a few moments trying to warm himself, Snatcher kicked at the embers and gave up. He walked out of the door, leaving it ajar.

Hanging from a short piece of string attached to Snatcher's waistcoat was a large bunch of keys.

Arthur crept out from behind the drapes and looked out into the hall. Snatcher stood in the archway facing the front door.

I have got to get those keys, thought Arthur. But how to do it—that was looking almost impossible. Then he heard a commotion from the passage.

"Come on, me lads! How many cheeses did we get in the end?" Snatcher called out.

"Eight, I think!" came the reply.

With a sinking heart, Arthur realized that the hunt was returning and that he needed to find a good hiding place—quickly.

"Put the mutts in my suite," Snatcher ordered.

The suite! Arthur glanced back at the velvet drapes and thought better of it. The dogs would sniff him out. Then he looked at the staircase. Perhaps he could hide upstairs? He crept to the staircase and started to climb as fast as he could. Behind him he heard more voices.

He crept to the staircase.

"The others made me be legs for the whole hunt!" It was Gristle.

"Stop your complaining and get upstairs and man the cheese hoist," Snatcher barked.

Arthur broke out into a cold sweat and increased his pace up the stairs. As he reached the top, he looked back. Gristle was just reaching the first step. Arthur rushed for the only door on the landing. In a second he was through it with the door closed.

He found himself in the roof space below the dome. Fenced pens filled with hay covered most of the floor. At the far end of the loft a pair of doors were open to the night sky—the doors that Bert had described.

At the far end of the loft a pair of doors were open to the night sky.

He heard Gristle again. "Oi! Master! Can you send me up some help? I'm knackered."

Arthur felt sick. He rushed to the open doors and looked down. Far below in the street he could see huntsmen and cheese-hounds milling about.

"Oi! Snatcher! I can't lift these cheeses on me own!"

The shouting was getting closer. Arthur looked up. Above his head was a metal beam that protruded out above the street. A pulley with a rope going through it hung from the end of the beam.

The door behind him opened. Arthur held his breath and jumped for the rope.

The Cheese Hall
Dome &
Attic
1/120 SCALE

Cross section of the Cheese Hall roof and dome.

chapter 23
OUT ON THE ROOF!

Arthur sat on the roof and caught his breath.

He had only just made it. Arthur sat on the roof and caught his breath. It was still raining, and a few inches behind him was a vertical drop to the street. He was not at all happy with the situation he was in.

Forcing himself to look straight ahead, Arthur shuffled along the bridge of the roof until he reached the statues below the dome. From inside the roof, he could hear muffled voices.

Then a metallic squeaking started. Arthur looked to see the pulley at the end of the beam turning, and the rope was slowly straining through it. Whatever it was lifting, it was heavy.

The plaintive bleating of cheeses grew louder.

"The poor things," Arthur muttered, then he looked up at the dome. If he could get up there, he might be able to signal to the Laundry.

Without his wings he would have to climb. Just the thought of this made him dizzy. It felt so different being up there but not able to fly. Still holding on to a statue, he stood up slowly and started to climb. Soon he was hanging onto the weather vane on the plinth.

Looking across the town he could just make out the mast of the Nautical Laundry. Black specks floated around it. Arthur guessed they must be the crows. He waved but was pretty sure they wouldn't see him. The rain grew heavier, and soon he lost sight of the crows. He looked down. Set into the dome were several small windows. He decided to have a look to see what was going on inside.

Arthur turned around slowly, lowered himself till he found a footing, and then released his grip on the weather vane. He slithered down to a narrow strip of stonework that ran around the base of the dome. One of the windows was just a few feet

He slithered down to a narrow strip of stonework.

from him. He eased himself along the ledge and peered in to see that the pens were now occupied by cheese. He moved around to the far window.

Several men were pulling something up.

Several men were pulling something up with the hoist. They pulled and pulled, and finally a net came into view. More cheese! Arthur could hear the bleating. When the net was level with the doors, one of the members took a long pole with a hook on the end and used it to swing the net into the loft. Then the doors were shut and the cheeses released from the net. For about a minute there was mayhem as the cheeses did all they could to evade capture. But trapped in the loft, they stood no chance, and soon they were all in pens.

Arthur peered through it.

The cheeses quieted down, and the members left. Arthur decided it was too dangerous to try to get back down with the hoist, but he had to get in somehow. He looked at the window in front of him and decided to try to force it open. It gave way fairly easily. Arthur smiled. Directly below him was a pen with a good covering of hay on the floor, which he thought might make a soft landing. Before he could talk himself out of it, he jumped. He hit the floor, just avoiding a cheese, and fell back into the hay. The cheeses in the pen started bleating noisily. Arthur sat still, hoping their noise would not bring any of the huntsmen back. But as the bleating died down, he heard footsteps coming up the stairs. He groaned, but quickly wiggled under the hay. Then he heard the door.

Arthur sat still.

"Them cheeses is making a right commotion! You'd think they knew what was going to happen to them!" said a voice. It was Gristle. "Let the cage down, and get them out of the pens. Snatcher says that the Great One is going to be right hungry after they give him a good zap!"

"What they going to use tonight?" asked another voice.

"Those awful trotting badgers. The sooner we cut them down to size, the better!" replied Gristle. "Did you see what they did to the Trouts?"

"Yes. Old Trout won't be able to sit down anytime soon, and Trout Junior is lucky he still has a nose."

"I am blooming glad it ain't us on lab duty tonight," muttered Gristle. "Anyway, they'll be done in there in about ten minutes, and so we better get on."

Arthur peeked out through the hay and saw Gristle standing by a pair of brass levers that stuck out of the wall.

"Move yerselves then," ordered Gristle. "Don't want to squash yer."

The other men cleared a space under the center of the dome, and Gristle pushed one of the levers. Arthur followed the men's gaze upward. A cage was descending from inside the very top of the dome. It clanked and shook as it moved slowly toward the floor of the loft. The cheeses were eerily silent. The cage settled on the floor and came to rest.

"Right!" said Gristle. "Get the cage door open, and let's get the cheeses in."

Gristle and the other man grabbed several cheeses.

While one of the men held the door open, Gristle and the other man grabbed several cheeses from the pens and pushed them into the cage. Soon the cage was full. The cheeses were so scared, they weren't even bleating.

"I do hope the Great One is hungry! Eight is an awful lot of cheese," said the doorman.

"Don't worry, he is getting huge!" smirked Gristle.

"Snatcher says he will be ready real soon. All we have to do is keep up the supply of cheese and monsters."

Arthur felt cold when he heard this. Supply of monsters?

"Oi! Gristle! D'yer think they're ready yet?"

"The music ain't started! They 'ave to 'ave the music before the cheese goes into the pit. Otherwise it wouldn't be a Cheese Ceremony, would it?" Gristle bellowed, annoyed. "Just keep your ear out for the din."

No sooner had he said that when strange music started to waft up from somewhere below. Arthur had never heard anything like it. It was a crazed drumming and blowing of horns. It reached a crescendo, then stopped.

Gristle raised a hand, then whispered, "'Ere we go!" He pushed down the second lever. With a bang, a trapdoor beneath the cage opened. The cage full of cheeses shuddered. Gristle pushed the first lever down again, and the cage started to disappear down through the hole.

After about thirty seconds Gristle cried out, "Look! The chain's gone floppy. It must have hit the fondue!"

"Let it sink slowly, then after about a minute haul it up," whispered one of the others. "Don't want no half-cooked cheeses hanging about!"

Arthur watched the men in silence. After a minute or so Gristle brought the cage back up . . . empty. Just a few strings of molten cheese hung from its bottom. Arthur was horrified. Gristle stopped the cage, then snapped the trapdoor lever up.

"Done!" said Gristle. "Now time for tea and biscuits."

The members trooped out of the loft. Arthur had witnessed something awful, but he was not sure quite what.

Just a few strings of molten cheese hung from its bottom.

Kipper suddenly burst through the door with Tom on his platform.

chapter 24
BACK AT THE SHIP

Mildred telling her news to Willbury, Marjorie, and the captain.

In the captain's cabin Mildred had finished telling her news to Willbury, Marjorie, and the captain, and they were all waiting rather anxiously over cups of cocoa when Kipper suddenly burst through the door with Tom on his platform.

"He's inside!" said Kipper.

Willbury looked at Tom and Kipper. Then his face fell. "Where's Arthur?"

"He's INSIDE!" repeated Kipper.

"Not the Cheese Hall?" said Willbury. He was met with silence. "I don't believe it. Why is Arthur inside the Cheese Hall, and you're here? You're supposed to be looking after him!"

Tom bit his lip. "After Mildred left, we started to follow them, but Snatcher came back. So we hid in the alley, and Snatcher left the door open while he went to get something . . . and Arthur says to me to distract Snatcher's horse . . . and he would sneak in . . ." Tom paused and looked even guiltier. "So I did. . . ."

Willbury closed his eyes and shook his head.

The captain sternly took over the questioning. "And then?"

The captain sternly took over the questioning.

Tom and Kipper both looked very upset. Kipper stared at the floor and told him, "Well, Arthur rushed in, and a few moments later Snatcher comes out and locks the door. Then he gets on his horse and rides off. . . ."

Tom followed on. ". . . So I says to Kipper that we better wait for Arthur to come out again. So we wait in the alley for about an hour or so. . . ."

"Yes . . . ," the captain prompted.

". . . then the hunt came back. . . ." Tom's voice quavered.

"Do you mean Arthur's trapped inside there, with Snatcher and his mob?" Willbury exclaimed, leaping to his feet.

"Yes . . ." Now Tom was looking at the floor too.

"What on Earth are we going to do now?" Willbury fumed. "Even if Arthur doesn't get caught, I think he's trapped."

There was a knock at the window. The captain opened it and two crows hopped in.

"'Scuse us, Captain!" said the crows. "But we've just seen something over at the Cheese Hall." Everybody in the room turned to look at the crows. "We think we just saw Arthur on the roof. He's not there now but we're pretty sure it was him."

"Can you fly over there and see if you can find him?" asked Willbury.

"Surely," said the crows. "We'll go right now."

With that, the crows hopped out of the window and flapped off.

With that, the crows hopped out of the window and flapped off.

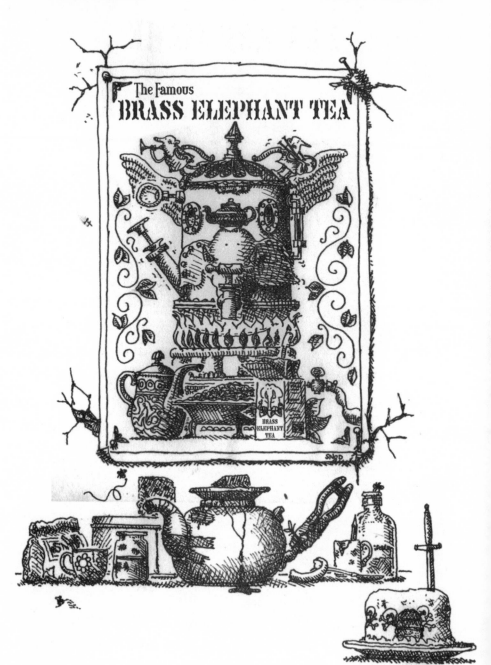

Inside the tearoom.

chapter 25
TEA AND CAKE

He could hear distant laughing and the chinking of crockery.

Arthur climbed out of the pen, crept up to the door at the top of the stairs, and opened it a few inches. He could hear distant laughing and the chinking of crockery. He closed the door again.

He wondered what he should do next. If he went down now, he was sure to get caught.

He looked at the cage that stood in the center of the floor. It was a very sad sight. Arthur climbed back into one of the pens and lay down in the hay to think.

He had to get back downstairs to rescue the underlings. . . . And what was he going to do about his wings? *I'll never be able to put them back together without Grandfather . . .* Arthur sat up and pulled out his doll. Grandfather! He'd forgotten about Grandfather.

He wound the doll and called his grandfather's name.

"Arthur!" His grandfather sounded both agitated and relieved. "Where have you been? Where are you? Are you all right?"

Arthur sat up and pulled out his doll.

"I'm all right, Grandfather . . . but I am in the loft above
the Cheese Hall."

"WHAT? You're in the Cheese Hall?" Now Grandfather
sounded angry.

"Yes . . . ," said Arthur, then he explained what had happened.

"Oh, Arthur! Why can't you do what you're told? I'm very
cross with you . . . and Mr. Nibble. He should never have let
you get into this trouble."

"Oh, Arthur! Why can't you do what you're told?"

"It's not his fault," Arthur said quickly. "He told me not to take any chances, and I disobeyed him . . . and you."

"Well, we will talk about this later, young man! But for now, we'll have to get you out of there. You say you've seen your wings?"

"Yes, the spars and leatherwork have been mended, but all the workings in the box have been taken to pieces."

"That's not a problem. I can tell you how to put them back together, if you can just find a way of getting your hands on them," Grandfather said, calmer now. "Then you'll be able to escape!"

A few tools.

"What do you think they are up to?" asked Arthur.

"I am not sure . . . but I am pretty sure it's no good!" There was worry in his voice. "Something strange is going on. This Great One that needs cheese . . . and they said they needed more 'monsters,' as they call the poor underlings. And those things you saw in the lab. It's all very peculiar."

"What should I do now?" asked Arthur.

"If you hide for a while, I bet the members will go to sleep before too long. Then get down to the lab and find a way of getting the wings. I'll guide you through rebuilding the motor."

"All right, Grandfather. And how are you doing?"

"This damp is getting worse and all my joints are aching. About an hour ago I heard some rumbling. It sounds as if some of the caves are starting to crumble. I don't know what those blasted boxtrolls think they are playing at. They are supposed to keep this place dry and shored up."

"Are you going to be all right?" Arthur asked worriedly. He wondered if Grandfather should perhaps come up from underground.

"I'll be fine. My boy, you get some rest! Contact me as soon as you get hold of your wings."

"I will . . . and Grandfather, keep warm!"

The crackling from the doll stopped and Arthur lay back in the hay. He tried to concentrate on the noise downstairs, but soon his eyes closed and he dropped off to sleep.

He awoke with a start. Something long and yellow was pecking his nose. He sat up, and as he did, two black shapes flapped up and settled on the edge of the pen.

Something long and yellow was pecking his nose.

"Sorry if we startled you." It was a pair of crows.

"You did!" replied Arthur as he rubbed his nose. "But I'm pleased to see you!"

"We're from the Laundry. Thanks for leaving that window open! The captain and the others are very worried about you."

"How did you know I was here?" Arthur asked.

"We saw you on top of the dome earlier, and we reported it to the captain and your friends. They asked us to fly over here to see if we could find you."

"Thanks," said Arthur. "Can you take a message back to them for me?"

"No problem!" cawed one of the crows.

"Tell them that I've found the underlings in the dungeon under this place. And Snatcher and the members have built some huge, weird device . . . and they are doing really nasty things to cheeses. Oh! And I have found out where my wings are. . . ."

"You've been busy then. Is there anything else we can do?" asked the other crow.

Arthur thought for a moment, then listened. There was no noise from downstairs. "Yes. Do you think you could fly down the outside of the building and check through the windows to see if Snatcher and his mob are asleep?"

"No sooner said, than done! It won't take a jiffy." The crows set off through the open window in the dome. Within a minute they returned.

"We flew around the whole building and looked in every window."

"It's all clear. We flew around the whole building and looked in every window we could. They're all asleep in a big room at the front. Looks like they've had a right feast of cake. Even that Snatcher is in there, snoring away."

"Good!" said Arthur. "I'm going to try to free the underlings and get my wings back."

"Anything else?" asked the crows.

"No. Just tell them what I've told you . . . and tell them we'll all be back soon."

The crows disappeared, and Arthur set off down the stairs.

When he reached the bottom, he crept across to the tearoom. As quietly as he could, he opened the door. About thirty men were strewn across sofas and old armchairs, surrounded by the debris of an enormous feast of tea and cake. On the far side of the room in the largest armchair, slumped the sleeping Snatcher.

About thirty men were strewn across sofas and old armchairs.

A cold sweat broke out on Arthur's forehead. He would have to be very, very careful. Trying not to make the slightest noise, he wove his way between the furniture, toward Snatcher. With each step, he tried to avoid the abandoned teacups and plates on the floor. Slowly he got closer. The legs of one of the members lay across his path, and Arthur stepped over them. As he did, the hem of his vest brushed the member's foot.

The hem of his vest brushed the member's foot.

"CAKE!"

Arthur jumped forward and turned. It was Gristle.

". . . Just one more slice. . . . I love cake. . . ." Gristle's eyes were still closed. He was talking in his sleep. Arthur closed his eyes for a moment and swallowed. He checked about the room and saw that nobody else was stirring, so made the last few steps to Snatcher.

The key ring still hung from Snatcher's waistcoat. There was a gentle jingling as Snatcher's enormous belly moved in and out.

Among a few crumbs on a cake stand that stood on the floor by Snatcher's chair was a knife. Arthur picked it up and gently, gently took hold of the keys. He held the knife to the string, and as Snatcher's belly moved, the knife cut slowly into the string. The string separated, and for a moment Snatcher's belly wobbled. Arthur held his breath. Snatcher snorted . . . but didn't wake. Arthur put the knife down and crept out of the room to the lab.

The knife cut slowly into the string.

Once in the lab he decided that it would be better to get his wings before releasing the underlings. Grandfather

was right—if he got caught, it would be all over. He just hoped that Snatcher's key ring had all the keys he needed. Arthur rushed to the shed. Searching among the keys, he found one that fit the door. He slid it in the lock and turned. There was a satisfying clunk and the door opened. Arthur pulled out his doll. "Grandfather! Are you there?"

"Yes, Arthur."

"I'm in the lab with the wings. Can you help me put them back together?"

"Certainly, dear boy. Can you find a small screwdriver and an adjustable wrench?"

Arthur looked about the bench and found the tools he needed. "Yes! I've found them."

Over the next hour, Grandfather instructed as Arthur rebuilt the wings' motor.

Over the next hour, Grandfather instructed as Arthur rebuilt the wings' motor. Occasionally Arthur would look up to check the door to the entrance hall or would have to break off to wind up the doll when his grandfather's voice started to fade. But finally the motor was back together, and Arthur felt immense relief.

"I suggest you put the wings on and wind them up . . . just in case," Grandfather told him.

"You're right," replied Arthur as he strapped them on. "Now—I've got underlings to rescue before Snatcher wakes up!"

"Very well, Arthur," said Grandfather. "But call me as soon as you are out of there! And please, please try not to take any unnecessary risks."

Arthur put the doll away and wound up his wings. Then he locked the shed and headed back downstairs. He peered in nervously at the members, but they were all still snoring away. Arthur prayed that they would stay asleep long enough. Tiptoeing on, he headed back toward the dungeon.

Arthur strapping the wings on.

Arthur looked down the length of the dungeon.

chapter 26
An Escape?

Fish nodded his head and gave him a thumbs-up.

Arthur looked down the length of the dungeon and stopped in his tracks. The door of the trotting badgers' cell stood open. He glanced across to his friends' cell. The four of them were still pressed up against the bars, obviously waiting for him to come back. They looked incredibly happy to see him. He silently pointed to the open cell door. Fish nodded his head and gave him a thumbs-up.

Arthur sighed with relief, but as he passed the open door, he remembered what the members had said about the badgers. The cell looked so very empty, and he felt an odd sensation of pity as he walked past it. Then he reached his friends' cell.

"Thank goodness you are still here!" Arthur exclaimed.

The underlings bounced up and down joyfully.

"I'm going to get you out of here," Arthur said, and produced the keys. He unlocked the door, and the underlings ran out and hugged him. Arthur hugged them back.

The underlings ran out and hugged him.

"Now," said Arthur, "we had better unlock the others."

Fish pointed to the cells that contained the other underlings and nodded.

"What about the boarded-up cell?"

The underlings looked toward it and shook their heads.

"Why not?" asked Arthur.

As before, they started to jump up and down and quietly made *bonk! bonk!* noises.

"I'll trust your judgment," Arthur said, eyeing the cell. "It might be very dangerous to release whatever is in there." The underlings looked relieved.

Arthur unlocked the other cells, and his friends went in to reassure the other creatures that they could trust Arthur. Soon they all gathered at the bottom of the stairs.

"Come on!" said Arthur. "We have to get out of here quickly . . . but remember, keep very quiet." The underlings nodded, and set off following Arthur.

He guided the underlings up the stairs and out through the lab to the door to the entrance hall. They stopped, and

Arthur checked that the coast was clear.

Arthur opened the door just enough to check that the coast was clear. Arthur was about to lead them out into the entrance hall when there was a loud cheese bleat from the passageway to the front door. Arthur and the underlings froze. The door of the tearoom opened and a bleary-eyed Gristle walked out.

A voice called out after him. "It'll be the milkman. Tell 'im to leave fifteen pints and that I will pay 'im next week." It was Snatcher.

The door of the tearoom opened and a bleary-eyed Gristle walked out.

Arthur watched as Gristle headed for the main entrance. Then he heard him shout, "'Ave you got the keys to the front door?"

Arthur felt a lump in his throat. He looked from the archway to the passage across to the tearoom.

There was a pause, then Snatcher's voice boomed from the tearoom. "Someone's nicked me blooming keys!"

Arthur swung the door the rest of the way open and ushered the underlings forward. "Up the stairs! Run for your lives!" he urged them.

Just as they started to scuttle across the hall, Snatcher stepped through the door of the tearoom. Arthur looked at Snatcher in horror. This might be the end of everything. Unable to control the panic in his voice, he shouted to the underlings:

"RUN!"

Arthur looked at Snatcher in horror.

The underlings rushed up the stairs. Arthur pushed the buttons on the front of the wing box and jumped. Up he went; oh, was it good to be able to fly again!

"It's that blasted boy. And he's stolen my wings!" bellowed Snatcher. The other members were now piling out into the entrance hall. They looked from Arthur to the underlings fleeing up the stairs.

"Get 'em!" screamed Snatcher, pointing to the underlings. He grabbed a walking stick from the coat stand by the door and raised it to throw at the underlings. Arthur threw the keys hard. They caught Snatcher in the nose, and Snatcher wailed at Arthur, "You little swine. Just you wait till I get 'old of you!" For the first time in a long time, Arthur grinned. He was already too far off the ground for Snatcher to reach.

They caught Snatcher in the nose.

Some of the members were gaining on the underlings. Arthur adjusted his wing speed and flew up to one of the alcoves and grabbed hold of a statue. Then he pulled it hard. The statue toppled over. Below, the members saw what was happening and ran back down the stairs to get out of the way. The statue crashed down.

Snatcher screamed again while frantically waving his walking stick. "Don't let 'im stop yer! Get those monsters!"

The statue toppled over.

Arthur flew to the next statue and waited till some of the members were brave enough to start mounting the stairs again, then he pulled on it. Again there was a crash as the statue hit the stairs, and again the members ran back to avoid it.

The members saw what was happening.

The underlings were just reaching the door to the loft. Arthur came down on the landing, turned off his wings, and ran through the door behind them, slamming it closed. As he did, a walking stick clattered against the door behind him.

The underlings stood in the loft looking scared out of their wits. Arthur looked around—they needed to barricade the door. His eyes fixed on the cage. He turned on his wings again, flew to the top of it, and unhooked it from its chain.

"Quick! Push this against the door!" Arthur shouted to the underlings.

The underlings obeyed and soon the cage crashed against the door. Arthur flew to the pair of doors at the far end of the loft and yanked them open. The net was hanging from the end of the beam.

The cage crashed against the door.

"Fish, help me get the net into the loft!" Arthur ordered. Fish quickly untied the rope and let a little play out. Arthur grabbed the net and pulled it in. He turned off his wings and spread the net out on the floor.

"Everybody but Fish get in the net." The underlings looked horrified and didn't move.

"Quick!" Arthur said urgently. There was a crash as the members threw themselves against the door. "This is our only chance! Please get in the net," Arthur pleaded. But even Fish looked scared.

More pounding and shouting came from the stairway door. Reluctantly the underlings climbed into the net, and Arthur joined Fish at the rope and they pulled the rope in. The pulley made a fearful squeak and moan, and the net swung out over the street.

The net swung out over the street.

"When you get to the ground, make for the canal," Arthur called out to the underlings. He felt Fish nudge him. He realized Fish was uncertain whether he was going to be left behind.

"Don't worry, Fish. You and I are going to fly," Arthur reassured him. And slowly they played the rope out, lowering the frightened creatures.

The crashing at the door grew louder, and Arthur and Fish let the rope out faster.

Finally it went limp.

"Right, Fish. Let's be off." Fish backed away from Arthur as the cage behind them toppled over, crashing to the ground, and the door flew open. Arthur grabbed Fish by his box corners and pushed him forward, toward the drop to the street. He turned the power knob on his box to full and hit both buttons.

"Get them!" screamed a voice. The members were racing across the loft. Arthur jumped and pushed Fish over the edge.

For about two seconds they dropped. Fish let out a howl, but the wings began to beat and their descent slowed. Below they could see the underlings running up a street in the direction of the canal, except for the lonely stoat, who was disappearing in the opposite direction, looking miserable. From above, they heard screams of rage.

"Stop them! Thieves! Kidnappers! Underlings! Monsters!" Then Arthur heard Snatcher's voice. "Get downstairs and go after them. They're not to get away!"

For about two seconds they dropped.

But Arthur wasn't worried. He had his wings. He asked Fish if he wanted to be put down on the ground.

Fish, turning his head to look at Arthur, shook his head. He was smiling.

"So you enjoy flying?"

Fish nodded and started to gently flap his arms.

"Right, then; I think we better catch up with the others."

So they set off through the early morning light, back to the Laundry. After they had gone a few streets, they heard the sound of dogs.

"They are coming after us!"

The lonely stoat, who was disappearing in the opposite direction, looking miserable.

"Back to the laundry! Follow us."

chapter 27

ATTACK ON THE SHIP

Arthur and Fish kept low as they flew.

Arthur and Fish kept low as they flew. They caught up with the underlings and Arthur shouted to them.

"Back to the Laundry! Follow us."

Arthur was surprised at how fleet-footed the underlings were, but still the sound of the cheese-hounds grew louder. Soon they turned onto the canal bank, and before them was the Laundry. The rain had stopped and the washing was blowing in the wind. A joyful shout rang from the deck, followed by a commotion.

"Are you all right?" Arthur asked Fish. There was a happy gurgling.

The other underlings ran along the towpath and Arthur landed by the gangplank. As he landed, he released Fish.

"Arthur! Fish! Egg! Shoe! Titus! You got out!" Arthur looked up to see a very happy Willbury standing at the top of the gangplank with Kipper, Tom, Marjorie, and the captain.

Arthur looked up to see a very happy Willbury.

"Yes! We're all right!"

"Thank goodness, and well done!" Everyone looked delighted, and Kipper and Tom looked especially relieved.

Then a shout came from somewhere on deck. "Dogs ahoy!"

Arthur and Willbury turned to see cheese-hounds rushing onto the towpath.

Arthur and Willbury turned to see cheese-hounds rushing onto the towpath.

"Quick, get the underlings aboard!" Willbury cried. Fish, Shoe, Egg, and Titus led the underlings up the gangplank. Arthur scrambled onto the ship after them.

"Draw up the gangplank!" shouted the captain. Snatcher and his mob were now running down the towpath behind the dogs, roaring in anger. The crew hauled the gangplank up just as the first of the hounds leaped at it.

"Load the cannon!"

"I told you, Captain, we ain't got any gunpowder!"

"Okay, okay! Prepare the knickers!" Crows flew down from the crow's nest to the underwear section of the rigging, unpegged six pairs of the largest knickers they could find, and then descended to the deck. The pirates quickly tied the knickers to various points on the gunwales of the ship.

Crows with a particularly large pair of knickers.

From below deck came a scampering, and rats appeared carrying oddly shaped lumps, each the size of a tennis ball.

Rats appeared carrying oddly shaped lumps, each the size of a tennis ball.

"What are those?" asked Arthur.

"We thought we might be attacked so Tom suggested that we make something to give the enemy a real surprise," said the captain. "We mixed all the gunge from the bilge pumps with glue, then rolled it into balls. They were very sticky so we coated them in bread crumbs and fluff. We tested one earlier. . . . It's disgusting; when they hit you, they burst and cover you in slime. It stinks and it is almost impossible to wash off."

"Knickers loaded, Captain!" came the cry from the crew.

"Prepare to fire!" ordered the captain. Rats pulled the knickers back to form catapults.

The knickers were pulled back to form catapults.

On the towpath everything went quiet; then a voice called out. It was Snatcher's.

"Board the Laundry!"

As the cheese-hounds continued to jump up and down on the towpath, baying, the members approached the ship. As they did, the captain bellowed.

"FIRE!"

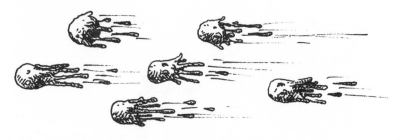

"FIRE!"

The twanging of six enormous pairs of knickers could be heard, followed by a whizzing, a splodging, and disgusted screams. The cheese-hounds ran back down the towpath to a safe distance. The members looked as if they wanted to run too, but Snatcher was having none of it.

Snatcher was having none of it.

"Go on, you weak-willed, yellow-bellied varmints! BOARD the Laundry!" he shrieked.

The captain shouted "Fire!" again, and another volley flew over the side of the ship. More screams could be heard. This time one of the screams was Snatcher's.

"Retreat!" shouted Snatcher.

The members didn't need telling twice. They ran back down the towpath to join the hounds, and the crew of the Laundry cheered.

The members didn't need telling twice.

"I think we have got them on the run," said the captain.

"They'll think twice about attacking us again," agreed Arthur.

"I hope you're right. . . ," said Willbury thoughtfully.

Along the towpath a meeting was being held, Snatcher seemingly doing all of the talking. Everybody on the Nautical Laundry watched uneasily. After a minute or so, one of the members ran off down the towpath and disappeared. Snatcher walked a little way back toward the ship, and shouted, "You may have beaten us back, but it's not over yet!"

"Err hmm!" Arthur heard the captain urgently clear his throat. "Did you see Pickles and Levi at the Cheese Hall?"

Arthur looked at the captain, who was waiting nervously for his reply.

"I am afraid I didn't," Arthur said sadly.

"No rodents at all?" asked the captain.

"Just a pair of tiny mice in Snatcher's room. And they were hardly big enough to be mice. . . ."

The captain sighed and turned away.

"Just a pair of tiny mice in Snatcher's room."

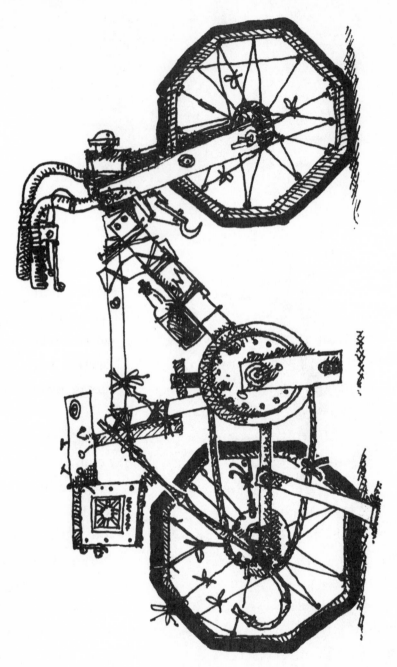

A Dodgy Tanner.

chapter 28
THE POLICE

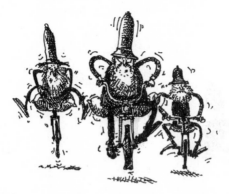

The Ratbridge Irregular Police Force on "Dodgy Tanners."

The bicycles that the Ratbridge Irregular Police Force rode were known as "Dodgy Tanners." This was because of the shape and number of their wheels. They had two wheels the shape of thru-penny coins. If one added together two thru-penny coins, one would have sixpence, and a sixpenny coin was known as a "tanner."

"Penny Farthing" bicycles had perfectly round wheels like the coins they were named after. Thru-penny coins were many-sided. Wheels this shape did not make for the good humor of the riders. On hard surfaces such as cobbles, the policemen could be heard a long way off as they let out little cries of pain at every turn of the wheels. Many a burglar had made an early escape because of the warning noises of an unhappy, approaching rider. Some policemen even took to wearing cushions strapped to their bottoms to prevent bruising. But not all could afford padding, so the Irregulars were known locally as "Squeakers."

*Many a burglar had made an early escape because
of the warning noises of an unhappy, approaching rider.*

The Squeakers now came down the towpath as fast as they could without causing themselves too much discomfort. Emergency calls were rare, and as the Squeakers were paid by the number of incidents they attended and arrests they made, they were in a rush to get to the scene. As they approached, all fell silent.

The Chief Squeaker dismounted his bike, unstrapped his cushion, and asked authoritatively, "Hello, hello, hello. What's going on here?"

The Chief Squeaker dismounted his bike and unstrapped his cushion.

The members and the pirates all looked very uneasy.

Snatcher replied first. "We are being attacked by this bunch of cutthroats and robbers!"

"Attacked, you say?" replied the officer.

"Yes! We were out for a peaceful stroll when these scalawags started firing at us. They need locking up!"

The sound of twenty pairs of iron handcuffs being prepared could be heard.

The sound of twenty pairs of iron handcuffs being prepared could be heard.

"This sounds very serious!" replied the Chief Squeaker with a smile. "It sounds as if a lot of arrests might need to be made!"

"That is balderdash!" called Willbury from the deck. "We are just defending ourselves. I am a lawyer and . . ."

The Chief Squeaker raised his hand. "A LAWYER!" He went bright red. "I don't think this is the sort of thing a lawyer should be mixed up in, but I expect no better. Officers, arrest that man!"

There was a rush for the ship.

"Stop!" cried Willbury. "And I'm a circuit judge!"

"WHOA!" cried the Chief Squeaker. "I am very sorry, my lord, I did not realize that you were so obviously honest. Men, arrest the party on the towpath."

The policemen turned to the members, still brandishing their handcuffs. But then Snatcher walked forward. "The difference between me an 'im is 'chalk and cheese,'" he said. Then he made funny little signs with his hands.

Then he made funny little signs with his hands.

The police stopped in their tracks. The Chief Squeaker now asked in a quavering voice, "Did you say 'chalk and cheese'?"

"Yes, I did!" replied Snatcher.

"What kind of cheese is that?" As the Chief spoke, his hands made a number of strange gestures.

Snatcher replied, "That would be a BIG CHEESE!" And he made the same gestures.

"Why is he doing that?" asked Arthur.

"I am not sure," said a hesitant Willbury.

Marjorie sidled up to them. "I think they are 'brothers'! Members of the Guilds."

"What's that?" asked Arthur.

"Secret organizations. They are making secret signs to each other and using code words to let each other know they are members."

"Why don't they just recognize each other?" Arthur asked.

"It's a very big organization, and there are lots of smaller parts of it. The police probably have their own section," said Marjorie.

The policemen looked at one another and then fell to their knees. They bowed their heads, and whispered, "We smell strong cheese! We smell strong cheese! It is overpowering. We respect it for it is the most flavorsome, and we are humble. What would it have us do?"

"We smell strong cheese! We smell strong cheese! It is overpowering."

Snatcher smirked at the policemen fawning before him, then told them, "I think you will find that 'm'lord' might well be retired. He holds no power now—and he is harboring a thief who has stolen a pair of mechanical wings from me. From me—A BIG CHEESE! I think that the right course of action would be to arrest the rapscallion who has stolen my wings and return them to me!"

The Chief Squeaker stood up and looked at Willbury.

"Is this so, sir? You are no longer a judge?" he asked.

"Technically that is true . . . ," replied Willbury.

And before Willbury had a chance to go any further, the Chief Squeaker cut in. "Right! Drop your gangplank, sir! Any failure to do so will be seen as hindering the police in the course of their duties and may force me to arrest you and your entire crew."

Willbury looked taken aback. "I think we'd better do what he says, otherwise we are going to get into real trouble."

The pirates reluctantly lowered the gangplank and the Chief Squeaker shouted out, "Arrest the boy!"

The policemen on the towpath rushed onto the ship. Kipper and the other pirates looked as if they were ready for a fight, and the policemen looked nervous.

"Hold back, crew!" said Willbury. Then he whispered to Arthur, "Quick! Fly!"

But there wasn't time. The policemen grabbed him and snapped handcuffs around his wrists. "Willbury!" Arthur cried, but the police marched him off the ship before Willbury could do a thing to help. The Chief Squeaker removed his wings.

The policemen grabbed him and snapped handcuffs around his wrists.

Arthur's heart sank. He thought he'd done so well to get himself and the underlings safely out of the Cheese Hall—he couldn't believe this was happening. Just when he'd got his wings back, to have them taken away from him again! And for the police to be on Snatcher's side! It all seemed so unjust. But there was no point struggling now. Perhaps he'd find a way to convince the police of his innocence.

"Right! I want a couple of you to take him back to the station," the Chief Squeaker addressed his men, "while the rest of you maintain order here. Let the respectable gents on the towpath go about their lawful business, and keep a close eye on that ex-lawyer and his bunch of pirates. If any of them try to get off their ship . . . arrest them!" The Chief Squeaker winked at Snatcher.

"Here, sir!" he said as he handed the wings over. "And if we can be of any more service to you?"

Snatcher turned the wings over in his hands, and gave Arthur an oily smile. "I was wondering how we were going to put them back together. You have done us a service. There are a few questions I would like to ask you. . . ." Then he turned to the Chief and spoke in a sly voice. "I know how understaffed you are at the police station. I think it might be as well if you were to let me help you out by keeping the boy." Snatcher smirked.

"No! You can't do that!" shouted Willbury from the deck.

"Oh, yes I can!" replied the Chief Squeaker. He then placed a hand on Snatcher's shoulder.

"By the powers invested in me, I now pronounce you a Temporary Jailer, Class 3. Please take custody of this criminal on behalf of the Ratbridge Police."

Snatcher gave a slight bow. "Oh, certainly officer. Anything to help out the police!"

"Oi, you two! Grab him!" the new Temporary Jailer, Class 3, snapped at a couple of rather sorry-looking members.

The two approached Arthur. The older one was bandaged from waist to knee, while the younger one's nose was covered in sticking plaster.

"It's them! The Trouts!" Marjorie shouted from the deck. "Those are the men who stole—"

The older one was bandaged from waist to knee,
while the younger one's nose was covered in sticking plaster.

The Chief Squeaker cut her off. "Any more trouble from you lot, and I shall have all of you locked up."

Willbury grabbed Marjorie's arm.

"Yes. Any more trouble, and I'm sure the police will want to give us the power to administer punishment to our prisoner as well," said Snatcher, eyeing Willbury.

"Quite right, sir," responded the Chief. "It is so nice to find a cooperative member of the public like yourself."

Snatcher then spoke to the Trouts. "Take the boy back to the Cheese Hall!"

Arthur looked nervously back at Willbury as he was led away. "What am I going to do?" he cried. The thought of trying to escape from the Cheese Hall again filled him with despair. And what on earth would they do to him once they got him there?

"We'll get you back!" called Willbury after him.

"I am sure your diligence will be well rewarded," Snatcher said with a smirk to the Chief Squeaker. "I will arrange for some 'paperwork' to be delivered to you later."

"Oh, thank you, sir!"

The Chief Squeaker mounted his bicycle and set off down the towpath.

The Chief Squeaker mounted his bicycle and set off down the towpath, leaving his men guarding the Laundry.

"Just when I thought things were getting better!" muttered Willbury. "Poor Arthur—it was so brave of him to rescue the underlings and get his wings back. Now he's worse off than ever! What are we going to do?"

A Squeaker on guard.

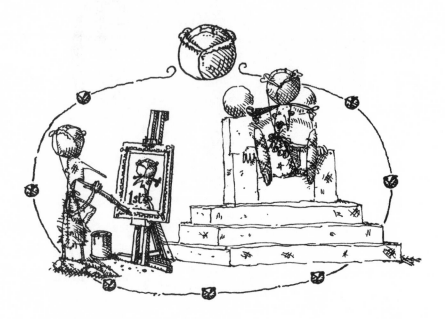

The queen very much enjoyed having her portrait painted, and would sit two weeks for new sets of stamps. For those who couldn't read, the value of the stamp was defined by the size of cabbage she wore on her head.

chapter 29
Exodus

*They assembled before the throne on the high
stone platform at the end of their cavern.*

Back in the Underworld, all the remaining cabbageheads
had gathered together. They assembled before the throne on
the high stone platform at the end of their cavern. The floor
of the cavern was now under several feet of water, and the level
was rising very quickly.

The queen adjusted the enormous cabbage on her head,
and then gave a haughty cough. She was the only cabbagehead
who ever spoke louder than a whisper. "We have brought
you here today, for we have unfortunate tidings to impart.
Pursuant to the ever-rising levels of ill, commodious abla-
tive liquids, we believe sustainable brassica production ceases
to be feasible. Therefore I decree that henceforth we must
sojourn to an alternative affiliated venue. Hey nonny nonny,
we have spoken!"

The other cabbageheads looked at one another, confused.
None of them knew what she was talking about.

Then a very old cabbagehead made his way up the steps to the throne and whispered in the queen's ear. She gave an embarrassed nod and spoke again.

A very old cabbagehead made his way up the steps to the throne.

"In alternative parlance, it is too wet to grow cabbages here anymore, and we'll have to find somewhere else to grow them."

There was a lot of nervous muttering among the cabbageheads.

The old cabbagehead whispered in the queen's ear once more. Then she spoke again.

"'Tis brought to one's attention that vertically positioned below dales, some few leagues beyond the confines of the above populace, is a sufficient aperture that we may abide. Thus we might alight and henceforth meander to yonder aperture to re-establish a harmonious, intergraded monarchical community, and go forth with our troglodyte agriculture."

There was more muttering from the "common" cabbage-heads, and the old cabbagehead once more spoke to the queen. She went a deeper red.

"There is another cave not far from here where we can move to and grow cabbages," she said rather awkwardly.

A small cabbagehead approached the throne and whispered to the old cabbagehead. He in turn whispered to the queen, and she spoke again. "It would appear that one's subjects who are currently absent from one's realm while . . ."

The old cabbagehead gave the queen a steely gaze and the queen started again. "One . . . We need someone to go and find Titus and the others and tell them where we've gone."

Two younger cabbageheads raised their hands.

"Very good," said the queen. "Now, follow one and one's assistant," she said, indicating the old man, "and don't forget one's seeds!"

Two younger cabbageheads raised their hands.

She surveyed her kingdom of water and bobbing cabbages one last time.

The crowd all patted their pockets and giggled. The old cabbagehead descended the steps and led them up a tunnel away from the platform.

The queen found herself sitting alone and feeling rather disgruntled. She surveyed her kingdom of water and bobbing cabbages one last time, and then followed.

THE DUNGEON UNDER THE CHEESE HALL

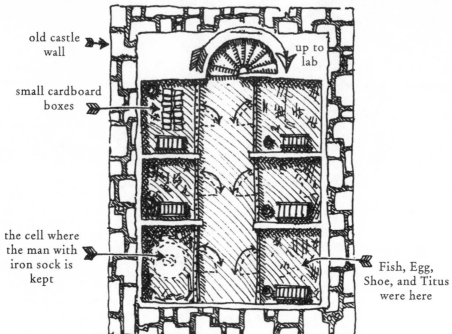

old castle wall

up to lab

small cardboard boxes

the cell where the man with iron sock is kept

Fish, Egg, Shoe, and Titus were here

The dungeon under the laboratory has a long and gruesome history, and predates the Cheese Hall by hundreds of years. It was constructed in 1247, as the dungeon/torture chamber/nursery/food cellar/rubbish tip for Ratbridge castle. In 1453, revolting peasants destroyed the castle. Eight babies and three hardened criminals survived—trapped in the dungeon for two years before they were discovered by a team of local builders, who were redeveloping the site as a shoe shop. For the next hundred years, the dungeon was used as a storeroom for shoes, and the equipment left over from the torturing came in handy for fitting shoes to those who lied about shoe size.

During this period, a small cheese shop was built next door, and due to foul and sharp practices, became very successful. When the shoe shop failed, it was bought up by the cheese shop owner and was used as a secret workshop where date-expired labels were filed off cheeses and newly forged ones applied. The cheese shop became wholesalers and gained control of the cheese trade in the area. Other cheese traders had to become members of a cheese guild (set up by the wholesalers) to be allowed to trade, and the empire expanded.

In 1712 the Cheese Hall was built and a laboratory was built behind it to further the "science" of adulteration. The dungeon found much use for the storage of those who caused any problems for the cheese guild, and long-term storage of failed experiments.

chapter 30
BACK BELOW THE CHEESE HALL

In the dungeon the members surrounded Arthur.

In the dungeon the members surrounded Arthur.

"What are we going to do with you, my little thief?" asked Snatcher.

"I am not the thief!" snapped Arthur.

"Oh yes, you are! You took my wings!"

"Those were my wings. You stole them from me in the first place."

"That is as may be, but they are mine now. And for all the grief you've caused me, I think pretty much everything of yours is as good as mine." Snatcher glared at Arthur. "Search 'im!"

The members descended on Arthur and emptied his pockets.

"Not much here, sir!"

Then one of the members noticed the bump under Arthur's shirt.

"He's got something up his jumper!"

"Get it!" ordered Snatcher.

Arthur tried to defend his doll with his cuffed hands, but he was overpowered and the doll was pulled from him.

"What have we here?" asked Snatcher. "The little boy has a little dolly!"

"Ahhhh!" scoffed the members.

"The little boy has a little dolly!"

Arthur grasped frantically for the doll. Snatcher laughed and threw it on the floor.

"By the time I've finished with you, that dolly is going to look like your big brother."

The members laughed.

"What do you mean?" asked Arthur, squirming.

"Haven't you guessed yet? Have you not realized why we are collecting big creatures and why only little creatures leave here? We are nicking their SIZE!" sneered Snatcher.

Snatcher laughed and threw it on the floor.

Arthur froze. "Size?"

"Yes!" Snatcher laughed. "It so happens that we have come by a certain device . . ."—he stopped and winked at the Trouts, who were holding Arthur—"that can extract the size from things. All your little friends who came our way are now your even littler friends."

Snatcher and the others burst out laughing.

"But what's the point in doing that?" Arthur asked.

"That is for us to know. It is part of our BIG plan." There was more laughter. Then Snatcher's face changed, and his voice turned nasty. "And if was not for you, things might be progressing a lot faster. I needed them monsters you freed. Perhaps you might like to donate some of your size instead?"

Arthur did not reply.

"Yes. I thought that might shut you up. You've put a wrench in the works. Now we have to go and find a load more monsters to shrink!" snarled Snatcher. He turned to the Trouts. "Throw him in a cell. We'll sort him out the next time we fire up the machine." Then he grinned horribly. "And next

time I go out on a little selling trip, I am sure all the ladies will be falling over themselves to buy a miniature boy!" He looked directly at Arthur, put on a silly face, and spoke in the unmistakable tones of Madame Froufrou: "I 'ave only one of zese little creatures, for sale to zee most fashionably rich lady of all!"

Arthur gaped. So that explained why Madame Froufrou had reminded him so strongly of Snatcher! And the clothes in the desk! Was this man behind everything sinister in the town?

Sniggering at the look on Arthur's face, the Trouts threw him through the door of the cell that had contained the trotting badgers. Snatcher locked the door. Arthur noticed that the keys were now attached to his waistcoat by a heavy metal chain.

Arthur noticed that the keys were now attached to his waistcoat by a heavy metal chain.

"When are we going to fire up the machine?" asked Gristle.

"The sooner the better," replied Snatcher. "But there is no point doing it just for the boy; we'll get some more monsters to put in it."

"Does that mean we have to go down . . . below?" Gristle said with a grimace.

"Don't worry, Gristle. I am sure somebody will hold your hand." Snatcher smirked. Arthur noticed the other members also looked worried.

A quick cup of tea.

Snatcher sighed deeply. "I think a quick cup of tea is in order," he said, then all the members set off up the stairs, leaving Arthur alone in the dungeon.

Arthur alone in the dungeon.

The police had set up camp on the towpath.

chapter 31
THE STANDOFF

Kipper was standing with Tom on the deck, watching the Squeakers.

Back at the Laundry there was a standoff. The police had set up camp on the towpath, and the crew stood about looking dejected. They were running out of food. Normally the crew would have gone shopping late on market day (to pick up bargains), but with all the excitement yesterday, they had forgotten, and now they were not allowed off the ship.

Kipper was standing with Tom on the deck, watching the Squeakers tuck into the eggs and bacon they had cooked over a fire they had started on the towpath. The smell of the bacon wafted over the side of the Laundry.

"This is torture!" muttered Kipper.

"I think they must be doing it to wind us up," replied Tom.

The boxtrolls were also becoming uneasy, sniffing the air and gurgling to one another. Fish stared hard at the feasting Squeakers. One of the new boxtrolls joined Fish and whispered something to him.

*The Squeakers were tucking into the eggs and bacon
they had cooked over a fire.*

"I can feel my energy sapping away," said Kipper. "If I
don't get something to eat soon, I shall just fade away."

Tom looked up at Kipper's belly. "The chance of you
fading away is pretty remote. It's us rats I am worried about.
We have a very high metabolic rate you know." Tom stopped
and tugged on Kipper's arm. Then he pointed at Fish who was
moving very slowly down the gangplank toward the bank.

"What's he doing?" whispered Tom.

Kipper shrugged and they watched, perplexed, as Fish
reached the bank and walked nonchalantly straight past the
Squeakers. The Squeakers glanced up but seemed to pay
the boxtroll almost no attention at all.

"Why didn't they grab him?" Tom asked.

Kipper watched as the Squeakers returned to their eggs and
bacon. "It's townsfolk. I think it must be that they hold underlings in such low regard that they just don't notice them."

Fish continued a little farther down the canal bank, then began waving to the other boxtrolls on deck to join him. A small procession of boxtrolls marched down the gangplank, passed the Squeakers (who hardly gave them a second glance), and joined Fish.

A small procession of boxtrolls.

"Well, blow me down!" muttered Tom. "Where do you think they are off to?"

"Off to find themselves breakfast," said Kipper, sounding very sorry for himself. "I wish I were an underling!"

Twenty minutes later Willbury and Titus were sitting in the captain's cabin, when Titus, playing with the miniature cabbagehead by the window, gave a squeak. Willbury got up and joined him at the window. Back along the towpath came the boxtrolls, and they were all carrying sacks.

"Oh no!" said Willbury. "Now what's going on?" He rushed up on deck just as the boxtrolls walked straight past the policemen and up the gangplank.

Marjorie was up on deck, watching. "Good, isn't it?"

Willbury looked baffled.

"Them Squeakers just don't pay them any attention," explained Kipper. "So used to thinking of them as nothing, they just don't seem to notice them."

Titus looking out of the window.

Fish and his group of friends emptied out their sacks. Piled in the middle of the deck was a large stack of cakes, biscuits, treacle, boiled sweets, toffee, shortbread, pasties, anchovies, pickled onions, raspberry jam, and lemonade bottles. The crew's eyes lit up, and the pile soon disappeared under a crowd of bodies.

Willbury, however, frowned. "You know that Titus and the other cabbageheads don't like this sort of food. Didn't you think to bring anything for them?"

The boxtrolls looked a little grumpy. Shoe picked up a small sack that was still lying beside him and threw it huffily forward. Willbury emptied it, revealing a pile of fruit and vegetables. He smiled at the sulking boxtrolls.

"Thank you; that is very thoughtful of you. I'll take these down to the storeroom to keep them safe for later."

Once he returned, Willbury stood a few feet away from the melee, watching the crew gorge themselves on

Fish and his group of friends emptied out their sacks.

the food. Marjorie joined him. She was tucking eagerly into a doughnut. "Aren't you hungry?" she asked.

"How could I be hungry at a time like this?" Willbury said fretfully.

Marjorie looked carefully at Willbury, then said in a low voice, "I have a dreadful feeling that this is all my fault!"

"What do you mean?" asked Willbury.

Marjorie led him away from the group. "It's my invention. I think I know what has happened to it. I'd an idea, but when the Trouts turned up with Snatcher, I knew. . . . I just knew."

"The Trouts?" said Willbury, looking puzzled.

"Didn't you see the men who had hold of Arthur?" asked Marjorie.

"Not really—I was so focused on Arthur himself."

"It was the Trouts; I swear it. They looked pretty rough, but I am sure it was them."

"So Snatcher has your invention?"

"Yes."

"Are you sure?"

"Yes. It's all these little creatures."

"The little creatures?"

"The invention that was stolen from me was a resizing machine," whispered Marjorie.

"A RESIZING MACHINE!" Willbury was flabbergasted.

"Yes, I discovered how to take the size out of one thing and put it into another. In the wrong hands it could be very dangerous . . . and I think it has definitely got into the wrong hands." Marjorie looked mournful.

"How does this machine operate?" asked Willbury, staring at Marjorie.

Willbury was flabbergasted.

"It consists of two parts. If you have two objects of equal size, one side of the machine drains the size out

of one object, and the other side of the machine pumps the size into the other," Marjorie explained.

"Do you mean it shrinks one thing and makes the other thing bigger?" asked Willbury.

"Yes, exactly. And Snatcher and his mob have got hold of it. I don't know quite what they are doing with it, but I bet it's something rotten."

Willbury thought for a moment, and then said, "Well, we know what they're doing with it. They're shrinking the underlings!"

"Do you mean it shrinks one thing and makes the other thing bigger?" asked Willbury.

"Yes . . . but that's only half of it." Marjorie paused. "Where is all the size going?"

Willbury thought to himself, then muttered. "Oh, my word! I hadn't thought of that." Then he asked Marjorie another question.

"Why underlings?"

"It only works on living creatures. I guess they thought that nobody would notice or care if they used underlings."

"Then I wonder why they have been blocking up the holes to the Underworld," Willbury pondered. "Surely that would stop the underlings coming aboveground and falling into their clutches."

"I've been thinking about that too. I think they must be blocking up the holes to help trap them in some way. Perhaps there is only one hole still open, and they lie in wait for the underlings there, knowing it is their only way to the surface. . . . I don't know," answered Marjorie.

"This is truly awful. What ever possessed you to build a machine that could resize living creatures?"

Marjorie looked very embarrassed.

"Truthfully?" Marjorie looked very embarrassed. "I was very interested in the scientific principles involved in making it. I just wanted to see if it would work. I hadn't really worked out what it was going to be used for," said Marjorie.

"I wonder what it is they are making bigger," Willbury asked again.

"I don't rightly know. And I have been trying to work out how the cheese comes into it."

"It must somehow." Willbury then spoke in a determined manner. "I have a very bad feeling about this. We have to get Arthur back and stop whatever is going on! Let's call a Council of War!"

The man in the iron socks.

chapter 32

The Man in the Iron Socks

Against one wall was a bed.

Alone in the cold, dank dungeon, Arthur looked around his cell. Against one wall was a bed. It had probably not been very comfortable even before it had been used by the trotting badgers, but now it was covered with bite marks, and he thought he would get peppered with splinters if he tried to use it. Shreds of an old blanket had been used to form a kind of nest in one corner of the cell. This did not look very inviting either. It looked full of fleas, Arthur thought.

The only other things in the cell were a filthy bucket and a few strands of straw scattered about the floor. Arthur looked out the bars. About six feet away lay his doll!

If only I could reach it, I could get in touch with Grandfather, and he might be able to help me, thought Arthur.

He dropped to the floor and reached as far as he could. If only he could get the doll back. It lay a few feet from his grasp, almost as if it had been positioned deliberately to taunt him. He looked about his cell to see if there was anything he could use to help him. There was nothing.

"This is useless!" he moaned. Feeling completely at a loss, he got up and kicked the bed in frustration. After a second or so, there came a distant, dull thump in return. Arthur was puzzled. What was that?

It lay a few feet from his grasp.

He waited for a few moments but there were no more sounds, so he kicked the bed again. There was another thump. He didn't think it was an echo, but to be sure, he kicked the bed twice in rapid succession. After a couple of seconds came a *Thump! Thump! Thump!*

"It can't be an echo then!" He kicked the bed again. The thumping started again but did not stop. Arthur pulled the bed from the wall and put his ear to the stonework. The thumping was coming from the next cell. There was definitely someone— or something—in there. Then Arthur realized that the cell next to him was the boarded-up cell that the boxtrolls had been so frightened of. He began to wish he hadn't attracted the attention of its occupant. He half wondered if it was starting to come through the wall.

The thumping got louder and louder. Arthur looked down and noticed one of the bricks in the wall moving toward him.

It is! It's coming through! Arthur panicked. He jumped over the bed, then smashed the brick as hard as he could into the wall, sending it shooting back in.

Someone shouted "Ouch!" and the thumping stopped.

He jumped over the bed, then smashed the brick as hard as he could.

Arthur waited.

There was a muffled cry, an even louder thump, and before Arthur had time to react again, the loose brick flew out of the wall and almost hit him.

There was a pause; then a hand holding a stub of candle appeared through the hole. Arthur froze.

"What's all this noise about? Can't a prisoner get any sleep around here?" came a very grumpy voice. "I'm the only one around here allowed to make a din."

Arthur bent down and peered into the hole. A face covered by a mask peered back.

"Who are you?" asked Arthur.

A face covered by a mask peered back.

"I'm Herbert!" came the reply. "And who are you? You are not one of these cheese wallahs, are you? Can't stand cheese or anything to do with it! Used to love it, but you can have too much of a good thing!"

"No, my name is Arthur."

"Where you from?" Herbert asked curtly. "And what are you doing here?"

"I'm from the Underworld. But I've got stuck up here in Ratbridge, and now I've been caught and put in this cell."

"Blimey. You're in for it. I've heard what they's up to. Blooming evil! You's going to get shrunk!"

Arthur peered through the hole. "Did you make this?"

"'Course I did! I make lots of holes. Trouble is that when I do, it makes so much noise that the cheese wallahs always come and fill them in again. Never seems to get me anywhere. Been trying to get out of here for years, but never been lucky. If I could get these socks off, they wouldn't be able to hold me."

"Socks?" asked Arthur.

"Yes. The cheese wallahs shoved me into a pair of iron socks to slow me down. They still don't dare come too close!"

"Why is that?"

"The cheese wallahs shoved me into a pair of iron socks to slow me down."

"They is scared of me, what with me mask and me walloper. I made me a mask out of a bit of my old boots, and a big walloper out of me bed, and if they come near me . . . wallop!"

"What's a walloper?"

"It's me big mallet! It's great for all kinds of walloping. I love it!"

"You wallop them with it?"

"I wallop everything with it! Trouble is, the cheese wallahs got tired of it and fixed up a way of stopping me walloping them."

"I wallop everything with it!"

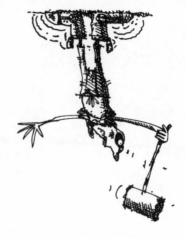

"So if I cause any trouble . . . they just turn the magnet on . . . boink!"

"How?"

"They stuck these socks on me and a huge electromagnet in the ceiling above me cell, so if I cause any trouble . . . they just turn the magnet on . . . and boink! I stick to the ceiling. Blooming iron socks!"

"Is that painful?" asked Arthur.

"Only when they turn the magnet off! I drops to the floor, you see . . . Bonk! But I still usually manage to wallop one or two of them."

"Why are you locked up here?" Arthur inquired.

"Me? Can't remember. Something to do with me and hmmm . . ." Herbert's voice trailed off.

"How long have you been here?"

"Can't rightly say. But I know that I have walloped more that a hundred and thirty of them over the years!"

"A hundred and thirty!" declared Arthur.

"Well, some of them might be the same person I walloped a few times. It was much easier in the early days before they put me in the socks. These days I am lucky to get even one of them!"

"Do you know what they are up to?"

"Well, I know they are shrinking underlings what they trap and steal," Herbert told him. "Don't know why."

"You say that they're *trapping* underlings?" asked Arthur.

"Yes, I heard them talking about it when they brought some in. They got some kind of way down into the Underworld . . . and they set traps."

"Do you know how they get into the Underworld?" Arthur asked, his interest rising.

"No, but I think they must have some way down from 'ere at the Cheese Hall, 'cause it don't take 'em long."

Arthur's mind began to whir. If there was a route between the Cheese Hall and the Underworld, then maybe there was a way for him to get back to Grandfather after all. If only he could tell Grandfather what he had learned, perhaps they could come up with a plan.

If only he could tell Grandfather what he had learned.

*Snatcher climbed onto a table and took a look out
through the boards that covered the tearoom windows.*

chapter 33
GOING DOWN!

"You worry too much."

Snatcher climbed onto a table and took a look out through the boards that covered the tearoom windows. It was raining again.

"Well, is it raining?" asked Gristle.

"No!" Snatcher lied, and climbed back down off the table.

"I still don't like it. It's getting very wet down there. Last time we were up to our knees in water."

"You worry too much." Snatcher chortled at the nervous-looking members assembled before him. They didn't look convinced. "One more load of them monsters and a few more cheeses, and all will be tickety-boo for our plans for Ratbridge."

"The traps were nearly empty on the last two trips."

"I know," said Snatcher. "Why else do you think I got you to grab them rats and monsters from the shop? Now, get on with you!" Snatcher fixed on Gristle with his good eye. "Or perhaps I could come up with a substitute for monsters. . . . If you get my drift?"

"Last time we were up to our knees in water."

Gristle turned pale. "No . . . err . . . I'm sure we can find something in the traps."

"Very good. Just make sure you do!" said Snatcher. "The Great One needs 'em, and we need the Great One. Our plans rely on 'im. If you get a good haul, this will be the last time, and after that we can seal up the Underworld completely."

"Promise?"

"Promise!"

The members looked happier.

"All right then!" said Snatcher as he walked over to a large cupboard and opened its doors. "First trapping party inside!"

A small group of the members carrying sacks reluctantly entered the cupboard. Snatcher gave them a wink and pushed the doors closed. Then, taking hold of a bellpull next to the

*A small group of the members carrying sacks
reluctantly entered the cupboard.*

cupboard and giggling, he said, "Going down!" and pulled.
There was a grinding noise, then muffled screams that quickly
faded away. After a couple of seconds there was a distant
splash, followed by a bell ping.

"Maybe it *is* a little wet," Snatcher guffawed. Still, he waited
for a few seconds before tugging the bellpull again. Soon
there was another ping, and Snatcher opened the doors. The
cupboard was empty, apart from two inches of dirty water that
ran out onto the carpet.

"Second trapping party, please," he ordered.

The members looked very, very nervous and all shuffled
backward.

*The cupboard was empty, apart from two inches
of dirty water that ran out onto the carpet.*

"Second trapping party, PLEASE!" Snatcher snapped.

Reluctantly, the remaining group stepped into the cupboard.

"Not you, Gristle!" Snatcher said. "You can go down on the last load with me." He closed the cupboard and sent the members on their way. Then he turned to Gristle and took a banknote out of his pocket. "But first I want you to pop down to the shops quick and get me a pair of wellies."

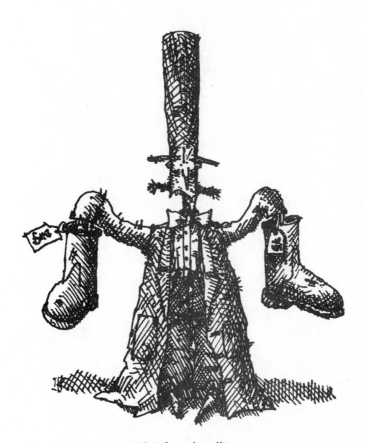

Gristle with wellies.

Kipper and Tom disturb the meeting in the hold.

chapter 34
THE COUNCIL OF WAR

Willbury, Marjorie, and the captain sat behind an ironing board.

It was early evening and it was raining . . . again. In the hold of the Laundry all the dirty clothes had been pushed to one end to make space for the Council of War. Willbury, Marjorie, and the captain sat behind an ironing board, facing the crew and underlings. Even Match, the miniature cabbage-head, and the freshwater sea-cow were there. The freshwater sea-cow had been adopted by some of the crew and was swimming about in a small barrel on wheels among her new guardians, who kept sneaking her lumps of cucumber. The only ones missing were Kipper, Tom . . . and Arthur.

Willbury looked about, and then asked the captain, "Where are Kipper and Tom?"

"We needed someone to act as watch on deck, and as it was raining, I gave them the duty as punishment. They should never have let Arthur go into the Cheese Hall alone."

"Oh . . . right then. Well, then we better call the meeting to order and get started." Willbury stood up, and the hold fell quiet.

The freshwater sea cow had been adopted by some of the crew.

"My friends, we have a number of problems. Firstly, we have to get Arthur back from the Cheese Guild and return him to his grandfather. And secondly, I think we must find out what Snatcher is up to and put an end to it." Willbury paused. "I have some disturbing new information. Snatcher, we think, is in possession of a terrible new invention."

Marjorie shifted uncomfortably.

"It is a machine that resizes things!"

There were gasps from the crowd.

"Yes! And I believe Snatcher and his mob are responsible for the tininess of our tiny friends."

Match and the little cabbagehead who was sitting on a step-ladder among the underlings squeaked loudly at that.

"We don't know what he is doing with the size he takes from the creatures—but I think we can be pretty certain that whatever it is, we're not going to like it. We *have* to get into the Cheese Hall. Does anybody have any ideas?"

Willbury looked around expectantly, but there were no replies.

At that moment, Tom and Kipper suddenly burst through the door, drenched.

Match and the little cabbagehead were standing on a stepladder.

"Willbury!" cried Tom as he and Kipper scanned the surprised faces. "We've just spotted cabbageheads on the towpath! Two of them! What should we do?"

"We've just spotted cabbageheads on the towpath!"

"Cabbageheads!" said Willbury. "Where could they have come from—all the cabbageheads from the Cheese Hall are down here with us, aren't they, Titus?"

Titus nodded, looking excited.

"Then I think you had better go up and find out what's happening."

Titus stood and dashed past Tom and Kipper and up the stairs to the deck. Tom and Kipper followed, along with the other cabbageheads and Willbury.

As soon as he reached the deck, Titus ran to the side of the ship and down the gangplank, past the police, and along the towpath till he approached two cabbageheads who were in the shadows. The cabbageheads came forward, and the three seemed to be holding a conversation. Then Titus turned back toward the Laundry, followed by two new cabbageheads who held hands and looked about nervously. Titus led them past the Squeakers, who ignored them completely, and up the gangplank.

Titus turned back toward the laundry, followed by two new cabbageheads.

The cabbageheads all ran to meet one another, hugging and whispering. After a few minutes the huddle broke up, and Titus, looking extremely agitated, came over to Willbury and began whispering in his ear. When Titus had finished, Willbury threw up his arms. "Oh, dear me! The cabbageheads have all fled their homes. It seems that the water level underground has driven them out!"

The cabbageheads all ran to meet one another.

"How did they get up here if the holes are all blocked?" asked Kipper.

Willbury looked puzzled. "That is an excellent question. I—or rather Titus—shall have to ask them."

Titus scampered over to where the cabbageheads stood, and they formed another huddle. After a few moments he returned and whispered in Willbury's ear again. Willbury turned back toward the others with an expression of surprise on his face.

"They came up through the rabbit women's tunnels."

"They came up through the rabbit women's tunnels! Arthur had told me about the tunnels, but he didn't know where they were. Apparently they come up in the woods just outside town."

Kipper grinned. "Well, that's how we get into the Cheese Hall then. We get under the town and burrow up!"

Tom and Willbury turned to look at Kipper in surprise. "You're right, Kipper! You're not as green as you are—no, that would not be very appropriate," said Willbury. "Titus, would your friends show us the way to the rabbit women's tunnels?"

The Squeakers who were still drinking tea and looking very wet and grumpy.

Titus returned to the new cabbageheads and whispered to them. They nodded.

"But how do we get off the boat?" asked Tom. He looked across at the Squeakers, who were still drinking tea and looking very wet and grumpy. Any attempt to get off this laundry by the crew was going to be noticed.

"I'm not sure . . . ," said Willbury. "Why don't we go tell the others about the tunnels and get out of this rain? There has to be a way to get past the Squeakers."

Tom and Kipper looked sheepish. "We are supposed to stay up here and keep watch."

Willbury smiled. "I don't think anybody is going to attack us in this rain. Why don't you come down with us?" he said kindly.

Everyone looked at them expectantly when they got below deck. Willbury began immediately to apprise them of the new developments. "Gentlemen, the cabbageheads who have joined us have just come up from the Underworld. They have found tunnels that are not blocked, which come up just outside the town walls, in the woods. Kipper has suggested that we use these tunnels to get under the town and burrow up into the Cheese Hall."

There were murmurings of approval when he told them of Kipper's plan.

"It's going to take a lot of burrowing," Bert reminded them.

"Yes . . . yes, it is," Willbury agreed. "We'll need as many hands and paws as we can muster. Volunteers?"

A sea of hands and paws went up, followed by a cheer.

"Good. But we still have a major problem. How do we get off the Laundry?" asked Willbury.

"We could jump over the side and tie up the Squeakers, then throw them in the drink!"

"We could jump over the side and tie up the Squeakers, then throw them in the drink!" said Bert.

There was another cheer.

"I don't think so, Bert. There are a lot of policemen, and they might win in a fight. And if they didn't, if even one of them got away, he could warn the Cheese Guild we were coming."

They all sat back down to think this over.

"Boxtrolls!" Kipper suddenly cried.

"What do you mean, 'boxtrolls'?" asked Willbury, a puzzled look on his face.

"Seeing as the boxtrolls and cabbageheads can get on and off the ship, we dress up as boxtrolls. Then the Squeakers won't pay any attention to us."

"You don't think the Squeakers might notice we're not real boxtrolls?" mused the captain.

"Well, they're not too bright," said Tom.

"And if the disguises were good, then we might get away with it," said Willbury with a chuckle.

"Don't you think they'd notice if there was no one left on the ship?" asked the captain.

"I think that we might be able to get around that," said Marjorie. "Leave it to me."

Soon everybody was busy.

Soon everybody was busy. In a storeroom where the crew kept things for recycling was a stock of folded cardboard boxes. Under the guidance of Fish and the other boxtrolls, the crew prepared these. They found that economy-size

Stainpurge boxes were just about the right fit for humans and that Blotch-B-White boxes fit the rats. Meanwhile the rats set about making troll teeth out of the vegetables and fruit, while Marjorie constructed dummies and some strange rigging device out of ropes and laundry. By late evening everybody was below deck and ready. Fish and the other boxtrolls, happy having so many new "boxtrolls" about them, chortled to themselves.

Willbury raised his hands and shushed the crowd. Then he said, "Arr arware bawaee waaee."

"Whaa?" came the reply.

Willbury took out his new orange-peel teeth.

"I said, is everybody ready?" There was a lot of nodding and giggling. "Well then, I think it may be best if we leave the Laundry in ones and twos, then meet up by the West Gate. Let's bring a rope ladder so we can climb down from the town wall."

Tom found a rope ladder and Kipper stowed it inside his new box. With his parsnip teeth, Kipper looked like Fish's bigger brother.

"Is your distraction ready?" Willbury asked Marjorie.

Marjorie nodded. "I have arranged a party—powered by the beam engine—for the policemen to watch. It should stop them noticing that the ship is empty. It's going to take a few minutes to really get going, but I don't see why we can't start sneaking off."

The captain handed out candles, which would be needed in the dark tunnels. Then the first group went up onto the deck, followed by Marjorie.

The "boxtrolls" then worked their way down the gangplank in small groups and walked straight past the policemen.

On deck Marjorie adjusted the beam engine, and the flywheel started to turn. She'd piped some of the steam from the boiler to a small harmonium, and the crows had agreed to stay behind and play the instrument. As their beaks hit the keys, steam and a great deal of noise burst from the back of the keyboard. The crows were delighted. Before long, terrible tunes could be heard up and down the towpath. The Squeakers covered their ears and moaned.

As their beaks hit the keys, steam and a great deal of noise burst from the back of the keyboard.

"It's working!" Marjorie cried.

She pulled a handle on the side of the beam engine, and a number of ropes fixed to pulleys tightened. Strange cloth figures appeared and started to dance about the deck. The

Squeakers were straining their necks to see the dancers, but they were obviously unwilling to get too close to the awful noise. More boxtrolls made their way up on deck and sauntered past the police, unnoticed. After half an hour only Marjorie and Willbury were left on board.

Strange cloth figures appeared and started to dance about the deck.

"This is really ingenious, Marjorie. I hope it will give us the time we need!" said Willbury.

Marjorie looked sad. "It's the least I can do to help. I still feel terrible that my invention has caused so much trouble. I'll do anything to put things right."

"You mustn't blame yourself," said Willbury, putting a hand on her shoulder. "You had no way of knowing what would happen. All we can do is to do our best to thwart these awful people and stop whatever it is they're up to. Now, I think it's time for us to go. How long will this dancing and 'music' last?"

"Well, if the crows can keep stoking the boiler, it could go on all night." Marjorie smiled.

"I don't think that will be very popular with the locals!" said Willbury.

"You never know. The crows might get better!" Marjorie chuckled. They put their teeth in and set off.

The West Gate.

chapter 35
UP AND UNDER!

When Willbury and Marjorie arrived at the
West Gate, Tom rushed up to meet them.

When Willbury and Marjorie arrived at the West Gate, Tom rushed up to meet them, snatching his teeth out of his mouth so he could talk.

"Quick! Bert has just seen town guards. They're coming around on their patrol, and they'll be here in a minute."

Then Willbury took out his teeth. "They won't bother us if we are dressed as boxtrolls, will they?"

"Yes, they will! They're not like the police—they're always on the lookout for boxtrolls. They know who's responsible for 'borrowing' things. They hate them!" Tom told him.

"Let's get over the wall then," suggested Willbury.

Tom looked up at the town wall. It was a good ten feet high. "How?"

Willbury followed his gaze. "Oh my. We didn't work that out, did we!"

"We've got to do something," Tom said urgently.

"I ah . . . ah." Willbury started to panic. Then he felt a tapping on his box. It was Fish.

Fish pointed at the real boxtrolls who were settling themselves outside a sweetshop.

Fish pointed at the real boxtrolls who were settling themselves outside a sweetshop that stood next to the wall. They crouched down, then pulled their heads and arms inside the boxes. They looked like a pile of boxes outside the shop. Fish led Willbury over to the shop and indicated to him to do the same.

"Fish wants us to pretend to be boxes. Quick! Do as he says!" Willbury whispered to the others.

With the help of Fish they assembled themselves in stacks outside the shop. Fish settled down beside them, and the cabbageheads hid behind the stack. Footsteps approached.

"An I sez to 'er, if our girl Sonya did that to—'Ello? What we got here?" said a voice.

"Looks like someone made a late delivery to the sweet-shop," said the second. "They wasn't 'ere an hour ago."

The two guards approached the boxes. One of them rubbed his chin and looked about.

The two guards approached the boxes.

"I am rather partial to sweets. Mind you, Stainpurge doesn't sound that tasty. Still, you never know. Do yer think anyone is going to miss one of these boxes?"

"Nah, 'course not! There must be at least twenty or thirty of them, and if one goes missing, that's only five percent! You must expect natural wastage when you leave something lying about, don't you think?"

"Oh, I should think so. Do you think that if we got a cart, then maybe twenty or thirty percent natural wastage might be acceptable?"

"I should think that if we got my brother Big Alf's wagon, then almost a hundred percent natural wastage might occur!"

"You stay here and I'll get the wagon!"

Off went one of the guards while the other kept watch
on the stack of boxes. After a few minutes there was a clattering of wheels. A large wagon appeared and stopped by the
wall, and the guard jumped down. With difficulty the two
of them heaved the boxes onto the wagon. When their backs
were turned, the cabbageheads jumped up and hid among the
boxes now on the wagon. When the guards had finished, they
stopped for a breather.

A large wagon appeared.

A head popped out of one of the larger boxes and looked
about. It was Willbury. The top of the town wall was just
inches above him, and he smiled. For the second time, he
removed his troll teeth.

"RIGHT! Everybody over the wall!" he shouted.

The two guards looked round and fainted at the sight of a
cartload of boxes all standing up at the same time.

They all clambered onto the top of the wall. Kipper got out
the rope ladder, hooked it to the top of the wall, and lowered

it over the other side. Climbing down dressed in a cardboard box was not easy, and several of the pirates ended up dropping off the ladder and crumpling their boxes. This was distressing to the real boxtrolls, who prodded at their fallen comrades' boxes, trying to push out the dents.

The two guards looked round and fainted at the sight of a cartload of boxes all standing up at the same time.

When everybody was down, Titus whispered in Willbury's ear.

"We'll follow our cabbagehead friends—they'll lead us to the rabbit women's tunnels," said Willbury. The party set

off following the new cabbageheads. It made a strange sight, with the moon casting long shadows across the landscape.

Once in the woods, the new cabbageheads wandered about a bit before they found an old oak tree. They ran to its base and pulled back some undergrowth, revealing a large hole between the tree's roots. Everybody gathered around as the new cabbageheads whispered to Titus. Titus then whispered to Willbury, and after some moments Willbury spoke to the group.

"This is the entrance to the rabbit women's tunnels. Our new cabbagehead friends don't want to go any farther." Willbury smiled at the cabbageheads. "They are rather frightened of what's happening down there and want to catch up with the other cabbageheads who are apparently making their way to a new cave in the hills. I think it is totally understandable. We don't really know what we are going to find down there."

They ran to its base and pulled back some undergrowth,
revealing a large hole between the tree's roots.

There were some nervous murmurings from the crowd.

"Yes, I think we should thank them for bringing us this far."

The new cabbageheads looked rather chuffed and gave a little bow. Titus approached Willbury again. When he'd finished, Willbury told them, "Titus says that the cabbageheads that Arthur freed are going to go with them, but that he himself would like to stay with us and help find Arthur." Willbury clasped Titus's hand. "You are very brave, Titus."

The murmurings in the crowd grew louder, and Titus took Fish's hand. The other cabbageheads took one last look at the hole, waved, and raced rapidly into the woods.

The other cabbageheads raced rapidly into the woods.

The strange party stood around the hole.

chapter 36

THE RABBIT WOMEN

The captain lit his candle.

The strange party stood around the hole. It was much, much larger than a rabbit hole, but it would still be a tight fit for a large pirate dressed in a stiff cardboard box. There was an air of trepidation among the group—if the cabbageheads were so frightened of what they would find down the hole, was it really a place that the rest of them wanted to go?

"Who is going to lead the way?" asked Willbury.

There was a pause. Then Fish and Titus put up their free hands.

"Very well," said Willbury. "Everybody get out your candles."

The captain produced a box of matches, and lit his candle.

"Right then, me hearties!" he said. "Form an orderly queue!"

Then, one by one, each member of the queue took a light from the captain's candle and slid down the hole. Some of the larger pirates took quite a bit of shoving to get them down, but soon they were all in without too much damage to their boxes.

Once underground the tunnel opened out, and even Kipper could stand up and move about with ease. There was a warm, earthy smell in the passage.

The procession set off. After a few hundred yards Fish held up a hand, and the procession ground to a stop. Fish turned to Willbury and put his finger to his lips. Then Titus whispered something to Willbury, and Willbury turned to Kipper and Tom.

Even Kipper could stand up and move about with ease.

"Fish wants us all to be quiet, and Titus wants us to put our teeth in. Pass it along." The message passed down the line, and soon all that could be heard was the sound of teeth being put in. Fish and Titus put their candles down and disappeared into the darkness.

"Aat oo ooh iiink aaye rrr oooht ooo?" Kipper whispered.

"Iiierrrt!" snapped Tom.

After a minute or two, they heard voices from somewhere ahead. The voices grew louder, and small green lights appeared. Before long Willbury could make out Fish, Titus, and some other shapes coming toward them.

As they got closer, the candlelight revealed that Fish and

Titus had returned with two rabbit women. The women were both dressed in knitted one-piece suits with long ears, and they carried glass jars full of glowworms.

The women were both dressed in knitted one-piece suits with long ears, and they carried glass jars full of glowworms.

The rabbit women bounded up to Willbury and smiled in welcome. The one in a gray suit spoke first. "Your friend Titus has told us that you'd like us to guide you through our tunnels so you can get under Ratbridge?"

Willbury nodded.

The other, who was dressed in brown, answered, "We'll show you the way but you'll have to be very careful."

Willbury nodded again, and the rabbit women beamed. Then the one in brown gave Kipper a funny look.

"You look rather big for a boxtroll." Then she looked down at Tom. "And you look rather small."

Titus trotted over to her and whispered.

"What's he say, Coco?" asked the gray-suited rabbit woman.

"Well, Fen, he says they're a different type of boxtroll. Just visiting."

"Well, that explains it!"

"I suppose so. But I think they need to see a dentist." Willbury blushed.

"Come this way please, and please remember to be careful!" The rabbit women headed back from where they came.

After a short walk the tunnel became lighter, and Willbury could hear more voices. They rounded a bend and were confronted by a wooden door. In the center of the door was a notice.

A wooden door.

Please close the door after you.
Remember
There are trotting badgers about, and
we don't want to lose any of the old folk!

"Mind where you walk!" warned Coco, then she opened the door of a large, low cavern. Hundreds of jam jars filled with glowworms were tied to roots that hung from the ceiling, and a pale green light fell on the scene below. There were small groups of rabbit women working at looms and spinning wheels, and tending raised vegetable beds. All around them were thousands of rabbits. By each group of workers sat a rabbit woman reading aloud.

There were small groups of rabbit women working at looms and spinning wheels, and tending raised vegetable beds.

Fen told the group, "Please be very careful not to step on our parents. They are not very bright, but we do love them."

Marjorie was grinning from ear to ear despite her vegetable teeth. She was obviously very impressed by the rabbit women, Willbury thought. As Fen closed the door behind them after shooing some rabbits away, Marjorie moved over to Willbury and furtively removed her teeth.

"They're fantastic," she whispered. "Just who are they?"

Willbury checked to see that nobody was watching and slipped his own teeth out. "The story I heard was that they were abandoned babies or little girls who fell down rabbit holes. The rabbits took them in and brought them up as their own. I guess as they grew up, they took charge and now look after the rabbits."

Willbury and Marjorie both quickly put their teeth back in as Coco pointed to the various vegetable plots. "We can grow most things here, but we avoid greens. Sometimes the old folks manage to burrow into the plots, and greens don't agree with them."

Fen noticed Willbury looking at the readers.

"We are very fond of books. You can learn nearly everything from them that rabbits can't teach you."

"We are very fond of books. You can learn nearly everything from them that rabbits can't teach you."

Willbury was dying to take his teeth out again and ask questions, but he didn't want to give away that he was not a boxtroll. So as they were led through the cavern, he listened and tried to make out what was being read. There were some passages from the *Country Housewife's Garden*, some Greek, mathematics, and even bits of Tristram Shandy and Jane Austen.

These rabbit women are very well educated! he thought.

The procession reached a door at the far side of the cavern, and their guides led them through it, then closed it behind them.

"We do have to be so careful as we have a problem with trotting badgers. Last month someone left this door open, and Madeline's stepparents were eaten. It was very upsetting," said Coco.

They followed the rabbit women through a maze of passages till finally they reached one that tilted down at a steep angle. The passage emerged in a stone cave and the rabbit women halted. The floor of the cave was awash with water.

Coco held her jar aloft.

Coco held her jar aloft.
"It's getting higher!" said Fen.

"Yes, but it will have to rise a good deal further before it gets close to our burrows. It's the cabbageheads and you boxtrolls that I am worried about." Coco gave them a concerned look. Then she pointed into the darkness.

"At the other end of this cave is a tunnel that takes you under the town. I am sure Titus and your friend Fish can lead you from here."

Willbury smiled through his vegetable teeth and bowed in thanks. The others followed his lead.

"Our pleasure. And good luck," said Coco, and she and Fen turned back up the passage. When they had gone, Willbury took out his teeth.

"Fish and Titus, are you all right leading us from here?"

Fish took a very long smell at the air, smiled, and then nodded.

A rabbit woman gardening underground.

Herbert and Arthur.

chapter 37
THE DOLL

"Do you think you could lend me your walloper?"

Back in the dungeon Arthur was determined to find a way to escape.

"Do you think you could lend me your walloper?" he asked through the hole in the wall.

"You! Borrow my walloper! I should think not!" snapped Herbert. "Anyway, what do you want it for?"

Arthur pleaded. "A doll that I need is in the corridor outside the cell and I can't reach it. I need something long to reach it with."

"Well, you can't borrow my walloper," replied Herbert.

"Have you got anything else I could use?" asked Arthur.

"Might have!" Herbert was not an easy man. "What's in it for me?"

Arthur thought for a moment. "If I can get the doll, it might help me find a way out of here. And if I get out, I'll see if I can get you out as well."

There was silence for a few moments, then Herbert replied, "Is a bit of string any good?"

Arthur looked across at the doll. "It might be. How long is it?"

"About six feet."

"That ought to do it."

"Well, how much do you want to borrow?"

"Enough!" snapped Arthur in frustration.

"Well, would two feet do?"

"No!" barked Arthur. "If you want to get out of here, why don't you just lend me all of it?"

"Oh, all right! But don't get funny with me. It is my string!" came back a very grudging voice.

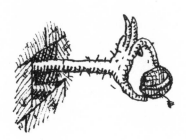

There was a scuffling sound and a ball of hairy string appeared.

There was a scuffling sound and a ball of hairy string appeared in the hole. Arthur took it with thanks. Then he unwound it, tied a noose in one end, and swung the lasso through the bars at his doll. After a few attempts he managed to get the lasso around one of the doll's arms and hoisted it into the cell.

"I've got it!" he cried.

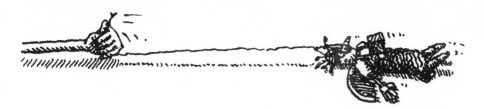

*After a few attempts he managed to get the lasso around
one of the doll's arms and hoisted it into the cell.*

"Can I have my string back?" Herbert asked, worry in his
voice.

Arthur unknotted the lasso, rolled up the string, and held
it out toward the hole. Herbert's hand darted out and snatched
it from him.

Arthur sat on the edge of his bed, winding the handle on
the doll; he called, "Grandfather! Grandfather! Are you
there?"

There was a popping, some static, and then he heard what
he was hoping for.

"Arthur, where are you?"

"I am locked up in a cell below the Cheese Hall."

"WHAT!" cried Grandfather. "They caught you?"

"No," said Arthur. "I escaped . . . but the police handed
me over to Snatcher. He accused *me* of stealing my wings
from *him*!"

"Archibald Snatcher!" Grandfather sounded angry. "He's
up to his old tricks again."

"I am sorry, Grandfather."

"You're not to blame. With that shyster involved, nobody
is safe," his grandfather said. "We have to get you out of there,
and soon. Are you on your own?"

"Well, almost. There is a man called Herbert in the next cell."

"Pardon? Did you say a man called Herbert?" asked Grandfather, sounding astonished.

"Yes!" said Arthur.

"Ask him if his nickname is Parsley!"

Arthur leaned down to the hole. "Is your nickname Parsley?"

"Don't you know it's rude to call your elders by their nicknames?" came the voice from the hole.

"That's him all right," said Grandfather. "Arthur, would you let me speak to Herbert?"

Arthur held the doll out close to the hole, and he saw Herbert's masked eyes staring at it.

Arthur held the doll out close to the hole,
and he saw Herbert's masked eyes staring at it.

"What are you doing there, Parsley?"

There was a silence from the hole, then Herbert's voice asked in a quizzical tone. "Is that you, William?"

"Yes!"

"What are you doing talking out of a doll?"

"I will tell you later, but you . . . Oh, Herbert, I can't believe it's you. Are you all right? Have you been in that dungeon for all these years?"

"I . . ." Herbert's voice trailed off. "I . . . can't remember . . . I am not even sure where I know you from . . . William . . ."

"Oh, Herbert. Don't you remember what happened?"

"No. Not really. My mind is so fuzzy."

"Don't you remember the fight?"

"No . . . just something vaguely about you, me, and . . . Archibald Snatcher. . . . It's all very confused."

"Maybe if I remind you?" came Grandfather's voice.

"Maybe . . . ," muttered Herbert.

Arthur's grandfather paused for a moment. "Arthur, you should listen to this too. It's time you heard the truth about why we live underground."

"My mind is so fuzzy."

Something was wrong.

chapter 38
WET!

Fish and the other real boxtrolls had a way of walking
with their feet a few inches up either wall to avoid the water.

Several inches of water ran through the tunnels as the procession made their way under the town. Fish and the other real boxtrolls had a way of walking with their feet a few inches up either wall to avoid the water, but even so, it dripped down from the ceiling onto their boxes. Willbury and the others were getting very, very wet, and the rats were complaining that the water came up well over the bottom of their boxes.

Tom came to a stop and took out his teeth. "It's not the water that I hate," said Tom. "It's the feeling of the soggy cardboard rubbing on my legs. It feels really horrid, like old wellies."

"It's the feeling of the soggy cardboard rubbing on my legs."

Rats with dripping boxes were lifted and carried aloft.

"We can do something about that," said Willbury, taking his teeth out. Then he shouted the order: "Large boxtrolls, please pick up small boxtrolls and carry them till it gets drier. And you can remove your teeth till further notice."

All down the line teeth were removed, and rats with dripping boxes were lifted and carried aloft.

"Thanks!" said Tom to Willbury.

The tunnels slowly rose up toward the town but remained wet. The real boxtrolls were now in familiar territory, and they didn't need their candles. Fish kept rushing ahead into the darkness and returning excitedly. After a few of these forays he seemed to grow pensive.

"Have you noticed the pipes along the tunnel tops?" asked Tom.

Willbury held up his candle to look. There were pipes . . . and most of them were leaking.

The tunnel leveled out, and Fish led them to an area of what looked like very old cellars. They went in, and turning a corner, saw an iron ladder fixed to a wall in front of them. The ladder disappeared up into darkness. Fish signaled to them to wait, then went up the ladder followed by the other real boxtrolls.

After a few minutes a distressed-looking Fish returned alone.

"What is it, Fish?" Willbury asked him.

Fish signaled to them to follow him up the ladder.

The group silently followed Fish up the ladder and through a hole onto a dry floor. There was a loud click, and above them a light came on. Shoe was standing on top of a huge pile of nuts and bolts, holding a chain fixed to some kind of glass ball, the light from which flooded the cavern. Everywhere there were machine tools, half-built pumps, broken bicycles, bits of wire, and pieces of metal of every shape, color, and description. The place was an Aladdin's cave of engineering scrap.

Shoe was standing on top of a huge pile of nuts and bolts, and holding a chain fixed to some kind of glass ball.

"This is the boxtrolls' nest!" exclaimed Willbury.

The boxtrolls nodded.

Marjorie was staring up at the glowing glass ball. "They've got electric light! Fancy that. I thought it might be possible one day."

Willbury looked about. "Where are the other boxtrolls?"

The real boxtrolls looked very sad.

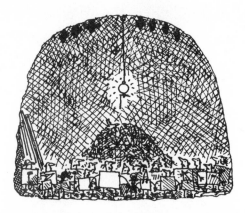

The place was an Aladdin's cave of engineering scrap.

Kipper whispered. "I think Snatcher has taken them. . . ."

Willbury took this in, then replied, "That may be it. But it would mean that he must have been capturing them somehow . . . down here!"

Fish turned to the boxtrolls. They nodded glumly.

Willbury spoke to them very gently. "You were captured down here?"

The boxtrolls nodded again, pointed back down the hole, and started burbling.

"Could you show us the way up to the Cheese Hall?" Willbury then asked.

They shook their heads and mumbled.

Titus whispered to Willbury, then Willbury turned to the others. "Snatcher and his mob put them in sacks after they were captured. But they think he has some sort of mechanical elevator, with an entrance down here somewhere. They say it shot them up to the Cheese Hall as fast as a rocket."

"They say it shot them up to the Cheese Hall as fast as a rocket."

"Do you think we could find it?" asked Tom.

The boxtrolls looked unsure, and Titus whispered again to Willbury.

"Titus says that this place is such a warren that the elevator could be hidden anywhere."

Everybody looked increasingly glum.

Willbury realized he needed to encourage them. "Come now, let's split up and search for the elevator. It shouldn't take long with so many of us. We'll meet up here in an hour."

It was agreed. Willbury stayed with Fish, Titus, Tom, and Kipper, while Marjorie teamed up with Shoe, Egg, and some other boxtrolls. As they waited for their turn to descend the ladder, Willbury told his group that there was something else he wanted to do before they started looking for the elevator. "I've got to find Arthur's grandfather. I am very concerned, as he must be running out of food."

Fish perked up and raised a hand.

"Do you know where he lives?" asked Willbury. Fish burbled something and Titus whispered something to Willbury.

"You say you have heard that there are some humans living in a cave off one of the large caverns?"

Fish nodded.

"Do you think you can lead us there?" Fish looked a little unsure but then nodded again.

"Well, let's try that!" said Willbury, clapping his hands together; then off they set back down the ladder.

Then off they set back down the ladder.

The evil crime.

chapter 39
The Telling

*"Don't you remember burning a hole in my mum's
carpet with the toy steam engine we tried to build?"*

In the cell in the dungeon Arthur listened as Grandfather tried
to jolt Herbert's memory. "Herbert, do you remember playing
with me when we were boys?"

"No." Herbert sounded utterly forlorn.

"What? You don't remember anything? Don't you remember the Glue Lane Technical School for the Poor?"

"Not really. . . . I do remember the name. . . . You're going
to have to remind me."

"Herbert, we grew up on the same street! We played
together, got measles together . . . and got our ears clipped
together. Don't you remember burning a hole in my mum's
carpet with the toy steam engine we tried to build?"

There was a pause. "Was the carpet a rather odd green color?"

"Yes! Yes it was!"

"I seem to remember something . . ."

"Do you remember sinking in the canal up to our waists
when we tried to cross the ice?"

"And the ice was so thin in the middle that it cracked and your dad had to pull us out?"

"Yes!"

"... It is coming back to me ... remind me of more."

"Do you remember sinking in the canal up to our waists when we tried to cross the ice?"

"Do you remember Tuesday mornings with the smell of the brewery? And cold nights in winter when the smell of the tannery filled the streets?"

"I loved the smell of the brewery, but the tannery smelled awful!"

"You are not wrong there!"

At first Arthur felt that it was not his place to be involved in the conversation, but now he asked a question.

"I know there is a tannery, but a brewery?"

"Not anymore. It went the same time as the cheese industry ... with the pollution."

"What happened?"

"Ratbridge was founded on the cheese, but when new industries came to the town, the smoke and waste they produced poisoned the water supply and a lot of countryside around

here. It got so bad that the local cheeses were decreed unfit to eat, and the cheese industry collapsed. The cheese barons went bankrupt overnight."

"The cheese barons went bankrupt overnight."

"I remember that . . . ," Herbert said. "Ain't that the reason that Archibald Snatcher turned up at the Poor School?"

"Yes," replied Grandfather. "His father was partly responsible for the ban."

"Why?" asked Arthur.

"He ran a mill that had always produced really dodgy cheese. They used all kinds of evil processes. One of their tricks was to boil down cheese rinds, extract the oil, and then inject it into immature cheeses. It was illegal . . . and cruel, but they had got away with it. What they didn't realize was that as the pollution got worse, making cheese oil was concentrating the poisons. Finally they got sued—their cheese poisoned the Duchess of Snookworth, and it was her husband who got the ban brought in. Archibald's dad lost his fortune and couldn't afford to have dear Archibald privately tutored anymore."

"And Snatcher turned up at our school!" Herbert nearly hollered. "He didn't take his fall from Ratbridge society well. Hateful little snob!"

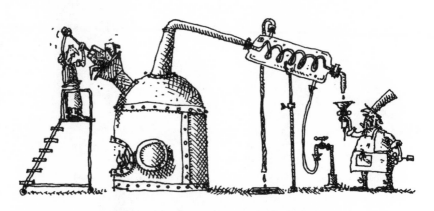

"One of their tricks was to boil down cheese rinds, extract the oil, and then inject it into immature cheeses."

Grandfather filled Arthur in. "Herbert and I were in our third year at school when Archibald turned up. He had spent his whole life being waited on hand and foot, so poverty came as a bit of a shock to him. He hated the school and everybody in it. Especially us!"

"Why?" asked Arthur.

"He seemed to think that Ratbridge had done him out of his rightful fortune, so thought it was his rightful place to do what he wanted and never lift a finger. But we didn't play that game," said Herbert.

Grandfather added, "But oh, was he cunning! Archibald took every opportunity that came his way to advance himself back toward his 'rightful place.' Smarming up the teachers, 'borrowing work,' a little blackmail, some bullying, and

extortion. When it came to the final-exam results, it was no surprise that he got the highest grades."

"Because he stole them!" interjected Herbert.

"On the strength of a bit of blackmail and his stolen results, he got a scholarship to Oxford. And that was the last we heard of him for a few years, till . . ." Grandfather's voice took a bitter tone. "Do you remember now, Herbert, what happened?"

"When it came to the final-exam results, it was no surprise that he got the highest grades."

"At the Inn?" Herbert replied slowly.

"Yes, at the Inn."

"Oooooooooh . . ." Herbert groaned, clearly remembering.

"What happened at the Inn?" asked Arthur.

"Herbert and I had just set up shop as freelance inventors and engineers, and the work was coming in. Then one lunchtime we went to the Nag's Head. We had just started eating a couple of pasties when we heard a raised voice at the next table. I looked over, and there sat Archibald Snatcher flanked by a couple of heavies.

"'Are you calling me a cheat, sir?' he said to a red-faced man across the table from him.

"'Yes, sir, I am,' said the red-faced man. 'It is not possible to have a hand of cards containing seven aces!'

"'It is, sir, for I am very lucky!' Archibald said.

"'Well today, sir, your luck has run out!' And the man reached inside his pocket. Thinking he was going for a gun, one of the heavies also reached for his pocket, and in an instant the bar cleared, leaving just Herbert and me watching the altercation."

"It is not possible to have a hand of cards containing seven aces!"

"Oh yes!" broke in Herbert. "The man had only taken out a notepad to ask for Snatcher's name and address. He wanted to report him to the police. But he didn't notice that one of Snatcher's men had taken out a catapult. . . ."

Herbert fell silent again, and Grandfather continued.

"That's right," he said. "And that's when Snatcher gave the order to the heavy . . .

"And that's when Snatcher gave the order to the heavy . . ."

"'Administer the treatment!' he said. Then a blur of something green whizzed across the table. It struck the red-faced man in the mouth. He went pale and slumped to the floor. Then we caught the smell. Oil of Brussels!"

"Oil of Brussels?" asked Arthur.

"It is poison distilled from sprouts. It is very fast acting and often lethal. Later I found out they had shot a small wad of cotton soaked in it down the man's throat," Grandfather told him.

"It is poison distilled from sprouts. It is very fast acting and often lethal."

"Awful!" added Herbert.

Grandfather went on. "Then there was the sound of police whistles outside, and Snatcher saw us.

"'Oh, look! A couple of old school friends,' he said. Then he threw something to me. The very moment I caught it, the bar door swung open, and a group of Squeakers ran in and saw the man slumped on the floor. Then Snatcher stood up and pointed at me.

"Then he threw something to me."

"'It was him! Officer! He has just poisoned that man. Look! He's still holding the evidence.' I looked down, and in my hand was a bottle of Oil of Brussels.

"'Arrest that man!' shouted one of the Squeakers, and they rushed to get me. So I panicked and made a run for it straight

"I managed to shake them off and climbed down a drain—"

through the back door to the street. The Squeakers followed me, but I was quite fit in those days, and I managed to shake them off and climbed down a drain—"

"Everything went green."

"I remember!" cried Herbert. "You ran out of the door with the Squeakers after you, then . . ." He paused for a long time, and then whispered, "Everything went green . . . and I woke up here."

"How do you think you got here?" Arthur asked him.

"They must have knocked me out or something, then kidnapped me . . . ," muttered Herbert.

"I knew you had disappeared, because that night I came up out of the drain and found posters up for our arrest for attempted murder. I just didn't know where you had gone. I grabbed some food from a garden, then went back underground to avoid being caught. I knew I would never be safe aboveground again unless I could find you as a witness to the truth."

"Attempted murder? So the man wasn't dead?" asked Arthur.

"No, he survived, but he suffered permanent memory loss from the poison and trauma."

"That's why everything went green. They must have had some more Oil of Brussels and smothered me with it. That's why me memory is so bad!" Herbert fumed. "And I guess we've both been prisoners of sorts ever since. . . ."

"Yes . . . it is true," replied Grandfather. "Mr. Archibald Snatcher has a lot to answer for."

"So, can you help us, William?" Herbert asked. But before Grandfather could reply, Arthur heard footsteps coming down the steps to the dungeon.

"Quick! Someone is coming. I'll speak to you later, Grandfather." He tucked the doll inside his suit, pushed the stone back in its hole, and shoved the bed against the wall. A member appeared carrying a bowl in one hand and a cudgel in the other.

"The guv sent me down 'ere with some nosh for you." He put the plate down, unlocked the door to Arthur's cell, slid the plate into the cell with his foot, then locked the cell door.

"Take your time boy! I got to wait for the plate, but I'm in no hurry. They ain't going to be back from the traps for ages." He sat down, leaned against the bars of the cell opposite, and watched Arthur eat.

*A member appeared carrying
a bowl in one hand and a cudgel in the other.*

They saw a small window in a wall of rock ahead.

chapter 40

A Glimmer at the End of the Tunnel

"It's rhubarb! We must be getting close!"

Fish led the way, and as they walked, water washed around their feet. The water level seemed to be rising all the time. Then a smell gently wafted into their noses. It was sweet and vaguely familiar. Something about it reminded Willbury of jam. They'd not eaten for a long time and the smell was almost too much to bear.

Willbury stopped. "That's it! It's rhubarb! We must be getting close!"

And sure enough, soon they saw a light in a window and a door within a wall of rock ahead. Willbury rushed forward and knocked.

The music stopped, there was some muttering, and the door swung open to reveal a stocky old man with a huge beard and glasses. He looked very damp.

"My word! You're big for a boxtroll!" Grandfather said.

Willbury had completely forgotten he was in disguise, and said in surprise, "I am not a boxtroll!"

"My word! You're big for a boxtroll!"

"Well, you will do until a boxtroll comes along. I have something I need you to help me with—urgently!"

"Of course we will do anything we can to help. I have spoken to you before, sir. I am Willbury Nibble."

"Oh! I thought you were a lawyer, not a boxtroll! It just shows that you shouldn't jump to conclusions. But I am pleased to meet you anyway," said Grandfather, his turn to look surprised.

"It's a disguise," said Willbury. "I *am* a lawyer. And I'm afraid I have some rather bad news for you about Arthur."

"I spoke to him just a little while ago," said Grandfather. "He called from the dungeon at the Cheese Hall. We have to do something to help him before it's too late."

"That is why we are here," said Willbury. "We believe there is a way up into the Cheese Hall from the Underworld. If we can find it, we can sneak up into the Hall and help Arthur escape."

"I see," said Grandfather thoughtfully. "I don't know of any such way—but there may be one. I also have an idea of how to help Arthur—but I can't do it on my own. I've been hoping for some underlings to come along and assist me, but they seem few and far between these days. But perhaps you and your friends . . ."

"Of course, we will do anything we can. Arthur has become very dear to us and we all want to get him back as soon as we can."

"Well, do come in," Grandfather said, taking a step back and gesturing Willbury into his home. "And bring your friends, the more the merrier!" said Grandfather. "If you like stewed rhubarb, I think I might have just enough to go around. Please help yourselves," he said, pointing to a saucepan on an old range.

There was a cheer and they set about serving the rhubarb. Very soon it was all gone and Grandfather brought them into the back room. There were puddles on the floor and water was dripping from the ceiling.

The small room was about the most crowded Willbury had ever seen. At its center was a brass bedstead. This was covered in a beautiful patchwork quilt. Surrounding the bed was a huge hodgepodge of wires, rods, cogs, pulleys, and other things that Willbury couldn't identify.

"If you like stewed rhubarb, I think I might have just enough to go around."

"Err . . . what is it?" he asked.

"It's something I have been working on for years. It's finished, but I don't seem to have the proper strength to operate it. However, we may be able to get Arthur out of his situation with it."

Grandfather explained his machine.

"It sounds amazing!" declared Willbury. "I only wish Marjorie was here to see it. But I certainly think we can help—obviously we need real muscle and some brains here," he continued, smiling at Kipper and Tom. "And I know just the pirate and rat for the job!"

Grandfather followed Willbury's gaze. "A pirate and a rat?"

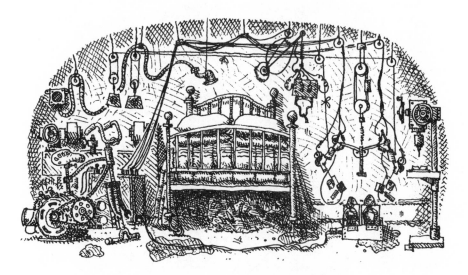

*Surrounding the bed was a huge hodgepodge
of wires, rods, cogs, pulleys, and other things.*

Arthur in the dungeon.

chapter 41
THE KEYS

He used his fingers to scrape it out of the bowl.

The porridge Arthur had been given was so cold it was almost solid, but he was so hungry, he tried to eat it. He'd not been given a spoon so he used his fingers to scrape it out of the bowl. It was a very slow process. As he ate, his jailer slowly drifted off to sleep.

"I give up!" Arthur muttered eventually. "I think I'd rather starve."

He looked over at the jailer, who was now starting to snore. Arthur coughed loudly, but the jailer didn't stir. Encouraged, he put the plate down quietly on the floor and retrieved his doll. Glancing nervously at the sleeping jailer, he quietly wound the handle and talked into the doll.

"Grandfather," he whispered. "Keep your voice down. One of Snatcher's mob is just outside the cell asleep."

"What's he doing there?" came a quiet voice from the doll.

"He just brought me some food."

"Did he have to unlock your cell?"

The jailer didn't stir.

"Yes. . . . Why?"

"So he's got a key?"

"Yes."

"Well, this might just be our lucky day. Where's the key?"

"It's in his right-hand coat pocket," Arthur whispered. "But how are we going to get it off him? He's right across the corridor; there's no way I can reach him."

"Listen, Arthur. I have a plan, but you need to do exactly as I say. I want you to wind up the doll till you hear it ping, then give the handle a few more turns until you feel the clockwork can't take any more. But be very careful and don't break the spring!"

Arthur did what he was told, jumping when he heard the ping. He checked that it hadn't disturbed the sleeping jailer, then carefully wound the handle a few more times until he felt it couldn't go any farther.

Arthur wound it very gently till there was a ping.

"Okay, I've wound it up."

"Right," said Grandfather. "Now reach out of your cell as far as you can and stand the doll up, facing toward the pocket with the keys."

Arthur stared at the doll in puzzlement but did what he was told.

In Grandfather's bedroom, Kipper and Tom were ready. Kipper sat on a bicycle that had had its back wheel removed and replaced with some kind of complicated pump. Tom was involved in something far more complicated. He was at the center of a web of levers and wires that stretched out from all over the room. On his head was a pair of goggles far too large for him, and fixed over the lens of the goggles was a box with wires sprouting from it.

Kipper sat on a bicycle that had had its back wheel replaced
with some kind of complicated pump.

Grandfather turned away from the strange trumpet mouth-piece he had been speaking into and said to Tom and Kipper, "It's time . . . and remember what I told you. You have to work together!"

Kipper started to pedal and soon a humming started to come from the pump. The levers and wires attached to Tom went taut.

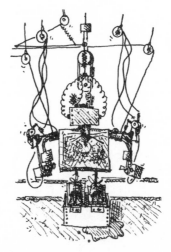

He was at the center of a web of levers and wires.

High above in the dungeon, Arthur watched the doll, wondering what his grandfather was up to. Something was happening! Arthur heard the ping and then a slow ticking. The doll's eyes lit up and cast two small pools of light toward the coat pocket.

The doll started shaking and fell over.

In Grandfather's bedroom Kipper was working the pedals as hard as he could and Tom was cursing.

"What's the matter?" Grandfather asked anxiously.

"It's fallen over!"

"What can you see through the goggles?" asked Grandfather.

Tom peered back through the goggles. "Just the jailer's boots, at the moment."

"Use the levers here to move the doll's arms. They should help you get it upright again," Grandfather instructed.

Tom started to slowly move the levers. After a moment he cried, "The doll must be moving! I can see all of the jailer now."

"Try moving your legs. The doll should copy your movements."

Tom felt the wires pull as he started to bend his legs.

Arthur watched in amazement as the doll started to move its arms. It seemed to be trying to get up . . . on its own!

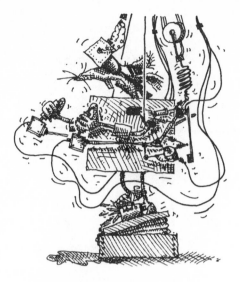

Tom started to slowly move the levers.

The doll's legs now moved as well, and it managed to stand again. Then its wings unfolded. Suddenly Arthur understood.

"Faster!" Grandfather shouted at Kipper. "Pedal faster! We need all the power we can get."

Kipper was already sweating but did all he could to increase his speed.

"I don't know if I can keep this up for very long. Please hurry, Tom."

"All right, all right!" said Tom. "I'm going as fast as I can, but it's pretty difficult operating this doll. You just concentrate on pedaling!" He adjusted a knob at the end of one of the levers strapped to his arm. The doll started shaking as its wings began to beat, then it slowly rose from the floor. Arthur watched as it wobbled and tried to keep upright. The lights from the doll's eyes flicked around the dungeon.

Its wings began to beat, then it slowly rose from the floor.

Finally it began to move across the corridor toward the jailer. As it reached him, it slowed to a wobbly hover over the pocket.

"That's it! I can see the pocket. But we need to lose height! How do I do that?"

"Kipper, ease off the power ever so slightly," ordered Grandfather. "Tom, you will have to tell him when you start to fall and when he needs to increase his pedaling."

"I shall enjoy easing off!" Kipper said, nodding vigorously.

The doll steadily descended till it was just an inch or so above the pocket.

"Steady, Kipper, steady!" whispered Tom. He gently pressed the levers in his hands and the doll moved forward till its arms entered the pocket.

"A little more power, Kipper!" said Tom, and he started to manipulate the levers, concentrating as hard as he could. For a few moments there was silence as he struggled to make the precise movements he needed. Then, suddenly, he gave a triumphant shout.

"Got them! Now, Kipper, give it everything you've got!"

Kipper began pedaling ever more furiously, wheezing and panting with the effort.

The doll rose and the keys lifted from the pocket. Tom shifted the controls, and the doll turned toward Arthur's cell.

"Please, I am going to pass out," moaned Kipper.

"Stop complaining, Kipper!" snapped Tom.

"Oh no! Something is happening!" cried Kipper in a panic.

"Shut up and pedal!" shouted Tom.

Grandfather and Willbury, however, were more concerned. Smoke was starting to rise from where the pedals joined the pump.

"Quick! Get the keys back to the cell!" Grandfather urged Tom.

"What's happening?" asked Kipper. "I'm going as fast as I can."

There was a crunching noise, and the pedals seized.

"It's bust!" shouted Grandfather. "Quick, before it dies!"

Smoke was starting to rise from where the pedals joined the pump.

In the cell, Arthur had watched mesmerized as the doll retrieved the keys. Now he stood horrified and helpless as it

started to fall toward the floor. Tom pushed both of the levers in his hands forward as far as they would go, and the doll tilted forward and dropped into a dive. As it neared the floor, Tom pulled the levers back and the doll pulled out of the dive and rushed toward the cell door. Arthur reached out his arms frantically; if only it could keep going until it got to him—but it didn't look as if it was going to make it.

Now he stood horrified and helpless as it started to fall toward the floor.

It didn't. The doll hit the ground about two feet from the cell. Arthur groaned, but in Grandfather's cave Tom made one last frantic effort with the levers. Just as it hit the floor, the doll let go of the keys and seemed to propel them desperately toward Arthur. They slid across the floor and through the bars. Arthur snatched them up.

"Grandfather! Grandfather! I've got the keys!" Arthur whispered gleefully, but no one heard him. The doll was dead.

They slid across the floor and through the bars.

Wet and miserable!

chapter 42
THE TRAPS

Wading around.

Meanwhile, deep underground, Snatcher and the other members had been wading around wet and miserable for hours. First they'd checked the traps closest to the elevator, but when they found nothing in them, they had to go farther afield to check their other traps. Water was everywhere, running over the floor, running down the walls, and gushing from the ceiling. And the sound of it was so loud they had to shout to make themselves heard.

"Maybe we already got all the monsters down 'ere," shouted Gristle.

"Well, you do remember what I said? You don't want to find yourself in reduced circumstance, do yer?" Snatcher replied.

"I think we should check the traps near the elevator again then," Gristle quickly suggested.

They made their way back toward the elevator. As they approached one of the traps, Gristle smiled.

"'Ere, guv. We got some!" He pointed to large net full of boxtrolls.

"'Ere, guv. We got some!"

"My word, we struck it lucky. And some of them is big 'uns!"

They lowered the net and bundled their haul into sacks. Then they eagerly set off to check the next trap, leaving a trail of vegetable teeth floating in the water. To Snatcher's delight and surprise, that next trap was also full of boxtrolls.

"Yes! You can never have enough size!" he shouted as he rubbed his hands together. "Get them down, boys! I'm starting to enjoy this!"

The members bagged up the boxtrolls and moved on. At each trap, they found more boxtrolls.

"This is blooming marvelous!" Snatcher chuckled. Gristle had never seen him so happy. "Makes you wonder where they all bin hidin'—we ain't seen so many for weeks! Right lucky for us, but unlucky for them—and Ratbridge!"

"Ain't we got enough now?" asked Gristle, struggling under the weight of a sack.

"Oh, go on. Let's check just one more trap. It ain't going to hurt."

"It's killing my back," complained Gristle.

"That ain't nothing to what it's going to do to Ratbridge!" gloated Snatcher.

"Ain't we got enough now?" asked Gristle,
struggling under the weight of a sack.

The Underworld.

chapter 43
DEEP WATER

"My bones are killing me," said Grandfather.

Willbury looked at Grandfather and sighed. "I guess we don't know if Arthur got the keys."

"No." Grandfather slumped onto the edge of the bed.

Just then Fish rushed into the room with Titus following behind. He started gabbling to Willbury.

"I don't understand," said Willbury. "I will have to get Titus to translate."

Titus hurried over to translate. Slowly he turned pale.

"Fish says that the water is starting to bring down the tunnel roofs! We had better get out of here quick." Willbury paused for a moment. "Let's go back to the boxtroll nest to see if the others have found the elevator."

He turned to Grandfather. "You had better come with us."

"Anything to get out of this damp. My bones are killing me," said Grandfather.

Kipper and Fish took Grandfather's arms and led him

Kipper and Fish took Grandfather's arms.

out of the bedroom, with the others following. When they reached the living room, Grandfather looked around.

"I shall rather miss this place." He sighed.

"We better hurry or goodness knows what's going to happen," urged Willbury. He grabbed a lantern, and they ran off toward the boxtroll nest as fast as they could through the water, which was starting to turn to a brown, muddy soup.

They were halfway there when they had to stop. The tunnel ahead was flooded.

"What do we do now?" asked Willbury. "We can't go back."

Grandfather looked worriedly toward Fish. "Do you know another route?"

Fish thought for a moment, then pointed to a side passage nervously. It, too, was flooded, but the roof of the passage was somewhat higher than that of the flooded tunnel.

The tunnel ahead was flooded.

Then Fish started to whimper.

"What's the matter, Fish?" asked Willbury.

Titus tugged on Willbury's cuff, and Willbury leaned down.

"Oh, dear!" Willbury exclaimed.

"What is it?" asked Grandfather.

"Fish is scared. It's the idea of having to swim. Boxtrolls loathe swimming. It is bad enough that their boxes got wet . . . but swimming."

Kipper waded toward Fish and smiled. "Don't worry; I'll carry you!"

Fish, however, did not look convinced. In the distance there was a sudden rumble and the sound of rushing water grew louder.

"Right. Fish, close your eyes." And before Fish could protest, Kipper picked him up and swung him over his head.

"Any room for a small one?" Tom asked hopefully.

"Go on then, climb on board," Kipper offered, raising his eyebrows. Tom scrambled up to join Fish, then Kipper turned to Titus. "You may as well hitch a ride. One more is not going to hurt."

Kipper carrying Fish, Tom, and Titus.

Titus looked at the passage ahead and made his decision. With Willbury's assistance he struggled up to join Tom and Fish.

Willbury frowned. "I think I can manage with Grandfather, but the lamp?"

"I can take that," said Tom, and Willbury passed it to him.

"Do you think you will be all right, Kipper . . . carrying that lot?" Willbury asked.

"With all the exercise I get from carrying washing?" he said with a smirk. He gave Willbury a wink and began wading into the tunnel. The water was icy cold, and Willbury felt his box go soggy as he hauled Grandfather along.

"Are you all right?" he asked the old man.

"I could do with a warm bath at the end of this, but don't worry about me. It's Arthur I'm worried about," Grandfather assured him.

*Kipper turned and waded into the tunnel ahead
and Willbury followed with Grandfather.*

Nonetheless, they were overjoyed to see that the passage angled upward, and they soon reached a point where the water became shallow.

"Do you mind if I have a breather?" puffed Grandfather.

"Let's have a rest on that rock—it looks dry," said Willbury, pointing to a large flat rock that was still above water. Everybody clambered up, looking forward to sitting down for a moment. But before they could even catch their breath, there was a twang and they found themselves hanging in a net from the ceiling.

"No!" cried Willbury. "It's one of Snatcher's traps."

There was nothing they could do but hang there and wait. Wet and miserable, they huddled in silence, too dejected even to talk. Several minutes passed before lights started to appeared.

"Keep quiet and pretend to be boxtrolls," Grandfather whispered. "I think they'll be taken in. But I'll have to take my chances."

As members approached, Willbury saw Snatcher grinning from ear to ear. "This one's full too!" he called back to the struggling members. "Sack this lot up, me lads, and we'll call it a day." Gristle lowered the net onto the rock and inspected the quarry. Then he cried out, "'Ere, sir. There's an old man in here with the monsters!"

"Well, I never," said Snatcher, leaning over Grandfather. "If it ain't me old school friend William Trubshaw!" Then he grinned. "So this is where you've been hiding all these years. How typical of you to be mixed up with all these wretched underlings."

"If it ain't me old school friend William Trubshaw!"

"Archibald Snatcher," hissed Grandfather. Some of the members close by heard this and giggled under their breath when they realized that "Archibald" was Snatcher's first name. Snatcher turned around and fixed them with a steely gaze.

"You think 'Archibald' is funny, do you?" They fell silent. "Shove him in a sack like the rest of them."

Then he leaned back over Grandfather. "You just wait till I get you back to the lab! By the time I've finished with you, you'll be wishing you were doing time for attempted murder instead!"

Members returning with their quarry by "Cupboard."

chapter 44
THE SHAFT!

Tea and cake.

Snatcher stood by the cupboard doors watching as the last of the members dragged their wet sacks into the tearoom. Flashes of lightning threw shafts of light through the cracks in the boards over the windows, and across the floor. Outside the rain fell hard on the streets of Ratbridge.

"Take 'em straight down to the lab and chain 'em to the railing. It'll make it easier for sticking 'em in the 'extractor.' Then we'll 'ave a quick cup of tea and some cake."

The members hiked the struggling sacks off to the lab. There they hastily chained their captives and raced back to the tearoom for cake.

Willbury looked around the railing and was shocked to see his fellow prisoners. There were the crew of the Laundry, Marjorie and the boxtrolls Arthur had rescued, Fish, Shoe, Egg, and Titus, and finally Grandfather. Everybody looked battered and very miserable.

Willbury noticed that Marjorie was anxiously studying the large funnel that hung above them. He took out his teeth.

"What is that thing, Marjorie?" he whispered.

Willbury looked around the railing and was shocked to see his fellow prisoners.

Marjorie looked crestfallen. "They have done it! They've built a copy of my machine . . . only much, much bigger."

"I thought you said it had two funnels?"

Marjorie pointed. "See the small one over there, on top of that cage by the shed? I think that is where they put the underlings to shrink them," said Marjorie.

"And the big funnel up there?" asked Willbury.

Marjorie looked at the large doors in the floor. "I'm not sure. . . ."

Footsteps approached, and they hurriedly put their teeth back in just as Snatcher and the members, all wearing their ceremonial robes, stomped into the room.

"Tonight, gentlemen, we have a special show," Snatcher announced. "Not only do we have enough monsters to finish our project, but also, as the grand finale, we shall for the first time use the machine to extract the size from humans. Please prepare the first boxtroll."

Snatcher and the members stomped into the room.

Marjorie was the nearest, and so they seized on her, unchaining her and pulling her across the room. She wailed and put up a good fight, but it wasn't long before the members had her inside the cage with the door shut. The underlings howled in despair. Willbury could stand it no longer.

It wasn't long before the members had her inside the cage with the door shut.

"Stop! This is inhuman," he shouted.

The members turned to look. Snatcher walked slowly over to where Willbury was chained.

"Human? What do you boxtrolls know about human?" Then he paused and eyed up Willbury. "Well, maybe you're a little more human than I thought!"

He put his good eye up very close to Willbury. "I know you! You are that Willbury Nibble, that lawyer we've had so much trouble with. We've got your little friend locked up downstairs. I think I'll have him brought up so you can get shrunk together."

Willbury froze. If Arthur had escaped, then Snatcher had not found out yet! If he hadn't, then the longer he stayed away from this machine, the better. Either way, delaying Snatcher from sending someone down to get him was a good thing. He decided to change the subject.

He put his good eye up very close to Willbury.

"This machine of yours is rather impressive. What are you using it for?"

"Wouldn't you like to know?" Snatcher grinned.

"It's not as if I can do anything about it. I'm sure your plan must be rather good."

Snatcher puffed up a little as his vanity took over. "You're right! You and your friends have already had your fate sealed, so there can be no harm in telling you my plan. We are going to reclaim our rightful place as the overlords of Ratbridge. The cheese barons shall rule again!" And he laughed madly.

"So how are you going to do that?"

"*This* is what is going to allow us to do it. We are creating a monster!" Snatcher paused for dramatic effect. "And in part, it's going to be with your help." Snatcher laughed again. "You know we have been shrinking your friends. Well, have you wondered where the size goes?"

Willbury tried not to look worried.

"AH! You have! Well, I can tell you . . . the size goes directly into a very special friend of mine, and as he gets bigger, he becomes more and more unstoppable!" Snatcher's good eye was nearly bulging in his excitement.

"Oh!" said Willbury, frantically trying to buy more time. "Your special friend . . . do we get to meet him?"

"Yes. Very shortly!"

"And . . . where does cheese come into all of this?" asked Willbury.

"The cheese! Cheese is central to it. To aid our monster's

growth we have been force-feeding him a fondue of molten cheese. It goes down very well." Snatcher guffawed. "A DEEP WELL!" And he laughed at his own evil joke.

Snatcher's good eye was nearly bulging in his excitement.

"Well, well," said Willbury.

"Very droll, Mr. Nibble. We have a heated pit that we drop cheeses into. This is piped directly to the Great One. Right down his throat. I think 'e rather likes it."

Willbury was horrified. What sort of monster could they possibly have created? "So, what happens now?" he pressed on.

"The boxtroll in the cage is about to donate some size to . . . the Great One, and after that the rest of you are going to do the same. Then, when you are all shrunk and the Great One is finally the size we want, it's time to unleash him. Boy! Are we going to have fun! I hate this town!"

Snatcher turned and called for a ladder. Soon he was on the top of the shed waving his duck stick about wildly in the air.

"To your places, gentlemen; we are about to start!"

Soon he was on the top of the shed waving his duck stick about wildly in the air.

The members scrambled to positions around the lab, tending different machines, while Gristle sat at the controls. Great whooshes of sound filled the air as the beam engine started to move, then generators started to hum and power surged through the sizing machine.

"Open the hatches!" Snatcher yelled above the noise.

Trout Junior operated a winch that wound in the chains connected to the doors, while Trout Senior took his place by the control panel on the rails and inserted a key. Soon the chains were groaning under the strain.

"More power, Little Trout!" shouted Snatcher.

Slowly the doors lifted and revealed a tiled shaft.

"Bring up the Great One!" screamed Snatcher.

Trout Senior turned the key in the panel and a great creaking came from below. The members stared toward the open shaft from their various stations, and everybody chained to the railings pulled back.

Trout Senior took his place by the control panel on the rails and inserted a key.

The creaking grew louder, and there was another sound, a hissing, sluggish breathing. It grew heavier as whatever it was rose up the shaft. Willbury and the others strained against their chains to no avail. Their chains were fast.

Snatcher peered down the shaft. Then he looked up at Willbury and laughed menacingly.

"You are about to meet my creation, Nibble. For all your meddling, it's done you no good. See what I am about to unleash on the world!"

Everybody chained to the railings pulled back.

A massive, bloated creature, larger than an elephant.

chapter 45
THE GREAT ONE!

What looked like a huge jelly covered in filthy gray, matted carpet started to emerge from the shaft.

A massive blob of what looked like a huge jelly covered in filthy gray, matted carpet started to emerge from the shaft. As it did, the smell of fetid cheese engulfed the lab.

Higher the great gray jelly rose, wobbling as it did. Something very long and rope-like was attached to one side of it, and on the other side . . .

Willbury gaped as a pair of door-size ears came into view.

"It really *is* a monster. . . ."

The ears were followed by great, red, dinner plate–size eyes. They swiveled about madly.

Willbury gaped as a pair of door-size ears came into view.

"No, it couldn't be!" cried Tom.

Still the creature rose. Its snout, bent and hairy, appeared.

Tom was jibbering, pulling wildly at his chain, "No! It can't be. It just can't!"

There was a loud clunk and the platform stopped as it reached the top of the shaft. Before them, in all its glory, was the Great One. A massive, bloated creature, larger than an elephant.

"What is it?" wept Willbury.

"I . . . I . . . I think it's a rat," moaned Tom. "And I think it's . . . Framley."

"YES! What was once Framley is now . . . the Great One!" cried Snatcher. "Once just nasty. . . . Now made monstrous by the hand of man!" Snatcher broke into hysterical laughter for a few seconds, then stopped suddenly to look directly at Tom.

"I'd been looking for someone really nasty, and when I saw dear sweet Framley in action, I realized what a perfect subject he would make."

"I . . . I . . . I think it's a rat," moaned Tom. "And I think it's . . . Framley."

Tom's gaze darted between the Great One and Snatcher. Framley had always had an unpleasant look about him, but now he just looked evil. As his huge eyes fixed on Tom, an enormous grin revealed great yellow tombstone-size teeth. Then one of the eyes winked . . .

"Now you will witness the fulfillment of my dream." Snatcher stamped on the roof of the shed and shouted, "Extract the size!"

Snatcher stamped on the roof of the shed

At the controls in the shed, Gristle threw a lever.

A flash of blue light shot from the cage. Willbury blinked, then blinked again. Marjorie was gone! Then he heard another cry from Snatcher.

"Gristle! Give the Great One what he needs!"

There was another flash, but this time from the great funnel above, and the Great One gave a great wobble.

Snatcher called out another order. "Next please! I think we will have the boy from the dungeon."

"No!" screamed Willbury and Grandfather simultaneously.

"Oh yes! You'll enjoy watching!" cackled Snatcher, then he

called after the member who had headed for the dungeon to fetch Arthur. "And can you bring back one of those shoe boxes down there. We need something to put all our friends in."

"You're going to pay for this!" Willbury shouted.

"Quiet!" replied Snatcher. "Or I'll turn up the voltage and you'll all be reduced to the size of ants!"

Willbury fell silent.

Snatcher spoke again. "Get the little creature out of the cage."

Trout Senior left his post by the railings, opened the door of the cage, and groped about the floor inside. Then he stood up with something in his hands.

"What shall I do with it?"

"Perhaps Mr. Nibble would like to be reunited with his friend?" Snatcher joked. "Show her to the lawyer."

Trout Senior walked over to Willbury and held out his hands.

Standing there was a miniature Marjorie, no taller than seven inches and looking very agitated.

Standing there was a miniature Marjorie,
no taller than seven inches and looking very agitated.

"Are you all right?" Willbury gasped.

"Yes!" came a squeak. Marjorie looked startled by the

sound of her new, high-pitched voice. Then she squeaked again. "I should never have built the prototype! I just never foresaw the consequences. What am I going to do?"

Trout Senior looked warily at the little talking boxtroll in his hands and lifted it up to take a closer look. Just as Trout realized who it was, Marjorie kicked him right in the eye. Trout screamed, dropping her. She scurried under one of the machines.

"Get back to your post!" Snatcher ordered Trout. "We'll let the hounds find it later."

Trout skulked off. Willbury looked about to see where Marjorie had gone, but he couldn't see her anywhere.

"Please, please find somewhere safe to hide." Willbury begged under his breath. "I couldn't bear it if you were eaten."

"Now, where is that blooming kid?" boomed Snatcher as he looked toward the dungeon.

She scurried under one of the machines.

A struggling Arthur appeared, being held by the scruff of his under-suit.

chapter 46

THE NEXT VICTIM!

There'd been quite a lot of noise from the dungeon.

No sooner had Snatcher said this than Arthur appeared at the entrance of the lab, struggling frantically, being held by the scruff of his under-suit. His captive was shorter than Snatcher remembered.

"Oi!" Snatcher bellowed. "You've forgotten the shoe box. Bring the boy here, then go and get it."

As Arthur was led through the machines, loud metallic footsteps reverberated through the room. Snatcher looked around, puzzled.

Grandfather and Willbury watched in despair as the boy approached. Arthur looked at the chained group in shock. Then Arthur and the member froze. They'd seen the Great One.

"Come on! Come on! We haven't got all night. Get a move on!" ordered Snatcher.

The member prodded Arthur toward the shed. As they passed, Arthur had an oddly intent look on his face, and

Grandfather noticed the member was holding something under his ceremonial robes. They paused just before the shed.

"What are you waiting for?" snapped Snatcher. "Shove 'im in the cage and go and get a shoe box."

"No," the member snapped back. "Get your own shoe box."

Snatcher was gobsmacked. No member had ever answered him back before.

"What!" he screamed. "Me! Get me own shoe box?"

"Yes, Archibald!" replied the member. "Get your own shoe box!"

Snatcher went red with rage and almost fell off the roof.

"You . . ." Snatcher roared as he waved his duck stick at the truculent member. Suddenly the member released his grip on Arthur and threw off his hat and robe. It was Herbert. In his iron boots . . . with his walloper.

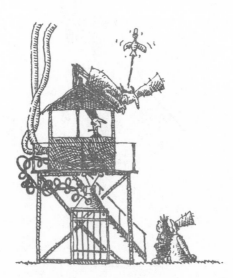

Snatcher went red with rage and almost fell off the roof.

The members froze and Snatcher went deadly pale.

"Oh my God! Get 'im!" Snatcher demanded.

The members didn't move.

"Get 'im!" Snatcher screeched again. Still the members held back. They all had experienced the walloper and weren't willing to get within range.

Snatcher was starting to panic. "All right! All right! Break out the weapons!"

As the members rushed toward a large cabinet on a wall of the lab, Grandfather shouted to Herbert. "Smash the railings!" Herbert grinned happily at his friend; then he raised the walloper and brought it down hard.

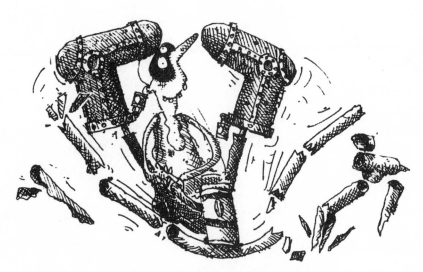

Then he raised the walloper and brought it down hard.

Crash! A massive section of the railing shattered. The blow was so hard that the Great One started to wobble violently and let out a low awful moan. Some of the boxtrolls were able to slip free, and Herbert moved on to the next section of railings. There was another blow and the Great One let out a huge bellow.

Snatcher was nearly apoplectic. "Faster!" he screamed at the members, who'd reached the cupboard and were fiddling with the keys.

With two more blows, all the railings lay shattered and the prisoners freed. Arthur ran to his grandfather and hugged him hard. Willbury smiled at the sight, then turned and shouted to Herbert. "Could you bash a hole in the wall so we can get out of here?"

Arthur ran to his grandfather and hugged him hard.

Herbert gave him a look. "Where I wallop is my business!" Then he winked at Willbury and made for the wall opposite of where the members were now arming themselves with blunderbusses.

Snatcher screamed. "They're going to get away! Open fire!"

The first shot sent bits of broken cutlery over them all. The second boomeranged off a machine, right back at the firer.

The first shot sent bits of broken cutlery over them all.

"Follow me!" Willbury shouted. "Kipper, help Arthur get his grandfather out of here."

Kipper saluted and ran to help.

Meanwhile Herbert, with two huge smashes, bashed a large hole in the wall. "Would you like it any bigger?" he asked Willbury.

"No," said Willbury, smiling. "An elephant could get through this. Well done!"

Herbert, with two huge smashes, bashed a hole in the wall.

Willbury guided the escapees through the hole.

Snatcher was dancing about on the roof of the shed in rage. "They're escaping! Shoot them!"

Volleys of marbles, nails, bits of china, and even old boiled sweets clattered against the wall of the lab as the escapees scrambled through the hole. The last out were Kipper, Arthur, and Grandfather.

"Make for the Laundry!" Willbury shouted. As they all began to run, Willbury stopped short and asked Herbert, "Can you bring down the wall? It might stop them from following us."

"A pleasure!" Herbert took a good long look at the wall and swung his walloper.

There was a dull thump, and for a moment Willbury thought it hadn't worked. Then cracks ran up the wall and a low rumbling started.

"Let's get out of here!" shouted Willbury.

Masonry crashed down as the wall collapsed, sending out huge clouds of dust.

As the dust settled, all that could be heard was the sound of rain and distant iron socks on cobbles.

Iron socks on cobbles.

Willbury and Herbert caught up with Kipper and Arthur just as they were helping Grandfather up the gangplank.

chapter 47

How Are We Going to Fix It?

Tom and the captain came forward to meet them.

Willbury and Herbert caught up with Kipper and Arthur just as they were helping Grandfather up the gangplank. The Squeakers had gone, the dummies on deck had stopped dancing, but the crows were still very happily playing the harmonium. They hadn't gotten much better.

"Is everybody all right?" Willbury looked to see that everyone had made it to the ship.

"I think so," Arthur said, helping his grandfather sit. "But where is Marjorie?"

Willbury gasped. "I forgot about her in the rush! She must still be hiding somewhere in the lab."

"We've got to go get her!" Arthur said, jumping up.

"We do," Willbury agreed. "And we also have to try to save Ratbridge from Snatcher and Framley."

"How are we going to do that?" asked the captain.

"I don't think we have any choice but to take them on, and the sooner we do, the better."

The captain agreed. "I don't really know how we take on Framley now that he's so monstrously big, but I suppose we do have to try." He turned to the crew and gave the order. "Okay! Gather all the weapons you can find!"

"Can we take off these stupid boxes?" asked Bert.

Fish looked very offended.

"I'm sorry," apologized Bert, "but damp cardboard . . . it chafes my legs!"

"Okay, everybody get changed! Then get the weapons," ordered the captain.

Kipper raised a hand. "May I keep my box on?"

"Oh, if you really want to!" replied the captain. Fish smiled at Kipper, who smiled back.

Herbert held up a foot. "And would you get me out of these darn socks?" he pleaded.

Kipper found a chisel, held it against the hinges of the boots, and with two careful blows of Herbert's walloper the socks were off.

Everyone stepped away a bit. Arthur held his nose.

He held it against the hinges of the boots.

"I think you had better go and wash those in the canal," Willbury said kindly. "And, Kipper, can you see if you can find some tin snips. Herbert needs to cut his toenails."

By the time the others had changed, Herbert had sorted out his feet and was back on deck.

"Do you need shoes?" asked Willbury.

"Nah! After years in those socks, me feet are as hard as granite! And by the way, you need some new tin snips."

"And by the way, you need some new tin snips."

The captain looked from man to man. Then he said, "Right. Herbert, I think you should lead the assault."

There was a cheer, and Herbert smiled.

Then Mildred came forward. "Is there any chance we crows could come too? We could play you all into battle."

Everybody went quiet, and then the captain took charge. "It would be splendid if you gave us a rousing send-off, but somebody has to have the important job of looking after, and err . . ."—the captain paused and raised an eyebrow—". . . entertaining Grandfather and the miniature underlings."

There was another cheer. The crows returned to the keyboard and tried to play a march.

Arthur suddenly grabbed his grandfather's arm. "Do

you realize that now that Herbert is free, you have a witness to what happened? We could clear your name . . . and live aboveground."

The crows returned to the keyboard and tried to play a march.

"Yes, Arthur, maybe we could. But first we need to stop Archibald Snatcher and whatever it is he's up to." He looked fondly at Arthur; then his expression grew more serious. "I'm not going to stop you from going back with the others to the Cheese Hall, but please think about it."

Arthur looked him squarely in the face. "I have to go back. I am not sure what's going to happen but I need to be there."

"All right, but . . ."

"I'll be careful!" Arthur smiled. "I haven't come this far to . . . well, you know?"

"Yes, I know," said Grandfather, and he winked. "Go on. Off with you!"

Arthur looked him squarely in the face.

"Careful now, Gristle; we don't want to hurt baby."

chapter 48
LET'S HIT THE TOWN!

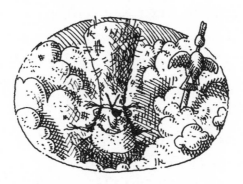

A smile spread over Snatcher's face.

As the clouds of dust settled, a smile spread over Snatcher's face. There was a massive hole in the wall of the lab.

"I was wondering how we were going to get the Great One out of here." Then he snapped out an order. "Ready the armor!"

Members ran to a corner of the lab and pulled dust sheets from a strangely shaped heap. Beneath the covers was a set of iron war armor. It looked like a cross between a giant snail shell and an old riveted boiler. Cannons were fixed above a small platform on either side, and in the center of the back was another platform for someone to ride on.

Beneath the covers was a set of iron war armor.

Inside the shed, Gristle flicked a lever and a crane moved across the floor to the armor. The members attached a hook from the crane to the armor so it could lift it from the floor. With the armor swaying in the air, the crane moved toward the Great One.

"Careful now, Gristle; we don't want to hurt baby."

When the armor was over the giant rat, the members maneuvered it onto him. Snatcher climbed down from the shed and inspected the armor for fit.

"It's a bit loose around the edges," Snatcher muttered, poking here and there. "We really did need the extra size from those wretched underlings."

Then he yelled out, "Gristle, lift the armor off for a moment and could the Trouts please go into the cage and check that the extractor funnel is correctly positioned. I am not sure it's working properly."

Snatcher followed the Trouts to the cage but stopped outside the door. Then in a blink, Snatcher snapped the door closed and locked it.

"Shrink 'em, Gristle!"

The Trouts looked horrified. "But Masterrrrrrrrrrrrrr . . ."

There was a flash from above the cage, and the Trouts' cries grew higher and higher pitched, until there was only an indecipherable squeak. Then there was another larger flash from the large funnel, and Framley gave a great wobble.

"That should do it!" Snatcher said, satisfied. "Can we try the armor for size again?"

This time the members had to push and prod to get the

armor back on the rat; then Snatcher inspected it again. "Marvelous!" he chuckled. "I knew he'd grow into it."

The Great One now looked fearsome. The members took the ladder and put it up to the platform on the back of the rat. Snatcher scrambled up, and a couple of members climbed onto the platforms on either side.

Snatcher scrambled up.

"Right, me lads. Gather round."

The members assembled, peering up at Snatcher and casting wary glances at the massive rat.

"Members of the new Cheese Guild, the time is here!"

There was a loud cheer.

"The Great One is ready, and Ratbridge is going to pay!"

There was an even louder cheer.

"Yes, my brothers! We shall use our leviathan to overthrow those that have held us down for so long. First we shall remove their government, then destroy their banks, smash their factories, and return Ratbridge to follow an open free trade in cheesy products!"

There was a silence, and then Gristle raised a hand. "Eh . . . what do you mean?"

"We're going to use the big rat to clobber them what done us down, blow up the council offices, rob the bank, knock down the factories, and then start flogging dodgy cheese again!" Snatcher replied.

There was an enormous cheer.

"Right! Let's hit the town!" shouted Snatcher, and he took hold of a pair of reins and pulled hard. Slowly his war machine rose and turned toward the broken wall. The members followed, carrying their blunderbusses.

"I've been looking forward to this." Snatcher smiled to himself.

The members followed, carrying their blunderbusses.

"Right, what's the plan?" asked the captain.

chapter 49

ATTACK ON THE CHEESE HALL

Herbert led the way.

Herbert led the way through the streets of Ratbridge. The sun was rising and was just breaking through under the dark storm clouds, and their footsteps were mixed with the rumble of thunder and rainfall. As Willbury surveyed the little army, he wondered about their selection of weapons. Some of the pirates carried large underpants and were accompanied by rats carrying the notorious gunge balls. This he understood, but the others . . .

The boxtrolls had selected screwdrivers and adjustable wrenches, Titus had found a small trowel and a bucket full of gravel, and the other pirates and rats had grabbed anything that was handy—mops, buckets, old fishing rods, in fact, anything that took their fancy. Willbury carried an umbrella that was keeping him dry and that he thought might be useful in a fight, while Arthur walked by his side carrying the doll.

The thunder drew closer as they stood in front of the Cheese Hall.

"Right, what's the plan?" asked the captain.

Kipper said eagerly, "Perhaps Herbert could 'open' the front door for us, and we could creep in that way and surprise them!"

"I don't think there will be much surprise after the noise of Herbert walloping down the door," said Arthur.

"If we wait for a flash of lightning and count a few seconds, then Herbert wallops the door, the thunder will mask the sound of the wallop," suggested Tom.

"That's a very intelligent idea!" Willbury sounded impressed.

They waited for a minute or so until the next flash of lightning came. Willbury held up a finger, counted for a few seconds, then gave the signal to Herbert. At the very moment the walloper struck the door, a loud clap of thunder filled the street. The front door was reduced to matchsticks. Everyone froze, waiting to see if the members were going to come rushing out. But there was still no sign of the members.

"I think we got away with it!" said Kipper.

"Right! Get the mobile knickers ready," ordered the captain.

Pairs of pirates stretched knickers between them, rats loaded them with the gunge balls, and each pair of pirates was joined by a third who stretched the knickers back, ready for firing.

"Everybody keep quiet and follow the knickers," ordered the captain.

Slowly, the pirates with the loaded knickers made their way up the passageway toward the entrance hall, the others following. As they reached the archway to the hall, one of the leading pirates peeked around the corner and signaled that the coast was clear. The little army made its way into the entrance hall.

Slowly, the pirates with the loaded knickers made their way up the passageway toward the entrance hall.

"Prepare yourselves," whispered the captain. "Now, Herbert, you wallop the lab door, and we'll let off a volley of knickers—" But before he could finish, the lab door started to creak open and everybody froze.

Around the bottom of the door a tiny person appeared. It was Marjorie.

Around the bottom of the door a tiny person appeared.

"I wondered when you were going to get here," she squeaked. "But you're too late. They've gone!"

There was a mixture of surprise, relief, and worry.

"Thank goodness you are all right," said Willbury, kneeling down and scooping Marjorie up.

"I am not hurt, but 'all right' is not exactly how I feel," Marjorie squeaked, her lower lip quivering. "Six inches tall . . ."

"Well, I'm not sure we can do anything about that right now," said Willbury sympathetically. "We've got to stop Snatcher first."

"They've taken the rat to wreak their revenge on the town. First they're going to destroy the Town Hall, then rob the bank, and after that they are going to destroy all the factories!" Marjorie said, her voice reaching an even higher pitch.

They all looked to one another in shock.

"C'mon, let's go!" the captain shouted.

"But how will we stop them?" Arthur had to ask.

"Knickers and a good walloping!" suggested Herbert.

The Laundry crew gave a cheer.

"I don't think even that could stop them now," Marjorie told them. "They've equipped the rat with some really heavy iron armor and cannons. And from what I can see, that rat is vicious and afraid of nothing now that he's enormous. It's going to take something really powerful to stop them now."

Everybody fell silent; then after a few moments Arthur had an idea. "Did you say 'iron armor'?"

"Yes," replied Marjorie.

"The same stuff Herbert's boots were made of?"

"Yes. Why?" Marjorie asked.

"I am not sure if it would work, but I have an idea," Arthur quickly explained. "There is a powerful electromagnet some-where above the roof of Herbert's cell. When they wanted to stop him from attacking them, the members would turn it on, and Herbert's boots would stick him to the ceiling. Couldn't we use that?"

Marjorie's eyes lit up. "If it was powerful enough, it might work."

Willbury looked perplexed and turned to Arthur. "I don't understand."

"We could use the electromagnet!"

"Don't you see? We could use the electromagnet!" said Arthur. "If Framley is wearing iron armor, we could turn on the magnet and pull him back here."

"Yes . . . but is the magnet powerful enough?" asked Willbury.

Marjorie grinned. "It will be by the time I'm finished with it!"

Everybody cheered.

"Herbert, can you pick me up and show me approximately where your cell was?" Marjorie asked him. "If we can find the spot just above it, we should be able to find the magnet."

Herbert carefully picked up Marjorie and looked toward the stairs to the dungeon. Then he made toward a space behind the beam engine.

As Herbert rounded a corner, Marjorie let out a squeak. "Here it is!"

On a cart sat a very large coil of wire.

On a cart sat a very large coil wire.

Willbury frowned. "Are you sure? It's just a large coil of wire."

"YUP! That's what it is until you put electricity through it," Marjorie squeaked with glee. "Now all we have to do is put enough electricity through it to give that rat a surprise!"

"What do you want us to do?" asked the captain.

"When we turn it on, we have to make sure the rat comes to the magnet, rather than the magnet going to the rat. If we make sure there is something really solid between the coil and the rat, that should stop the magnet from moving."

"How about a wall of the lab? The one closest to the Town Hall," suggested Arthur.

"Good idea," Marjorie said, nodding.

"What about all the machinery in here?" asked Willbury. "Won't the coil be attracted to that?"

"Mmmmmm. You have got a point. We'll have to fix the magnet to the wall. Some of the loose parts of machinery might fly toward it, but the heavy stuff should be bolted down firmly, I think."

Fish made a gurgling sound, and Titus came forward to whisper to Willbury.

"Titus says the boxtrolls are very good at that sort of thing and would like to help," Willbury said to Marjorie.

"Very good!" Marjorie squeaked, turning to the boxtrolls. "You lot move the coil and fix it to the wall."

The boxtrolls nodded happily, and Shoe made a burbling noise. Titus whispered to Willbury, and Willbury passed on the question to Marjorie.

"I don't really understand, but they would like to know if you would like them to rewire the cabling so you can have the switch up here, rather than down in the dungeon."

"Bless me! That would be grand," squeaked Marjorie. "Could we have the switch in the control shed, please? And wire the coil directly to the generators?"

Shoe nodded and the boxtrolls set to work. Marjorie then told the captain, "We need as much power as possible if we are going to stop that rat," she told him. "The beam engine that powers the generators will have to be running flat out. Is your crew any good stoking up boilers?"

"Be our pleasure!" said the captain. "We know all about stoking boilers. It's one of our specialties."

So the crew of the Nautical Laundry set to stoking the boiler of the beam engine. It didn't take long before the great arm of the beam engine was pumping up and down and the flywheel was spinning again.

Marjorie asked Willbury to bring her up to the shed. Arthur and Titus joined them. Willbury looked about the small room.

The strange device with two small funnels.

On the bench at the back were Arthur's wings and the strange device with two small funnels.

Willbury pointed to the design. "Is that yours?"

Marjorie sighed. "Yes. . . . Yes it is." Arthur was busy checking his wings.

"At least they haven't had time to take them apart again," he said in relief.

Willbury put Marjorie down on the control panel. She took a few moments to study the controls, then pointed to one of the dials.

"That shows the pressure in the steam boiler." Then she pointed to a lever. "And that lever engages the generators. Arthur, could you swing it to the upright position, please?"

Arthur obliged. As soon as he did, a gentle whirring started and built to a loud hum that filled the whole lab. A needle in another large dial in the control panel started to climb.

Arthur thought for a moment, then asked Marjorie, "How did they make the magnet work when the beam engine wasn't running?"

"Arthur, you really are as sharp as a knife." Marjorie smiled. "You saw all those glass tanks?"

"Yes," replied Arthur.

"Those are batteries. They store power, but not nearly enough for what we want. That's why I asked the boxtrolls to wire the coil directly to the generators," answered Marjorie. "Now all we have to do is wait until the needle hits the red."

"Are you sure that's safe?" asked Willbury.

"Err . . . no," confessed Marjorie. "But it should be all right for a bit."

The stokers were doing their work well. The beam engine kept increasing in speed and the generators hummed louder, and soon the needle reached the red.

"Arthur, can you tell the boxtrolls to stand clear of the magnetic coil, please?" asked Marjorie.

Arthur leaned out of the door and shouted, "We're turning the magnet on. Stand clear!"

The boxtrolls dropped their tools and ran to the other end of the lab as fast as their legs could carry them. Arthur poked his head back in the shed and told Marjorie, "They're clear!"

"Well then," Marjorie said, grinning at Arthur, "would you like to throw the switch?"

Arthur looked a little hesitant.

"Don't worry. What can happen?" She smiled.

Arthur paused, then grinned back and threw the switch.

Every piece of loose metal in the lab flew toward the magnet. Tools, nuts and bolts, pieces of machinery, a door handle, bits of chain, and several enameled mugs and plates whizzed past ducking heads as they made the most direct way to the magnet, where they formed a jumble on the surface of the coil.

"Strong, isn't it?" Marjorie said, pride in her voice.

"Strong, isn't it?"

At the head of the procession rode Snatcher high on the back of Framley.

chapter 50

MAGNETISM!

Shutters were thrown open by the townsfolk wondering what all the commotion was about.

Ratbridge was a strange town and had seen some very strange and fearful sights during its history, but none as strange and fearful as that making its way through its streets now.

At the head of the procession rode Snatcher high on the back of Framley. Following were the other members, carrying an assortment of blunderbusses and other weapons, and behind them ran the cheese-hounds. Sparks flew out from below Framley's belly as his armor grated on the cobbles of the streets. The noise drew people from their beds, and as the procession approached, shutters were thrown open by the townsfolk wondering what all the commotion was. Very quickly the shutters were closed and bolted again.

Very quickly the shutters were closed and bolted again.

Encouraged by the obvious fear they were generating, Snatcher chuckled to himself. He hadn't felt this good in years . . . or ever! Life felt wonderful.

"Just wait till I get to the Town Hall!" he sniggered. Looking ahead his eyes fixed on a row of shops. About half way down the row was a shuttered shop frontage with the three balls of the pawnbrokers' sign hanging above it.

"I wonder? . . ." he muttered.

As Framley drew level with the shop, Snatcher pulled hard on the reins. The Great One stopped. Snatcher swiveled around to the members, who had come to a sudden halt behind him. "I am sorry, lads, but I can't resist it!" He then pulled on Framley's reins and aimed the rat at the front of the shop. "Go on, my beauty! Let's see what you can do."

The shop did not put up much of a fight.

For a moment the rat didn't move; then, apparently realizing just how big he was and just how small the shop looked, he raised his head and swung it at the front of the shop.

The shop did not put up much of a fight. Within a fraction of a second the shutters and windows gave way and the contents of the windows spilled out. The members let out a mighty cheer and ran forward to gather up the treasures.

"This is going to be so easy!" shouted Snatcher. "Help yourselves, boys; there is going to be plenty more where that came from."

He pulled on the reins and set the mighty rat off again toward the market square. As they barreled through the streets, he set Framley upon several more unfortunate shops that took his fancy, and each in turn was reduced to a wreck in seconds.

Finally they crossed the market square and arrived outside the Town Hall. Snatcher brought the procession to a halt and turned to the members.

"This is where the real fun begins, lads! Prepare to charge!" Snatcher shouted.

Gristle shouted back, "Can't we use the cannons? I like a bang. Please, please let's use the cannons."

Snatcher looked down at Gristle benevolently. "Oh, all right, Gristle. As you have been so good, we'll use the cannons." Then Snatcher gave the order. "Prepare to fire!"

The members who were standing on the platforms on

There was a roar of cannon and blunderbusses.

the sides of the rat took out boxes of matches, and the other members leveled their weapons at the front of the Town Hall.

"Ready . . . fire!" Snatcher cried as he brought down his arm.

There was a roar of cannons and blunderbusses . . . but then something very strange happened, something that seemed to defy the laws of nature. The cannonballs and the nuts and bolts that

A member with a box of matches.

the members had fired hurtled toward the Town Hall, but then slowed . . . stopped . . . then turned back toward the members.

"Duck!!!" screamed Snatcher. The members hit the ground as the missiles whizzed over their heads and continued back across the market square in the direction of the Cheese Hall. Everybody looked baffled.

"Prepare to fire!" Snatcher screamed again.

The members tried to follow orders, but now their guns and ammunition seemed to want to go home and were pulling the members back toward the Cheese Hall.

The members hit the ground as the missiles whizzed over their heads.

"Master!" cried Gristle with fright in his voice. "Something weird is 'appenin' . . ."

"Stand firm!" ordered Snatcher, but the terrified members were now letting go of their blunderbusses and untying their

Their guns and ammunition seemed to want to go home.

ammunition bags from their belts to avoid being dragged across the square.

"Load the cannons!" cried Snatcher. The two members on the platform unstrapped cannonballs, but before they could load them into the cannons found themselves being dragged off the platforms and bouncing across the square, screaming.

"It's a curse!" cried one of the members.

"Run!" cried another. And they did in all directions.

Across Ratbridge most people were just getting up and might well have been very frightened by the noise of the blunderbusses and cannons, if it were not for the thunder and the fact that they had problems of their own. In every household, objects were coming to life.

Saucepans and cutlery had suddenly decided to stick to walls, and cooking ranges and iron bedsteads were going for walks. Several ladies who had slept in their steel reinforced

corsets now found themselves irresistibly drawn to join the saucepans and cutlery. One man who had invested in an expensive set of metal false teeth found himself hanging on as tightly as he could to the kitchen table to avoid being dragged through the house, while outside in the street, dogs with

Snatcher looked completely flummoxed.

studded collars found themselves sliding through the mud toward the Cheese Hall.

Snatcher looked completely flummoxed. A cart, riderless bicycles, garden furniture, and several old barrels were all making their way at high speed across the market square. Snatcher looked down at the head of the great rat.

"It's down to us Framley! Attack!" And Snatcher pointed toward the Town Hall.

The Great One let out an awful moan.

"Come on, my horrid!" Snatcher urged.

But Framley seemed very perturbed, for although his legs were scrabbling on the wet cobbles, he and Snatcher were not moving forward. In fact, they were starting to slip backward.

Inside the lab Arthur and the others listened nervously to the strange noises coming from outside. There seemed to be a pattern. Each started with a distant whizzing or clattering that grew louder very quickly, then stopped suddenly with a *thwonk*, *thud*, or similar sound.

"Do you think we'd better go and have a look at what's happening?" Arthur asked Tom.

"I think we know what's happening, Arthur. For the time being, I think we'd better stay safely in here. If the metal doesn't get us, I think there are going to be some very angry people out there," Tom replied, and then winked.

Snatcher watched the last of the cannonballs break from their lashings and fly off across the square. The rat was picking up speed, despite desperately trying to cling to the cobbles with its claws. There was a horrible scraping and grinding as the armor slid across the market square.

"Oh, my poor horrid!" Snatcher wailed. Framley just let out a mournful whimper.

On the way to the Town Hall, Snatcher had taken what he thought was the most direct route, but he now discovered that there was an even shorter route back—a straight line.

As the armored rat reached the edge of the market square, it was not a street that they met but a cobbler's shop. Snatcher, seeing what was going to happen, crouched down on the back

There was much surprise as a screaming, crouched man on a small railed platform came through the wall and moved rapidly across the room.

of the ever-accelerating rat and hung on. The shop, like most of the buildings in Ratbridge, was badly built and put up little opposition.

With a crash they disappeared through the shop frontage, leaving a large-armored-rat–shaped hole. In the apartment above the shop where the cobbler lived, there was much surprise as a screaming, crouched man on a small railed platform came through the wall, moved rapidly across the room, and went out through the back wall. The Great One then slid across the muddy back garden till it reached the next building and there was another crash.

The armor protected Framley as they smashed through

badly built building after badly built building, but Snatcher was getting rather bruised. And all the time they were picking up speed.

Finally with a great deal of splintering and crashing of masonry, Framley broke from the cake shop across the road from the Cheese Hall, shot across the street, and hit the lab wall in a puff of flour and cake crumbs.

The building shook.

"I think someone's arrived!" Marjorie squeaked. Herbert nearly skipped in joy. Arthur ran down to the floor of the lab. He found a wooden stepladder, placed it below a window near the magnet, and scrambled up. After a few moments he turned

"Framley is being squashed by his armor. He could burst at any moment!"

and shouted, "It's Snatcher and the rat! And they look really angry!" Everyone let out a cheer.

"We'd better keep them there then," Willbury advised.

Arthur took another look out of the window. "I'm not sure you want to do that!"

"Why not?" Willbury asked.

"Because Framley is being squashed by his armor. He could burst at any moment!"

"Can we reduce the strength of the magnet a bit, Marjorie?" asked Willbury.

Marjorie looked around uncertainly. The stokers were still very enthusiastic, and the generators were spinning faster and faster.

"The circuit is either on or off. The only way we can ease the power is to slow down the generators, and that's going to take a few minutes, even if we stop stoking the boiler and let off some steam," she said.

"Try it!" shouted Arthur, looking increasingly worried. "Framley looks like he could blow any second."

Willbury turned to Marjorie. "Well?"

"We could turn the current off for a few seconds," Marjorie

Marjorie jumped back.

suggested. "Herbert! Would you lift me up so I can turn off the switch?" Marjorie squeaked.

Herbert held her up and she tried to grab it. But the switch was red-hot and Marjorie jumped back.

"Let me try!" shouted Herbert. But he, too, had to pull back from the red-hot switch.

"I can't! It's too hot."

Willbury wrapped a handkerchief around his hand and tried. It was useless. . . . With all the current, the switch had fused solid. He looked at them frantically. "We have to get out of here!" he cried. "An explosion could bring down the rest of the lab."

Willbury grabbed Marjorie and ran out of the shed, followed by Herbert and Titus, and then he shouted from the top of the stairs.

"Everybody out! Run for your lives! No, no, don't use the hole in the wall! It's too close to the rat! Use the door to the entrance hall."

Willbury, Titus, the stokers, and the boxtrolls all ran for the entrance hall, but as Willbury reached the door, he turned to see Arthur making for the shed.

"Arthur! What are you doing?" he shouted.

"I've got to get my wings," Arthur shouted back.

He took the steps two at a time, grabbed his wings, and hastily strapped them on. Then he grabbed Marjorie's prototype from the bench and made for the door. As soon as he was outside, he wound the handle on the wings' motor as fast as he could. He had never wound it as fast in his life.

Willbury called him from the door to the hallway. "Arthur! Arthur!"

Arthur looked up—the last of the underlings and Laundry crew were disappearing out of the door, past Willbury. He adjusted the knob on the front of the box, pressed both buttons, and jumped.

He adjusted the knob on the front of the box, pressed both buttons, and jumped.

The big bang.

chapter 51
THE BIG BANG

The day was not going well for Snatcher.

The day was not going well for Snatcher. His attempt to return himself to his rightful social position seemed to have failed, the members had all run away, he'd been dragged through a number of buildings, and now rain was hitting him from above and small metal objects were hitting him from every other direction. How could things get worse?

Beneath him the iron shell that had protected the giant rat was now looking battered and flimsy. The Great One bulged out around the edges of the armor like a squashed balloon.

Then it happened.

Framley had not eaten since he'd had his last dose of "size," and even though he was extremely uncomfortable, he felt *very* hungry. And there on the ground, in the midst of rubble and cake crumbs, was a cream bun. It was not a

There on the ground, in the midst of rubble and cake crumbs, was a cream bun.

large cream bun, but it would do until he could get more cheese. He lowered his head, snapped up the bun, and swallowed. What followed was disastrous.

A clap like thunder broke as Framley burst and everything went yellow!

A large cream bun.

Everything went yellow!

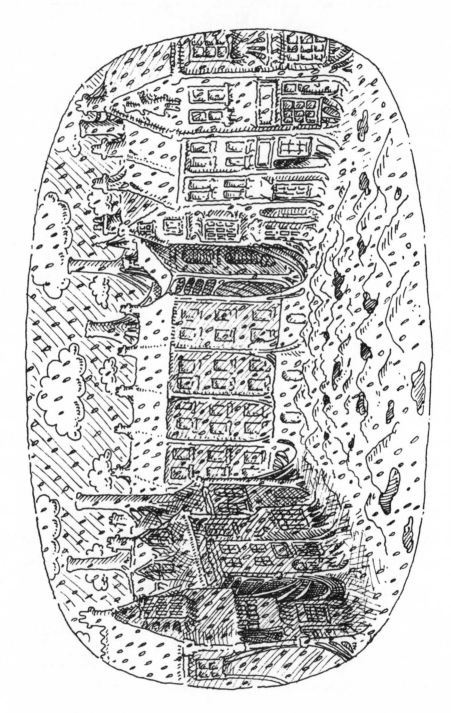

Everything was covered in a smooth film of elastic cheese.

chapter 52

SKINNED!

The two mice in the bottle.

Arthur flew straight toward the lab door where Willbury stood waiting. When Willbury was sure Arthur was coming, he turned and ran. Arthur followed.

Just as Arthur was halfway across the entrance hall, he remembered the two mice in the bottle. He swirled around and landed by the door of Snatcher's suite, ran in, and grabbed the bottle from the table. As he ran back toward the front door, he was hit by a blast from behind.

The blast shot him through the door. Just as he realized the front windows of the inn across the street were approaching him at a blinding speed, someone grabbed him out of the air and pulled him to the ground. Then he felt something thick and very sticky cover him entirely and everything went silent.

Arthur tried to stand up. He seemed to be under some kind of soft-elastic yellow tent. With a slight struggle, he freed his hands, and then with one finger he managed to poke a hole through the yellow skin. He stretched the hole until he could step out of it. Strands of cheese hung from his wings.

With one finger he managed to poke a hole through the yellow skin.

Arthur looked about. He was standing in a shiny yellow street. Everything was covered in the smooth film of cheese. He turned toward where the Cheese Hall had once stood. It was now just a low, shiny yellow mound. The buildings around the Cheese Hall now had yellow frontages but, apart from the bakery, didn't seem to be damaged.

Then Arthur remembered the others. He looked about on the ground close to where he stood. Odd shapes were wiggling under the cheese skin, and some were just starting to break through the film. Close to where he stood was the form of Willbury, lying flat with outstretched arms. Arthur ran over and started to peel the cheese film away from his friend.

"Willbury . . . Willbury . . . are you all right?" Arthur cried.

A muffled grunting came through the skin. Arthur tore at the cheese and soon had Willbury freed.

Arthur tore at the cheese.

"Thank you, my boy!" Willbury gasped as he tried to disentangle cheese strands from his wig. "We'd better help get everybody else out." Then he stopped.

"Have you seen Marjorie?"

"No!" replied Arthur. "When did you last see her?"

"I think I let go of her when I grabbed you."

They looked down at the smooth film that covered the cobbles. Arthur couldn't see any shape that resembled Marjorie, and then he turned toward the inn. In the middle of the front door was a perfectly formed molding of their friend.

A perfectly formed molding of their friend.

"Look!" cried Arthur, pointing. Willbury ran over to the door and unpeeled her.

She gave a splutter. "I hate cheese!"

Within a few minutes everybody was unpeeled. They all seemed shocked but okay, apart from the boxtrolls. Their boxes were now so damaged by the rain and blast that they were embarrassed to be seen in them.

Arthur then remembered the bottle and ran to where it lay, still under the cheese. He broke through the cheese and saw that the bottle was smashed. Close by, the bodies of the two tiny mice lay on the ground.

"Captain! Quick, over here!" Arthur called. "I think it's Pickles and Levi!"

The captain rushed over and knelt down.

He picked them up and looked at them very closely.

"You're right. I would recognize them any size," said the captain. "But they're not moving." He picked them up and looked at them very closely. "They are not quite the right shape though . . . sort of swollen up around the belly and there seem to be strands of cheese around their mouths." His eyes lit up. "But they're breathing!"

Levi and Pickles started to move and let out little groans.

"They must have gorged themselves on the cheese while under there," the captain said, bemused, and then carefully placed them in his pocket.

"What do you think has happened to Snatcher and Framley?" asked Arthur.

"I think we can guess what has happened to Framley," said Willbury, surveying the cheese. "But you're right. Where's Snatcher?"

Willbury led the group over the mound that had once been the Cheese Hall.

Willbury led the group over the mound that had once been the Cheese Hall, toward the place where the back wall of the lab had stood. Pools of water were now collecting on the surface of the cheese. At the far side of the mound they looked fruitlessly for signs of Snatcher.

They were just about to give up when a new noise started. It was a low rumble, and they could feel it under their feet. Beneath the town, the water had been doing its work. The foundations below the Cheese Hall had been almost completely washed away and, combined with the shock from the explosion, it was just too much. The rumbling grew louder and the earth began to shake. Arthur noticed ripples running over the surface of the pools of water.

"Look, Willbury! Look at the water!"

"Look, Willbury! Look at the water!" Everybody turned to stare.

"Quick!" Willbury urged, pulling the boxtrolls back. "Get away from the mound!"

The rumbling grew and the mound began to shake. They all backed even farther away, just as the ground issued a huge cracking noise and the mound suddenly disappeared.

In the same moment, all across the town, the iron plates covering holes to the Underworld were blown high into the air, and in the woods the trotting badgers were shot out of their tunnels and were last seen flying over the next county. Fortunately for the rabbit women, the doors they had constructed to keep the rabbits in were very well built and saved them from the blast.

Then everything was still. Everybody moved forward to look down the hole. It was some twenty or thirty feet deep and lined with the skin of cheese. Water was washing about in the bottom.

"If it were blue, it would look like a swimming pool," said Kipper.

"Yes!" Tom agreed.

"What's a swimming pool?" asked Arthur.

Willbury pulled them back from the edge. "Let's get back to the ship to see if your grandfather and the others are all right. Kipper can show you what a swimming pool is later."

Then he noticed how forlorn the boxtrolls looked.

"I'm sure we can find a few new boxes, and if not, I shall have you some made!" The boxtrolls beamed; they had never had brand-new boxes.

"It's all very well for them," said Marjorie mournfully. "But what about me and the other shrunken creatures?"

"Hang on a minute!" said Arthur, remembering.

Everybody moved forward to look down the hole.

the prototype. He rushed back around the edge of the hole to where it lay under the cheese skin. After a few seconds he managed to break through the skin and retrieved Marjorie's machine.

Marjorie squeaked with delight. "Oh, Arthur, thank you; you've got my sizer!"

"Where do you suggest we get your size back from?"

Willbury took the sizer from Arthur, gave it a long look, and then frowned. "I don't want to disappoint you, Marjorie, but where do you suggest we get your size back from, now that Framley is no more?"

Marjorie's eyes widened. "I hadn't thought of that . . ."

"There must be somewhere to get it from," said Arthur.

"Maybe," said Willbury. "We'll have to think about that."

As they set off for the ship, the townsfolk arrived to find out what all the commotion was. They formed small, puzzled groups, gawping at the newly decorated hole and buildings. The underlings had been through so much that now even Titus held his cabbage up in a very uncabbagehead way and walked straight past them.

What nobody noticed was that high above, just under the gables of the bakery, was what looked like a ship's figurehead of a very angry man wearing a top hat. The figurehead started to slide slowly down the wall.

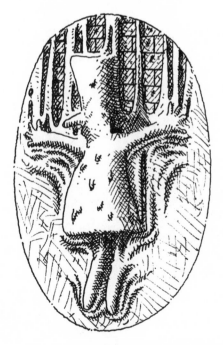

The figurehead started to slide slowly down the wall.

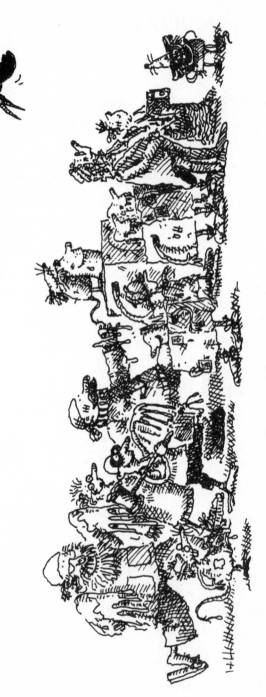

She swooped down to meet them.

chapter 53

REPAIRING THE DAMAGE

They saw Mildred flying toward them.

Weary and covered with bits of sticky cheese, but feeling proud and relieved, the group headed for the Laundry. The rain stopped and they saw Mildred flying toward them. She swooped down to meet them, circling a few feet above their heads.

"What's happened?" she cawed. "We heard an explosion!"

The boxtrolls bounced excitedly, and Willbury told her that they'd got Marjorie, Levi, and Pickles back and they had stopped Snatcher.

"Wonderful! Is everybody all right?" asked Mildred.

"I think so!" said Kipper. "Well, Marjorie, Levi, and Pickles are still little . . ."

"And Framley blew up!" added Arthur.

"That was the explosion you heard," said Tom. "We're not sure about Snatcher. He disappeared."

"And you say Framley exploded?" Mildred asked.

"It's a long story," said Willbury. "Let's get back to the ship; then everybody can hear it."

"I'll fly back and tell them you're on your way," Mildred offered.

Arthur had an idea. "If you'll wait a moment, I'll join you, Mildred."

Mildred looked surprised and watched as Arthur wound the box on his front until it pinged and he unfolded his wings.

"Cor! Like your wings," said Mildred. "What are those bits that look like cheese on them?"

"Cheese!" giggled Kipper.

"What are those bits that look like cheese on them?"

Arthur crouched down, jumped, and pressed a button. Mildred flapped out of the way as Arthur rose to join her.

"We'll see you in a few minutes!" Willbury called after Arthur. "And get the cocoa on!"

Arthur followed Mildred up above the rooftops. The streets were filling with people and many of them turned to stare up at Arthur as he flew over.

"Ain't they seen anybody fly before?" cawed Mildred.

They were joined by the other crows.

Arthur beamed. It was magnificent flying over the town by day, and with all the rain, the air was now clean and clear. As they approached the Laundry, they were joined by the other crows. Arthur spotted Grandfather standing on the main deck and waved. Grandfather waved back joyfully.

"Everything's all right!" called Arthur as he came onto land.

"Good!" replied Grandfather.

"Get the cocoa on!" said Arthur when he touched the deck. "The others will be back any minute."

Grandfather wrapped him in a hug. "It's good to see you in one piece!"

"Not bad to see you, either!" Arthur told the old man, hugging him back.

Grandfather released him. "We had better get the cocoa on. The milkman has been, and there's plenty of hot water as the boiler was on all night." Grandfather chuckled. "And then I expect a good story."

They arrived just in time to see the others returning. Soon

everybody was sitting on deck grinning, swapping stories, and drinking cocoa out of buckets. Even Marjorie seemed happier, poking and prodding at her prototype.

Then they heard a whistle from along the towpath. Everyone rushed to the rail. The Squeakers straddled their bikes below them.

"Goodness, will we never be given any peace?" sighed Willbury. The Squeakers dismounted from their bicycles and took out billy clubs and handcuffs. The Chief Squeaker approached the bottom of the gangplank, carrying a large sheath of papers.

Then he stopped, raised the papers in front of him, and declared, "I hereby arrest all presently residing upon this ship, formally known as the Ratbridge Nautical Laundry, under sections . . ."—he paused and shuffled through his papers—". . . C35 . . . D11 . . . Y322 . . . T14 . . . W24a . . . W24b . . . and Q56 of the Ratbridge penal code. I also charge you with . . ."—and he looked at his papers again—"riotously destroying a grade-six public building, escaping custody, playing music without license, causing a disturbance between the hours of eleven p.m. and six thirty a.m. . . . and about fourteen other charges."

Willbury raised a hand. "I think, sir, that it ill behooves one who has assisted in kidnap and wrongful imprisonment, handled stolen goods, aided in a plot for the destruction of the official offices of this town, been a member of an illegal organization, and connived with those who have been illegally hunting cheese and experimenting on animals without a license to cast the first stone."

"I hereby arrest all presently residing upon this ship."

The Chief Squeaker looked completely puzzled. "What do you mean?"

"I will explain it in court!" snapped Willbury. "And while we're at it, I have another case to talk to you about." He waved Grandfather and Herbert forward.

"Do you remember a case many years ago where a man was poisoned with Oil of Brussels in a local hostelry?" Willbury questioned the Chief Squeaker.

"Yes. I'd just joined the police, and it was the first crime scene I ever attended. Very nasty case. We chased the assailant but he disappeared," the Chief Squeaker replied.

"Well, do you remember that one of the witnesses also disappeared?"

"Yes. Archibald Snatcher said he had gone home for his tea. . . ."

"Was it not lunchtime? And was this not the man?" Willbury pointed to Herbert.

Herbert made a slight bow, and the Chief Squeaker gave him a funny look.

"I think, sir, that it ill behooves one."

"It could be. . . ."

"I am telling you it was. This man was knocked uncon-
scious and imprisoned by your good friend Archibald Snatcher
to stop him from giving true evidence and has lingered in a
miserable cell under the Cheese Hall ever since." Willbury
paused for a moment and fixed the Chief Squeaker with his
gaze. "It was Archibald Snatcher who was responsible for the
poisoning. Yes! That very same Archibald Snatcher whom
we all witnessed you investing with legal powers to justify
a kidnapping and the theft of a pair of mechanical wings. I
intend to sue whatever remains of the Cheese Guild on behalf
of my clients here, for compensation, and I am sure the full
story will come out."

The Chief Squeaker went very pale. "Umm . . . err . . .
I think there might have been a misunderstanding. . . ." He
lowered his papers. "Didn't you say you had retired?"

"I was retired but I now feel that it is my duty to return to the law," replied Willbury.

"Oh!" muttered the Chief Squeaker, and then he turned to the other Squeakers. "Back to the police station. Quick!"

Everybody cheered as they watched the Squeakers pedal madly down the towpath.

"You're rather good at this law thing," Arthur said to Willbury.

It was Willbury's turn to make a slight bow. Then turning to Grandfather, he said, "I think it's going to be safe for you to set up home aboveground now if you would like."

"Thank you," said Grandfather, and he shook Willbury's hand.

Everybody cheered.

The deck of the Ratbridge Nautical Laundry.

chapter 54
HOME

Snoozing in the morning sun.

On deck everybody had finished their cocoa, and with the Squeakers sent off with their tails between their legs, there was an air of relaxation. Some of the crew went belowdeck to get cleaned up, while others snoozed in the morning sun. Willbury wandered across to Arthur and whispered quietly to him.

"Your Grandfather is exhausted. It would be a good idea if he had a rest and time to recover. Why don't you and Herbert take him down to the captain's cabin and look after him while I get a few things sorted out."

"All right," replied Arthur as he looked fondly at his grandfather. Then he turned back to Willbury. "I don't like to ask this, but I'm worried about where we are going to live, and—"

Willbury cut him off. "You are not to worry about that. I have an idea. You concentrate on looking after Grandfather. I am sure he has missed you, and it would be good for both of you to catch up."

Arthur nodded and walked over to where Grandfather and Herbert were chatting.

"Willbury says we're to get you down to the captain's cabin so you can have a rest, Grandfather."

"Oh, all right. If I have to! I am feeling much better though, now that it's stopped raining and my bones have had time to dry out."

"Come on!" chuckled Arthur, as he and Herbert helped him to his feet.

He and Herbert helped Grandfather to his feet.

For the rest of the day Arthur sat by Grandfather, who insisted on telling him stories of Herbert's and Grandfather's youth. Herbert's memory continued to improve as story after story unfolded, and Arthur could hardly bear to tear himself away from them, but they kept needing fresh top ups of cocoa and biscuits from the galley. There were tales of learning to ride bicycles, disastrous experiments, pet frogs, and engineering projects.

By late afternoon when they were all growing sleepy, Grandfather patted the cushion beside him, motioning to Arthur to sit close.

"I am glad we have come aboveground, my boy," he told him. "I loved every moment I spent living in the Underworld with you, but it's not the best place for a child to grow up. You need sunlight, and you need friends. And now you are going to have both."

Arthur smiled contentedly and a quiet calm settled on the cabin.

About seven o'clock a knock on the cabin door woke them. They opened the door to see Kipper grinning from ear to ear and covered in splashes of paint.

"Sorry to disturb, but Willbury has called a meeting in the hold and would like you all to attend."

"Why have you got paint all over you?" asked Arthur.

"You'll just have to wait and see," Kipper replied mysteriously.

Herbert and Arthur went to help Grandfather, but before they got to him, he had stood up on his own.

"Come on, then," he said. "What are you waiting for; let's get to the meeting!" And he set off out the door. Herbert and Arthur grinned at each other and hurried after him.

When they arrived in the hold, Willbury sat behind the ironing board with the captain. In front of them lay the prototype resizing machine, with Marjorie almost hidden behind it.

Willbury saw Grandfather walking on his own and smiled. "Come join me here, William. There is a spare chair."

Grandfather nodded and made his way to the chair, while Arthur and Herbert joined Kipper to sit among the boxtrolls. Quite a few of the pirates and rats also had splotches of paint on them, and they were smirking at Arthur. Then Willbury began.

Splodges of paint.

"My dear friends. There are a number of important issues to resolve, and I think it best if I outline them, then we discuss how they might be solved." He addressed Grandfather. "I have already taken the liberty of asking my landlady if she would rent the vacant rooms above my shop to you and Arthur. She has agreed, and this afternoon I had Kipper lead a working party to clean and repaint them. There is even a small storage room that Herbert could use till he gets his own place. Kipper tells me he has sorted out some basic furniture, so you are welcome to move in anytime you like."

Grandfather clapped his hands together, and called to Arthur, "What do you think?"

"Yes, please!" answered Arthur with a huge grin. Kipper and Fish both patted him on the back.

There was a roar of approval from the others, and then Grandfather, his voice shaking, said, "I want to thank you from the bottom of my heart . . . but how are we to pay the rent? I don't have a job and I haven't got any savings."

"You're not to worry about that. This afternoon I filed a claim with the clerk of Ratbridge courts for compensation, on your and Herbert's behalf, against Snatcher and the Cheese Guild. Until it comes to court, if Arthur helps out with chores, I'll sort out the rent."

"I filed a claim with the clerk of Ratbridge courts for compensation, on your and Herbert's behalf."

There was another cheer. Willbury raised a hand and continued. "Now we come to our friends the underlings." He turned to where the underlings sat.

"The problem of the entrances to the Underworld has been solved, but . . . at the moment most of the Underworld is flooded. Does anybody have any suggestions?"

Marjorie stood up on the table and squeaked, "Easy!"

Willbury looked startled. "Yes?"

"We already have a beam engine on this Laundry. Pumping

water is what it was built for. All we have to do is drop a pipe down into the Underworld and pump out the water."

"I might be being stupid," said Willbury, "but where are we going to pump the water to?"

Marjorie looked flummoxed.

Marjorie looked flummoxed.

Kipper raised a hand. "How about the hole where the Cheese Hall was? That cheese seems to be pretty water-proof and would stop the water from leaking back into the Underworld."

"Would it work?" Willbury asked Marjorie.

Marjorie thought for a moment. "I think so . . . and once the underground becomes drier, the boxtrolls could repair their drainage system to stop it from flooding again."

The boxtrolls made gurgles of agreement.

Kipper raised a hand again. "Can I help them?"

"I see no reason why not," Willbury said. He looked toward the captain, who was nodding in agreement. Kipper beamed.

"Well, that just leaves us with one last problem," Willbury announced. "Size! We have our friends here who have been reduced in size, but we know there are many others, and some are in the hands of those who treat them as just pets. We have

to get them back, and we have to work out where to get the size to put them right. Does anybody have any suggestions?"

"How about we find the members what ran away and suck the size out of them?" Bert suggested. There were hearty cheers from the pirates and rats.

Willbury stood silently until the cheers died away. "I'm sorry, but I'll not countenance revenge shrinkings. We must not lower ourselves to that. No, we must find another way. Does anybody have any other suggestions?"

"Couldn't we use vegetables to suck the size from?" asked Tom.

Titus looked shocked, and Marjorie raised a hand to speak. "It doesn't work. You have to use living creatures. If you used vegetables, you might end up with some strange results."

"What, like half trotting badger, half potato?" asked Kipper.

Half trotting badger, half potato.

"Exactly," replied Marjorie, nodding.

"Might be an improvement," suggested Tom.

"I think we have to stick with getting the size from creatures," said Willbury. "But I am really not sure how."

"Couldn't we all donate a little bit of size?" asked Grandfather.

"You could, but with all the creatures we have to resize, it would leave you all pretty tiny," Marjorie responded.

"Well, let's think on it," said Willbury. "And there is the issue of how we get the other underlings back to resize them in the first place. They're in homes all over the town. If we do find them and just steal them back, we are going to start another whole round of trouble, and with the court case coming up, that is the last thing I want."

The hold fell silent and everybody looked rather glum. Finally Willbury told them, "Let's get some rest. It's been a tiring few days, and I am sure we'll think better after some sleep. We can all meet here tomorrow morning to start pumping out the underground. Marjorie, will you take charge of that?"

Marjorie nodded.

"Could those who are coming back to the shop meet me up on deck?" said Willbury.

The meeting broke up, and a few minutes later Arthur found himself on deck with the boxtrolls, Titus and the tiny cabbagehead, Grandfather, Herbert, Marjorie, and Willbury.

"Are we taking the little sea-cow with us?" asked Arthur.

"No, she is staying here for the moment. The crew has grown very fond of her," Willbury replied.

So they set off and soon arrived at the shop. Willbury opened the front door and stopped in his tracks.

"Oh, my word!" he exclaimed.

Willbury opened the front door and stopped in his tracks.

The shop was cleaner and tidier than Willbury could possibly have ever imagined. The walls and ceiling had been given a fresh coat of white paint, the old bookshelves had been righted and repaired and were tidily stacked with all his books, the floorboards had been swept and polished, and against one wall, stacked soap boxes formed open-fronted storage spaces into which the rest of Willbury's loose possessions had been neatly piled. His bed was freshly made and some extra blankets lay at the foot of the bed.

The shop was cleaner and tidier than
Willbury could possibly have ever imagined.

There was a popping noise and Willbury turned toward the fireplace. He smiled. In front of the blazing fire was his old armchair . . . and it also had been repaired.

Willbury turned back around. "Welcome home! Please come in."

The little group walked into the shop and Willbury closed the door, then took a key off his key ring and handed it to Grandfather.

"This is a spare key. Please feel free to wander through here whenever you like." Then he said to Fish, "Would you like to show our friends their new home?"

Fish eagerly led them through the door at the back of the shop into the hallway. Now it was Fish's turn for a surprise. Where once the hallway had been dark and dingy, it was now bright and clean. A lit ship's lantern hung from the ceiling, and every surface was painted white. Fish was just about to lead them up the stairs when he noticed there was something different about the back room as well. He ran down the hall and gave an excited gurgle. Arthur, Grandfather, and Herbert trotted after him.

The back room looked like a new ironmonger's shop. Cubbyhole shelving made from cardboard now covered the walls, and all the nuts and bolts that had littered the floor had been sorted and placed in different labeled holes.

Fish let out a whistle, then stopped still when he noticed a stack of folded . . . clean . . . brand-new . . . cardboard boxes on the floor. After a few seconds he walked forward slowly and bent down to stroke the top box. Then he turned and let out an enormous gurgling cry.

He walked forward slowly and bent down to stroke the top box.

There was a scrabbling of feet from the shop, and the other boxtrolls rushed past Arthur, stopped, and hooted at the sight of the boxes. The boxtrolls looked from the new boxes to one another, then to Arthur, Grandfather, and Herbert.

Fish came forward and gently shooed Arthur, Grandfather, and Herbert out of the room and closed the door. As soon as the door was shut, there was a frantic tearing of cardboard and whooping, followed by some chewing noises, then the door opened again. Fish and the other boxtrolls were wearing the new boxes and were grinning from ear to ear.

The boxtrolls were wearing the new boxes and grinning from ear to ear.

Fish swaggered along the hall and marched up the stairs, waving for Grandfather, Arthur, and Herbert to follow. As they reached the top, Arthur ran ahead. There were three doors. The first one opened to a tiny room with a hammock and another cardboard box. But this time the cardboard box had been tipped upside down to form a table. On it was a small vase of flowers and a cake.

"Is this my room?" he called over his shoulder.

"Is this my room?"

"No, that is the storage room for Herbert." Arthur nodded approvingly and opened the next door. There he saw a brass bed and, to his surprise, tools laid out on a workbench.

"Is *this* my room?" he asked.

"No!" came Willbury's voice. "It's Grandfather's."

Grandfather walked past Arthur, looked at the bench, and sat on the edge of the bed. "I do hope so," he said contentedly.

Arthur then turned to the last door. "Then this *must* be my room!" He swung the door open.

The room was a little smaller than Grandfather's and was painted completely white, including the floor. There was a cardboard-box table like in the smaller room, but there were also some shelves. On the top shelf, lying on its side, was a large bottle. And inside the bottle was a model of the Ratbridge Nautical Laundry—complete with tiny washing. Arthur ran forward to look at it and noticed a small plaque fixed to the bottle. Engraved into the plaque were the words TO ARTHUR FROM THE R.N.L. Arthur bit his lip and looked at the others wonderingly.

Inside the bottle was a model of the Ratbridge Nautical Laundry.

Herbert spoke. "Kipper had been making it since they arrived in Ratbridge, and when he heard that you had lost all your toys, he decided you would make a good home for it."

Arthur could barely speak, he was so moved. Finally he managed to say, "I shall treasure it always."

Then Arthur looked about the room again. A hammock hung from corner to corner. Arthur jumped in it and lay down. It felt very comfortable apart from a bump behind his neck. He reached his hand around to retrieve whatever was causing the discomfort, and to his surprise, he found he was holding his doll. Arthur was confused. He checked under his suit, but discovered that it, of course, was not there.

He found he was holding his doll.

He swung himself out of the hammock and ran to his grandfather's room.

"My doll? It was in my room!"

"Where else did you expect to find it?"

"But how did it get there?"

"You must have dropped it when you were caught in the explosion. Tom found it and brought it to me. Marjorie fixed it this afternoon."

Arthur held the doll up wonderingly.

"I'm afraid that it will never fly again, but you will still be able to speak to me through it."

They smiled warmly at each other, and Grandfather said, "I think we are going to be happy here."

"Cocoa!" came a call from downstairs.

"Yes . . . yes, we are," said Arthur.

They smiled warmly at each other.

Children swimming in Grandfather and Herbert's hole.

chapter 55

Measure for Measure

He helped the crew pump out the Underworld.

The next few weeks were very busy ones. Grandfather thought it would be a good education for Arthur to help with all the work that had to be done, so each morning Arthur set out for the Laundry. Some days, under the guidance of Marjorie, he helped the crew pump out the Underworld, and on other days he worked with the boxtrolls as they rebuilt the underground drainage system. He enjoyed those days most, as Kipper and Tom worked with the boxtrolls. Kipper still wore his battered cardboard box and now had learned to "speak" boxtroll. This made him even more useful and very happy.

Willbury, Herbert, and Grandfather spent their time preparing the compensation case against Snatcher and the Cheese Guild. When the day of the trial came, neither Snatcher nor any member of the Cheese Guild turned up to defend themselves, and the court awarded the hole in the ground to Herbert and Grandfather (as it was the only property left that Snatcher and the Cheese Guild owned).

That evening to celebrate, they all walked to view Grandfather and Herbert's hole. As they approached it, they noticed local children swimming in the crater.

"You're going to have to fence off your hole," said Willbury. "What would happen if a child got into difficulty?"

Herbert and Grandfather looked at the swimmers.

"Seems a pity. I suppose we could pay one of the pirates to keep an eye on the kids, but where would we get the money to pay him?" said Grandfather. "We still don't have enough money to pay you rent."

"Why don't you charge for admission?" Willbury suggested.

"What a brilliant idea!" Herbert and Grandfather agreed simultaneously. Willbury advised that it would still be a good idea to put up a fence, to stop any accidents. They trooped eagerly off to the Laundry and were greeted with friendly cries.

"Is the captain about?" Willbury asked Mildred, who had flown down to meet them.

"Yes! He's down in his cabin. You know the way."

When they got to the captain's quarters, Willbury opened the door and there sat Tom with the captain's hat on, behind a huge heap of laundry slips.

"Where's the captain?" asked Willbury, puzzled.

Tom smiled. "I got voted captain last Friday. It's rather nice being captain but I am looking forward to next Friday. I can't stand the paperwork. Anyway, what can I do for you?"

Willbury explained, and it was agreed that in exchange for half the profits, the Laundry would provide lifeguard cover every day between six a.m. and eight p.m., and they would help erect a fence around the pool. It was also agreed that

There sat Tom with the captain's hat on, behind a huge heap of laundry slips.

any spare hot water left over from the Laundry would be piped into the pool.

Soon the "Ratbridge Lido" (as the pool became known) became the main attraction in the town. Children swam there by day, and in the evening when it wasn't raining, the fashionable women paraded along its shores, while the pirates held raft races. Herbert, who was quite a swimmer in his day, taught Arthur, and once the water became warm, Grandfather could be found most days taking a dip.

All this time the question of the shrunken creatures had not been solved, but then something curious happened.

A Frenchwoman arrived in Ratbridge and found work in one of the cafes that had sprung up around the Lido.

The pirates held raft races.

She immediately became the center of attention for the fashionable women as she was from "Pari."

For days the ladies spent their time plucking up courage to ask her questions about the latest fashions till finally one Ms. Hawkins could bear it no longer and stormed into the cafe.

"May I ask you about the Pari fashions, my dear?" Ms. Hawkins asked.

"*Certainement.* What do you want to know?" replied the Frenchwoman.

"Is it true that hexagonal buttocks are going to be the rage this year?" said Ms. Hawkins knowingly.

"*Quel horreur!* What is it with zee Ratbridge ladies and their fascination for ridiculous buttocks?"

Ms. Hawkins dropped her pet boxtroll and fainted. When she recovered, she went straight to her friend who wrote the fashion articles for the *Ratbridge Weekly Gazette*. The following Friday a special edition of the paper came out with two main articles.

The first reported in detail what Snatcher had been up to and the second reported the fact that buttocks were "OUT!"

The next morning as Arthur made his way to the Laundry, he found the towpath thronging with the ladies of the town, trying to get on the ship. After a struggle he managed to push past them till he reached the gangplank. Kipper and a number of the bigger pirates were holding back the crowd. When he

"Quel horreur!"

saw Arthur, Kipper grabbed him and lifted him up onto the deck. Here Arthur found Tom and Marjorie pacing back and forth worriedly.

"What's happening!" shouted Arthur over the noise of the crowd.

"We are not sure, but it has something to do with my resizing machine. They've heard we've got one here," squeaked Marjorie.

"Quick! You've got to come and deal with them!" Kipper shouted from below. "We can't hold them back for much longer!"

"What do they want?" asked Arthur.

When he saw Arthur, Kipper grabbed him and lifted him up onto the deck.

"I don't know . . . ," Marjorie admitted, panic in her voice.

"Let one of them up here and see what they are after?" suggested Tom. "It might be the only way to stop a riot."

They nodded quickly and Tom called out to Kipper to let one of the ladies through. A moment later, a very cross-looking woman strode up the gangplank, and as she did, the din died down.

"How can I help you?" Marjorie squeaked.

"I've read that you have a machine like the one that Snatcher scoundrel had, that can shrink things." It was Ms. Hawkins.

"I want you to shrink my buttocks!"

"Err . . . yes?" Marjorie prompted.

"I want you to shrink my buttocks! And that is not a request but an order!" said Ms. Hawkins.

Everyone else on deck looked astonished. "Umm . . . are you sure?" Marjorie finally squeaked.

"I am not leaving here till you do," Ms. Hawkins replied. "You can use my boxtroll to put the size into." She thrust the tiny boxtroll toward Marjorie.

"All right, if you insist," Marjorie said, smiling slowly with realization. "But I do charge!"

"I don't care. I want my buttocks reduced at any price," Ms. Hawkins insisted.

"How about ten groats a pound . . . and your boxtroll?" Marjorie said.

"Done!" Ms. Hawkins snapped, and took out her purse. "Who'd want a big boxtroll anyway; it's only the small ones that are fashionable!"

"Very well then!" Marjorie squeaked. Then, raising her eyebrows at Tom and Arthur, she asked them, "Can you rig up a screen for the ladies to go behind? It will need a hole in it big enough for the funnel on my resizer."

They hurried off. Marjorie turned back to Ms. Hawkins. "I've got to go and get my machine. I'll be right back."

While Tom and Arthur put up the screen, one of the pirates found a pair of scissors and cut a hole in it. Ms. Hawkins huffed, placed the boxtroll on the deck, and then slipped behind the screen.

Tom finished putting up the screen with the aid of the crows.

Marjorie returned, struggling with her machine. "Tom, can you get one of the pirates to operate the resizer? I don't think I am big enough."

Tom found a volunteer and Marjorie ordered him to push the funnel through the hole in the screen.

"Are you ready now? Please place your right buttock against the funnel!"

"Ready!" came the cry from behind the screen.

"Extract the size!" Marjorie ordered the pirate. The pirate pulled the trigger and there was a flash and puff of smoke from behind the screen. This was followed by a delighted titter.

"Please place your second buttock against the funnel!"

"Ready!"

Where her buttocks once had been, her figure was now as straight as a board.

"Extract the size!" There was another flash and puff of smoke from behind the screen and yet another titter of delight.

Moments later Ms. Hawkins appeared from behind the screen to gasps of admiration from the women standing at the top of the gangplank. Where her buttocks once had been, her figure was now as straight as a board.

With no word of thanks, she marched past her fashion rivals, flaunting her nonexistent buttocks, went down the gangplank, and disappeared.

There was another flash and instantly the boxtroll grew about three inches.

Marjorie now instructed the pirate to point the other funnel at the tiny boxtroll.

"Do you understand what we are doing?" she asked the boxtroll. The boxtroll nodded and hopped up and down.

"All right, release the size!" Marjorie ordered. There was another flash and instantly the boxtroll grew about three inches.

"Well done!" Marjorie said to the boxtroll, who was looking very pleased.

Over the course of the day many ladies were treated, including a large number who didn't have underlings as pets. This enabled Marjorie to get all of the creatures back to their original size. Several women turned up with buckets

On deck there were swarms of full-size underlings.

containing freshwater sea-cows. These proved a little more difficult to resize, as they had to be taken out of their bucket and kept wet during the process, then lifted carefully over the side and lowered into the canal.

By late afternoon Arthur had had to find somewhere to put all the money. He now had a large barrel almost full of banknotes and coins. On deck there were swarms of full-size underlings, and there was still a queue of ladies on the towpath, but none of them had pet underlings.

"Where are you going to put the size?" asked Arthur, looking around.

"We need to find some more shrunken underlings," Marjorie told him.

"Why don't I go and get Match from the shop, and the little cabbagehead that Titus is looking after?" Tom suggested.

"Yes! And what about the freshwater sea-cow that was here on the boat?" Marjorie asked.

"We did her hours ago," Tom said.

"Well, what shall I do while I am waiting? There are still loads of ladies on the towpath . . ."

"Isn't that obvious?" asked Tom.

"No," replied Marjorie.

"Don't you want to get back to normal?" Tom asked.

Marjorie grinned at Willbury as he arrived.

Marjorie laughed, turning red. "Of course. It had gone clean out of my head."

Tom returned with everyone from the shop to see a full-size Marjorie standing on deck, accompanied by full-size versions of Pickles and Levi.

Marjorie grinned at Willbury as he arrived.

"I am not sure I approve of this," said Willbury.

"We didn't have much choice in the matter," said a much less squeaky Marjorie. "I think we would have been lynched if we had refused to cooperate. And look at the underlings!"

Willbury looked around at all the happy, big underlings milling about the deck.

He smiled. "Well, let's finish this off. Fish, please bring Match over. We are going to get his size back."

Fish placed Match in front of the screen, and Marjorie ordered the pirate to let another lady through.

Over the next few minutes the queue of ladies on the towpath disappeared, and Match and Titus's friend regained their size.

"That's the last one!" said Marjorie triumphantly. "Everyone's back up to full size!"

"Right!" said Willbury. "Now, Marjorie, could you lend me your machine for a minute?" Marjorie looked curious but handed the machine over. Willbury placed the machine on the deck.

"Herbert, could you do the honors with your walloper, please?"

"But . . . ," Marjorie cried, and started to move forward to get her machine.

Willbury raised a hand. "No! We have had enough of all this resizing. I am going to get Herbert to destroy the resizer, and I want you to promise you are not going to try to build a new one."

Herbert, walloping the machine.

Marjorie frowned for a moment and then slowly seemed to realize it was a good idea. "I suppose so. . . ."

"All right then. Herbert, wallop the machine!"

There was a mighty crash and the resizer lay bent beyond recovery on the deck.

"Thank you, Herbert!" Willbury said to his friend.

Marjorie looked from the smashed machine to Herbert. "Yes, thank you very much, Herbert," she said, resignation in her voice. Then Willbury noticed the barrel full of money.

"That's my girl. And look, you've made rather a lot of money out of this. Perhaps you could put it to some more useful purpose than just changing the size of things," he said warmly.

"And maybe something that causes less trouble," added Grandfather, looking up at the smog that was starting to settle over the town. "Have you ever thought about going into pollution prevention?"

"I did have an idea about how to distill oil and run a motor off it. It would be a lot cleaner than steam engines," Marjorie said, grinning.

That night a party was held on the Laundry.

"Do you think I could help?" asked Arthur.

"Of course you could. I need a bright assistant."

That night a party was held on the Laundry. The crows played harmonium, vast quantities of cocoa were drunk, everybody danced, and complaints were made about the noise to the Squeakers, who did nothing about it. As the party died down, Arthur wandered onto the towpath with his friends—Fish, Tom, and Kipper—for a little peace away from the crows' "music." As they walked along, they saw Willbury and Grandfather sitting on the bank with Titus.

"What are they doing?" asked Arthur.

"Looks like they're throwing weeds in the canal," replied Kipper.

As they approached, Willbury put his fingers to his lips to keep them quiet, then pointed out into the canal.

There were the mother freshwater sea-cow and her size-restored calves, feeding on the weeds that Willbury and Grandfather had been throwing in.

They watched until the sea-cows had had their fill and swam off down the canal. Willbury and Arthur helped Grandfather to his feet, and they all waved as the little group of sea-cows slowly disappeared into the distance.

"You know, for all its failings, I rather like Ratbridge," said Willbury.

"It's not all bad, is it?" replied Grandfather as he gave Arthur a wink.

It's not all bad at all. Arthur agreed. And he smiled.

www.here-be-monsters.com

Come in and explore the wonderful world of Ratbridge at our
Here Be Monsters! website. Inside Willbury's shop, you'll find
all sorts of bits and bobs to keep you as happy as a boxtroll in
a pile of nuts and bolts. Website includes:

- A crazy Here Be Monsters! animated game featuring
  cabbageheads, boxtrolls, and cheeses galore!
- Screensaver to brighten up your computer
- Animation clips of creatures from the book
- A downloadable toy theater—have the Here Be Monsters!
  characters live in your living room
- Maps of Ratbridge—investigate all those nooks and
  crannies and find out what happens when the book
  cover is closed

www.here-be-monsters.com